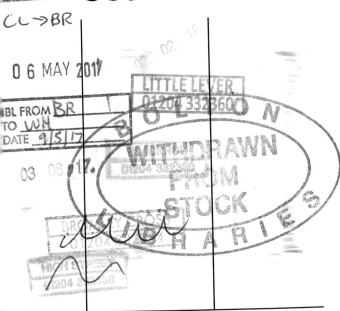

husky' His des...
opp...

D1355417

BT 1969661 2

"We can settle this between the two of us, no need for the police," he replied. **"For the last time, what are you doing here?"**

"And if I don't change my answer?"

Maddening. What a shrew. Her eyes flashed, and her chest rose and fell with her hot-tempered breathing. Ah, but she was sexy as all get-out. His gaze focused on the cleavage exposed by her deep V-neck shirt.

A leather-fringed, beaded necklace with some sort of woven charm settled in the space between her rounded breasts. He couldn't help it. Payton reached a hand out to touch it, his fingers lightly brushing her skin.

Heat sparked his fingertips and spread throughout his body, and he dropped his arm and stepped backward. For a brief instant, he caught a returning fire banked in Tallulah's widened eyes—until animosity again took its place.

"What's that on your necklace?" he asked, trying to break the tension.

"A miniature dreamcatcher I wove. And don't you dare touch me again like that."

Did he imagine it or did her voice sound a tiny bit husky—spike-doubled. Here was an opportunity. He dared, all right.

BAYOU WOLF

DEBBIE HERBERT

Debbie Herbert writes paranormal romance novels reflecting her belief that life, like nature, casts its own spell of enchantment. She's always been fascinated by magic, romance and gothic stories. Married and living in Alabama, she roots for the Crimson Tide football team. Her eldest son, like many of her characters, has autism. Her youngest son is in the US Army. A past MAGGIE Award finalist in both young adult and paranormal romance, she's a member of the Georgia Romance Writers RWA chapter.

Chapter 1

The creature had been watching her ever since she entered the forest, half-hidden in the lengthening shadows. Trees rustled in the distance. One small sapling bowed, bending over until the tip brushed the ground. It was too far away for even her keen eyesight to locate the creature's form or even a vague outline. But Tallulah sensed its energy emanating from the woods. A deer, perhaps? No, that wasn't right. Too bold for a deer. Whatever it was, it didn't appear to be a threat—for now.

Red feathers and black ribbons fluttered in the bayou breeze as she fastened the dream catcher to a cypress branch. Dozens of similar artifacts hung in varying states of disintegration, a shrine to her one and only love.

Bo had died here—832 nights ago—in this very spot. On this lonely patch of swampland, amidst the droning code of self-preservation that made them untrustworthy allies in the fight to keep evil contained in the bayou.

Maybe tonight's wolfish creature was an anomaly. Maybe she'd never see it again.

And maybe she'd grow wings and fly. Like Tinkerbell. She couldn't help snorting. Anyone who knew her for more than a day realized she was light-years away from a sparkly, bubbly, fairy-type personality—in truth, she more closely resembled a grouchy goblin. Those who cared for her called her *challenging* or *abrupt*, while those who cared nothing for her, which was the majority of people, merely called her *bitchy*.

Tallulah stuffed the slingshot in her backpack and slung it over her shoulders. "Bye, Bo," she whispered. "Love you forever."

This moment of saying goodbye always pinched her heart. Resolutely, she straightened her shoulders and hurried down the path. Experience had taught her it was best to keep the goodbye brief.

"Be back tomorrow," she called over her shoulder.

The silence of the woods mocked her words. And she couldn't shake the memory of the creature's eyes boring into her own, memorizing her sight even as it caught her scent. She hadn't seen the last of that one.

Vroom, vroom, vroom.

The loud whir of the skidder powered into the morning's quiet. The cab of the heavy engine rumbled as it lifted felled trees and transported them to the waiting logging trucks. Payton grinned at the familiar vibration that shook his body. It felt damn good to get back to work after the last week of moving from Montana and settling into the new place. A fresh start was exactly what they all needed. An escape from the unwarranted accusations and territorial disputes from other wolf packs.

Besides, being cooped inside too long made him feel caged and claustrophobic. The great outdoors lifted his spirits, even when it came to back-breaking work. Sitting in some cubicle in a monkey suit would be his idea of torture.

Payton expertly maneuvered the skidder, creating cleared trails on the new land they were harvesting for its wood. The twenty-three-ton machine bulldozed through the thick underbrush. Cautiously, he kept a watch for his pack members, all of whom worked with him in the same timber clearing crew. Most of them were on the ground, felling trees with chainsaws. Those unlucky bastards might have a few snake encounters in this swampy land. Not for the first time, Payton was glad to be ensconced in the cab. He'd take his chances on a rollover or a fallen log over a rattlesnake bite any day.

Their pack leader, Matt, served as the lumberjacking supervisor. He directed traffic around Payton, the other skidder operator, and the truck drivers parking their vehicles at the edge of the property.

Payton lifted the edge of his T-shirt and wiped the sweat off his face. Seven o'clock in the morning, and it was already hot as Hades. Adjusting to the Alabama weather would take some time. What would it be like two months from now in the heat of summer?

Sweat stung his eyes, and he blinked. What the hell was that in front of him?

A gorgeous, olive-skinned woman stood a mere ten feet from the skidder, hands on her hips and a fierce gleam in her dark eyes. He slammed on the brakes and waved his arms. "Get out of the way!"

She scowled more deeply but otherwise didn't budge an inch from her entrenched position. Was she crazy? Suicidal, perhaps?

Payton shifted to Neutral, settled the brakes and lowered the skidder's blade. "Gorgeous or not, she's a damn nuisance of a woman," he sputtered, unbuckling the seat belt and hopping to the ground. He strode in front of the machine, boots squishing in the wet, red-clay soil. "This is a logging site. You can't be here."

Her eyes narrowed. "Is that so? Well, I *am* here, and I'm not moving."

The heat, coupled with her defiance, stirred his temper. "Are you nuts? Move it, lady!"

She folded her hands across her chest. A beautiful chest, he couldn't help noticing.

"No," she said simply.

No? She had some kind of nerve. "What the hell do you mean? You trying to get yourself killed?"

"I'm trying to stop you from destroying our land."

Confusion knit his brow. "Excuse me, are you the owner?"

"Not legally. But—"

So she was one of those conservation types. They'd dealt with them before. Payton slapped on a fake smile and tried a placating tone of voice. "Look, lady, uh… what's your name?"

"Tallulah," she replied grudgingly. "Tallulah Silver."

He nodded. "Payton Rodgers. Now, unless you have a property title in hand, Miss Silver, you have no say in this matter."

"All of Bayou La Siryna once belonged to my people, the Choctaw. I'm not moving."

An uncharacteristic silence settled over the workplace. All the men had turned off their chain saws and regarded the intruder quizzically. A few were just plain getting an eyeful.

Payton had to admit the crazy woman was easy on the eyes—she was tall with lean muscles but all the right curves, long black hair and angular features. Her fierce don't-mess-with-me attitude was a characteristic some men found to be a welcoming challenge. Not that he was one of them. Nope. Give him a woman with a soft voice and gentle, feminine manner. Someone that didn't ask too many questions or make too many demands.

"Stay then. Suit yourself," he said, bluffing, as he climbed back into the cab and gunned the engine. He thrust the gears and moved forward a couple of feet.

Damn it to hell. She stayed rooted to the spot and regarded him defiantly, a smirk flirting at the edge of her full lips.

Payton sighed and jumped back out of the skidder. Heat flushed up his neck as the pack watched his defeat. "What do you want me to do?" he asked her, throwing up his hands. "You really gonna stand there all day?"

"As long as it takes."

Smart-ass woman. "You know you're wasting your time. We'll just work around you."

A flicker of uncertainty lit her dark brown eyes, and he felt momentarily guilty. Payton wasn't entirely unsympathetic to her cause. If anyone had the right to protest timber cutting, it was Native Americans. "We're only harvesting the wood," he explained, keeping his voice reasonable. "We'll plant new trees when the job is finished."

Tallulah lifted her chin. "I've seen what these crews do. You'll clear valuable hardwood, and when you leave, you'll replant only pine. Doing that destroys the wildlife habitat."

"The company we work for replants the same ratio of tree species as what we clear." This he could say with a clear conscience. He wouldn't do this work otherwise.

Miss High-and-Mighty only sniffed. "Like I'd believe you. Even if that were true, you're still disrupting our wildlife."

Payton shifted his feet. Yeah, he wasn't too wild about that, either. But if he didn't do it, someone else would. This was the employment his pack had chosen. In many ways, the job was perfect. Work in a transient crew a few months, and then move on. That way, no one had time to really get to know you and discover your big, hairy secret. And when trouble brewed with neighboring packs, you could always cut out for greener pastures. If he had twinges of guilt, that was his problem. A small price to pay for the pack's safety.

"Sorry you feel that way," he said stiffly. "But that doesn't change the fact that you aren't allowed to be here. It's dangerous."

"I have no fear of danger."

Because she was daft. He tried to appeal to her sense of self-preservation. "You might get sliced with a chain saw or run over by heavy equipment. You see all of us in hard hats and goggles? There's a reason for it."

Tallulah shrugged.

Maybe an appeal to her dignity would do the trick.

"Leave now, or the police will come out here and forcibly remove you," he threatened.

She didn't blink. "They can try."

He caught movement in his peripheral vision as Matt strolled over. Great, she'd make him look like an idiot in front of his alpha.

"Is there a problem?" Matt asked in his wry, quiet way. He signaled the others to get back to work, and a loud buzzing returned to the scene.

"Yes. I've got a problem with you destroying these trees." Tallulah tossed her mane of black hair and raised her voice over the whir of the chain saws. "Some of them have stood for decades."

"They're coming down," Matt said firmly. "Unless you have a court order to stop us."

She flushed. "I don't. Not yet. This project sure was kept on the down-low. I didn't know about it until I happened to drive past and heard the noise."

"I suggest you protest this through the court system," he murmured.

"By then, it will be too late," she spat out. "All the trees will be cut."

Matt didn't respond, but his powerful, firm energy was like a force of nature. Being the alpha came naturally to him.

Tallulah turned her attention from Matt and shot Payton a daggered look with narrowed eyes. "I'll be back," she promised. "And I won't be alone."

Payton removed his hard hat and ran a hand through his hair. He nodded at Tallulah, but she'd turned away, her spine ramrod straight as she made long, purposeful strides toward the county road.

Of course she'd return. What fun this job was shaping up to become. The long, hot summer stretched before him, full of conflict with the locals, high heat and humidity and increased guilt over the destruction of yet more land.

He wasn't the only one watching her ass sway in angry strides to her car. Eli, one of the ground cutters, approached and nudged his side. "What a looker. You get her number?"

Payton snorted. "I reckon she'd rather spit on me than exchange phone numbers."

"Oh, I don't know about that," Eli said with a slow drawl. "Where there's sparks, there's chemistry."

Huh. More like "where there's smoke, there's fire." And an opportunity to get burned again when it came time to pick up and leave again for the next job, the next town. No thank you.

Chapter 2

Dark clouds grayed the sky, and thunder rumbled through the woods. Fat, splatting raindrops dripped from magnolias and pines.

Tallulah didn't care. The increased gales cooled her hot skin and made her restless, hungry for action. Wisps would be out this evening—the storm energy called to their chaotic, wild nature. For the past week, they'd been more active. So had the Ishkitini, as they'd hooted and fluttered in the treetops, ever watchful, looking for an opportunity to swoop in and slash with their sharp talons.

It wasn't her imagination. Her brother, Tombi, and the rest of the hunters felt it, too. They'd be joining her during the next full moon's hunting. For now, they were busy with new lives, new loves. Tallulah tamped down the jealous twinges. She'd had a shot at domesticity last year when Chulah, a lifelong friend and hunter, had proposed marriage. She'd even had second thoughts about turning him down, but then he'd fallen for a fairy, and that was the end of that.

It was all for the best. No one could ever compare to Bo, and second best wasn't fair to anyone.

Whoosh.

Tallulah ducked and loaded her slingshot in one swift movement—but not before a talon swiped the side of her neck. Ignoring the pain, she released the stone. It thudded against flesh, and a lump of brown-and-gray feathers hit the ground.

Excellent. But the damn owl had got in a lick. Tallulah carefully touched the scrape and then examined her fingers, sticky with blood. Not too bad. Might not even need stitches. She dug in her backpack and unwrapped an antiseptic wipe. The alcohol stung a bit as she placed it on the gash, but nothing like a future infection would hurt. Quickly, she bandaged the wound and continued into the woods.

Where the Ishkitini appeared, the will-o'-the-wisps were sure to follow. The night would not be wasted if she killed a wisp. Every defeat ensured a safer, more successful full-moon hunt. She attuned her senses to the night, amplifying sight, sound and smell, then inhaled the scents of wet leaves and damp soil, and even the coppery smell of her own blood, which left a metallic taste in her throat.

Branches scraped bark. Little critters—squirrels, rabbits, mice—scrambled about the carpet of pine needles and the prickly underbrush of saw palmettos and stunted shrubs. Tallulah's vision adjusted to the gathering darkness, and she unerringly kept to the path leading to the center of the forest.

A teal glow burst through a gap in the oaks—a wisp. Her breath quickened. She needed to get a little closer. Soundlessly, she padded from tree to tree, pausing to hide her body while she edged nearer.

The glow dazzled her eyes. The wisp floated a mere ten feet away. She'd been spotted.

Tallulah loaded the slingshot.

It's useless, the negative whisper echoed in her mind. She had come way too close to the wisp. Close enough that it could invade her thoughts, inducing despair and misery and hopelessness. The wisps thrived on human suffering. It made them stronger, more deadly.

Death is imminent. Don't fight it.

No way. Tallulah's arm drew back the slingshot band, ready to strike.

Join Bo.

Her lungs squeezed, and her throat painfully tightened, as if a boa constrictor were wrapped around her chest. Her breath grew harsh, and her biceps quivered and strained on the band.

You know you want to see him again. It would be so easy. Give in.

Bo. It dared mention his name. She stared at the center of the wisp, where the blue-green heart pulsed. Where the imprisoned spirit lived its miserable existence. Because that's what wisps did. They killed humans and trapped their souls inside their parasitic bodies. That's what they had done to Bo—until she had killed the wisp host and set Bo free.

Bo was dead, but at least he'd passed over into the After Life.

"You lie," she growled harshly. She could never be with Bo again. Not in this life.

Hot, angry tears burned her eyes, but Tallulah got off her shot. Then another and another. Stones whizzed through the air at top speed.

The wisp collapsed upon itself, gray smoke from its dead form carried up to the skies by the storm's wind. Tallulah swiped at her eyes, wanting to see the soul's release. It was one of the few pleasures of being a shadow hunter.

From the dying, gray ash, the teal heart transformed to a small, pure white spirit, as tiny as the flick of a cigarette lighter. The trapped soul took wing, flying up to the After Life. Tallulah leaned against the nearest tree, watching. Praying. It was a sacred moment. A shame that April, the fairy, wasn't here. April had the ability to communicate with and identify the released souls. Whoever this soul belonged to, Tallulah wished it Godspeed on its journey to reunite with ancestors and loved ones.

Before Tallulah could pack her slingshot away, a chilling cry rent the air—the unmistakable cry of an animal in the throes of death. Once heard, it was never forgotten. Tallulah shoved off the tree, instantly wary, and tried to pinpoint the location. Such was nature— one moment divine, the next moment a brutal kill.

The question in her mind wasn't figuring out the kind of victim, but rather identifying the size and ferocity of the predator. Was she in danger?

Judging from the small size of the victim and the distance of the killing, probably not. She turned to go home. One Ishkitini, one wisp and one wound were enough for a day's work. And what an aggravating day it had been, right from the beginning when she drove to work and witnessed the trees being destroyed.

Payton's image flashed in her mind's eye. The challenging spark in his smoky gray eyes, the power of his lithe body... Not that she was interested in someone employed in that despicable occupation. Besides, she wanted a man like Bo—kind and sensitive and understanding. Domineering men like Payton held no charm.

So why was she thinking of him? Impatiently, Tallulah wiped Payton's image from her thoughts and quickened her step. If she hurried, she'd arrive at her cabin before the worst of the storm was unleashed.

The death cries continued. Nature was a cruel bitch, she mused. As quickly as they had begun, the pitiful squeals stopped—it was dead and done, and the knot in her shoulders relaxed. She might be used to the ways of the wild, but it didn't mean her heart was immune to its violence.

A crack of thunder rumbled, and she upped her pace to a light jog. Her mind calmed and jumped ahead to trivial matters—what to fix for dinner and what TV show to watch afterward. Another exciting evening alone.

Tallulah rounded a bend in the trail, only to find the wolfish creature from the night before blocking her path, twenty feet ahead.

She stilled and drew a sharp breath. It came with no warning. Perhaps she wouldn't have been caught unawares if she hadn't let her attention drift. *Focus.* That was the number-one rule of the shadow hunter—a basic tenet to avoid spirits and predators before you became their next meal.

Blood dripped from the beast's gaping mouth, and

bits of rabbit carcass hung from its back molars. Mystery solved as to the screams—the thing should be sated. Its eyes focused on her neck, and she touched the crusty bandage. Could it smell her blood from that distance? Anger replaced fear in pounding waves of adrenaline. She was bigger and smarter than the animal, and she was a skilled hunter with a weapon. If anyone had the upper hand, it was her.

"You want a piece of this again?" She withdrew her slingshot from her backpack.

The animal growled, but hung its head in submission. The cagey fellow remembered *that*, all right.

"Go on—git!" she yelled, and the beast snarled, but turned and trotted off.

Were there others like him? Was she in the midst of its territory? Impulsively, Tallulah followed it from a respectful distance, using all her tracking skills to move as soundlessly as possible. It never even looked back.

Curiosity killed the cat, you know.

She ignored the internal warning voice. In her experience, knowledge was king. Twice in two days, this animal had confronted her, and she vowed to learn more about it. Kill or be killed. That was the lesson of the wild.

Close to the end of the trail, the animal veered off the path into a clearing, a wide-open area recently planted with cotton. The quarter moon easily highlighted its movement down rows of ankle-deep greenery, allowing her to watch from a greater distance. Across the field, bright lights shone through windows at Jeb's old farmhouse. He'd vacated it last year and put it up for sale, preferring to live closer to town now that he was older and his sons had taken on most of the farming duties.

News to her that someone had bought the old place. It was large and old-fashioned, a wooden, three-story behemoth that over the decades had been a temporary home for many field hands. Nearly every house light blazed, and over a dozen cars and trucks were parked in the front yard.

The animal cut a direct path across the cotton field, straight to the back porch door. Was it a danger to anyone who might step outside for a smoke or a bit of fresh air? Tallulah jogged across the field, prepared to fight if needed, but the creature confidently climbed the back steps and nudged open the screen door with its broad snout.

Tallulah ran, blood pounding in her ears as loud as ocean waves crashing on shore. She'd never seen a wild animal so brazen, so indifferent to the danger posed by humans. At the edge of the property, she witnessed the animal squeeze into an extralarge doggie door and enter the farmhouse.

It was *in* the freaking house. She panted, hands on hips, trying to make sense of what she'd seen. The animal was *not* a dog. It more closely resembled a coyote. Actually…okay, she admitted to the fantastic notion, it appeared to be a wolf. It was much too large to be a coyote. Wolves weren't supposed to be in south Alabama, but she'd seen many stranger things in the bayou woods.

Her ears tingled, waiting for the inevitable shrieks and commotion from inside the house, but silence reigned in the woods.

She'd heard wolves were cagey, but this was ridiculous. A wild animal in the house was bound to make noise, would elicit surprise from the residents. Obvi-

ously, people were home—unless they had gone out
and left all the lights on.

Yes, that could explain it. Curiosity propelled her
forward until she crept in the hedges against the farmhouse. A jumble of male voices sounded in a back room
as she passed, and she raised up from her crouch by the
open window. Just a quick second was all she needed,
and she ducked back down in the hedge before she could
be spotted.

The den was packed with over a dozen men. Some
playing cards, some watching TV and a couple playing pool.

Not a wolf in sight. And no commotion among the
men.

Tallulah tiptoed to the driveway, determined to learn
as much as possible. Heat fanned across her face. Peep-
ing into windows wasn't exactly her normal modus operandi. *It was necessary. The wolf is a danger, and my
duty is to protect*, she insisted to herself. Still, the curiosity remained, and she decided to see if she recognized any of the cars.

A hodgepodge of pickup trucks and beater cars were
parked haphazardly in the front yard. Crouching, she
went from vehicle to vehicle. All of them had Montana
tags. Transient farm workers arrived from all over, but
usually they were from nearby states, and quite a few
came from elsewhere in Alabama.

Now what? Tallulah stood, debating her options. Perhaps a ruse could gain her entry. She'd knock at the
door and claim to be looking for her lost dog. But that
wouldn't be too smart. She was no frail flower, but a
single female approaching a group of strange men at

night would be a dumb move. No, best to leave and gather more information later.

A screen door creaked open.

Holy crap. Tallulah dropped to the ground behind a truck, and her heart thudded against her chest as she listened intently. Footsteps plodded down the front porch steps. What if this was his truck and he wanted to drive? She furtively looked around, seeking other avenues of cover. Fingers crossed that the guy just came out for a bit of fresh air or to smoke a cigarette.

Tallulah wrapped her energy tightly around her body, somewhat cloaking her scent—just in case the wolf made an appearance. It was a form of protection for the shadow hunters in seeking and destroying their prey.

Gravel and weeds crunched underfoot. Damn it, the man was headed straight in her direction. Another couple of steps and she was toast.

Danger.

The smell of human was faint but totally out of place, and Payton's wolf senses shifted to high alert. The scent teased his brain. He'd smelled it before—recently, too. Who the hell would be out in this remote area at this time of night? Someone up to no good.

No need to call the rest of the pack. Whoever the prowler was, he'd no doubt take off before backup arrived.

Payton unerringly followed his nose. Adrenaline pumped through his veins as he geared up for a fight. Danger had seemingly followed them for hundreds of miles. His fingers twitched at his sides, and he flexed them into his palms, his nails digging into calloused flesh. If he needed to shift to wolf form, so be it.

The human smell emanated from behind Darryl's pickup. The scent grew stronger—it was woodsy and green. His memory strained, almost grasping where he'd encountered it before. Another step closer, and Payton picked up the tart zing of citrus mixed with the other notes. Recognition slammed into his consciousness.

Well, I'll be damned. He walked swiftly to the rear of the truck, where the human huddled into a ball on the ground. "What the hell are you doing on my property, Tallulah Silver?" he demanded.

Her head slowly rose, eyes flashing in surprise. She stood and brushed the front of her jeans. "You found me." Her brow furrowed, as if she were puzzled. "How did you manage that?"

"Answer my question." No need to try to be friendly or placate the woman now. "Were you perhaps putting sugar in the gas tanks? Nails in the tires?"

Her chin jutted forward. "Of course not. Why would I vandalize your property? I'm no criminal."

"To run us off from our job." Conservationists could be a passionate lot. Militant, even. And she'd been extremely confrontational this morning.

"Don't be ridiculous," she countered. The arrogance in her manner had returned. "I was out for a walk and got spooked when you came outside. I'll be on my way now."

That woman, spooked? He snorted. "You're lying."

"Believe what you will."

She turned away, and he grabbed the handle of the backpack slung across her shoulders. Damn, it looked heavy, as if it were loaded with rocks. "Not so fast. What you got in there?"

"None of your business."

She tried jerking out of his grasp, but he held firm. "It *is* my business when you're sneaking around on my land."

"You got a property title? 'Cause I'm pretty sure this land belongs to Jeb. Not you." A nasty smile curled her full lips.

She'd cunningly boomeranged his own words from their earlier encounter. "A technicality. We're renting, which gives me a reason to legally be here. Now, why are you slinking around our home?"

"I told you already." With surprising strength, she pulled away from his grasp. "If you want to call the cops or something, be my guest. I happen to know the sheriff."

Terrific. She had connections with some Bubba local law enforcement dude. And trouble with the authorities was the last thing they needed. The locals here could call the cops in Montana, and information might get exchanged about a series of unsolved murders. He and his pack were innocent of wrongdoing, but it was as if a toxic miasma clouded their reputations.

"We can settle this between the two of us, no need for the police," he replied. "For the last time, what are you doing here?"

"And if I don't change my answer?"

Maddening. What a shrew. Her eyes flashed, and her chest rose and fell with her hot-tempered breathing. Ah, but she was sexy as all get-out. His gaze focused in on the cleavage exposed by her deep, V-cut shirt. A leather-fringed and beaded necklace, with some sort of woven charm, settled in the space between her rounded breasts. He couldn't help it. Payton reached a hand out, as if his bones were made of steel and the necklace a magnet pulling him closer. He touched it, his fingers lightly brushing her skin.

Heat sparked his fingertips and spread throughout his body, and he dropped the necklace and stepped backward. For a brief instant, he caught a returning fire banked in Tallulah's widened eyes—until animosity again took its place.

"What's that on your necklace?" he asked, trying to break the tension.

"A miniature dream catcher I wove. And don't you dare touch me again like that."

Did he imagine it, or did her voice sound a tiny bit husky? His desire doubled, and an erection began to strain against his jeans. Here was an opportunity. He dared all right.

Payton stepped closer to her, their bodies inches apart. She didn't retreat.

"You felt it, too, didn't you? A spark between us when we touched?"

She skirted the question. "I loathe everything about the work you do."

"But I'm not my job. I'm a man and I find you...very intriguing."

"Don't you mean *maddening* instead of *intriguing*?"

"Flip sides of the same coin. Can we call a truce?"

Tallulah crossed her arms. "I'm not one to back away from my principles, not for you, not for any man. Besides, there's something strange going on around here."

"Only strange thing from where I stand is that I found you slinking around in the dark with only a stupid story to explain your presence."

"It's not stupid. I often walk the woods in the evening," she insisted.

"Ridiculous and unsafe. Perhaps I can coax the truth from you," he said hoarsely. He bent his head, and she still didn't budge.

A sure sign she felt the same chemistry as he did.

Because of the transient nature of his job, he didn't allow himself to become too emotionally invested in any woman. But physically…that was another matter. What would this woman be like as a lover? Passionate, no doubt. If he could put up with her saucy tongue.

His mouth found hers.

Despite his calculated move, doubt assailed him. What the hell was he doing?

She pressed her full lips against his and groaned softly. The sound undid him—it had been too long since he'd been with a woman. He placed his hands on the sides of her waist and drew her even closer. Damn, she felt good. No, not good…great. Fantastic. They'd be perfect in bed together.

"Stop." Tallulah stepped out of his arms.

Payton blinked at the unexpected emptiness and his hands fell to his sides. Even for him, he'd assumed too much, too quickly. He'd been carried away with passion from a mere kiss. What was the matter with him? "Sorry. Too much, too fast?"

She regarded him for several heartbeats. "You don't know me. You don't even like me."

No denying that. He gave her a lopsided smile. "You're growing on me."

Her mouth trembled, as if she were about to smile, but she pressed her lips into a frown. "I have my own doubts about you, too. Am I crazy, or did a wolf enter your farmhouse about ten minutes ago?"

Chills doused the fever her body had created, and he

became aware of the rain running in rivulets down his arms and face. Tallulah's words plunged him back into reality. Apprehension replaced desire in a heartbeat.

"A wolf?" he repeated stupidly, buying time. "Not supposed to be any wolves in this part of the country."

She crossed her arms. "Exactly. That's what I thought. But I know what I saw."

So someone had slipped out into the woods and shifted. A violation of the new pack rules. As a precaution, Matt had ordered that they only shift in pairs. That way, if one of them developed the lycanthropic fever, it would be impossible to hide the symptoms of their bloodlust from each other while in wolf form. Yet someone had violated the alpha's edict. Why?

"You thought wrong," he stated flatly, trying to create doubt and throw her off. "A wild animal wouldn't let you get that close. It'd smell you a mile off."

How had she managed to see this? Now that he thought of it, her human smell had been faint when he stepped outside. It should have been much stronger. Tallulah held his gaze, unflinching and challenging. He rubbed his chin, studying her exotic beauty. She was a mystery, a most unusual female. "I've never met a woman quite like you."

"No," she quickly agreed. "You have not. Now about that wolf—"

"There is no wolf."

"Was."

"Wasn't."

The rain picked up, and leaves rustled in the heightened wind. They stared at each other, bristling like wary dogs.

"We appear to have reached an impasse," he said at

last. Apparently, there was no changing her mind with mere words.

Tallulah held up a hand and stared up at the rain. "For now. I'll be on my way."

He couldn't let her escape so quickly. *Know your enemy.* He had to win her trust, find out more about her. Ensure her silence if needed. "Wait. We started off on the wrong foot. It's ugly out here, let me make it up to you by giving you a lift home."

Tallulah hesitated. Was his presence so distasteful now that she'd rather wander home—alone at night—in the rain? "C'mon," he said cajolingly. "Don't be stupid."

Her chin jutted forward in a now-familiar gesture, and she opened her mouth—no doubt the precursor to some sharp retort. Calling her stupid was no way to win her over. Time for damage control. Payton flashed his most charming smile. "What kind of gentleman would let a lady walk home at night in a storm?"

"How about the same gentleman who called a lady *stupid*?"

He bowed gallantly. "My bad. Please let me drive you home, or I'll worry about you all night."

"Yeah, right," she said with a snort. "You're not exactly my idea of a knight in shining armor."

He kept his smile in place, although it took great effort. "I have a feeling your standards run extremely high. Besides, no one could mistake you for a damsel in distress."

"Damn right. I can take care of myself."

With that, she turned on her heel and started down the gravel driveway, her back ramrod straight. Same posture as that morning when she'd left the work site in a huff. The rain picked up, saturating her hair and clothes, making her appear sleek and even more sexy. Tallulah didn't even hurry her pace. A woman used to the elements, impervious to nature's nuances.

It appealed to his inner, primal wolf. That hidden part of himself that was also at one with the night and the land. His pulse raced as he imagined the two of them in some hidden forest glade, naked and wet, making love under a full moon as rain caressed their bodies.

He blinked, coming out of his hormonal trance. Damn, if she didn't do the weirdest things to his mind. Tallulah was already at the end of the drive and stepping out onto the road. Payton ran a hand through his soaked hair and dug the truck keys out of his pocket. Quickly, he jumped in the truck, cranked up the engine and eased out of the tangle of vehicles.

Tallulah never even turned around as he pulled up beside her on the road. He unrolled the passenger side window.

"Get in," he barked.

She kept her face forward, her angular profile set in stone. "No, thank you."

Son of a bitch. Payton shifted to Park, scrambled from the truck and marched in front of Tallulah, blocking her direct path. Just as she had blocked him this morning on the skidder. "C'mon, Tallulah. This is ridiculous."

It wasn't just a matter of getting wet. It was dark, and a member of the pack had violated house rules by roaming in wolf form, so who knew if others were doing the same, and damn it, he couldn't stand seeing a woman walk the streets alone at night. Even one as strong and stubborn as Tallulah.

A sudden thought floored him. "You aren't afraid of getting in the truck with me, are you?"

"'Course not." Her chin lifted.

Payton hid his smile and opened the passenger door. "Well then," he said, gesturing her to enter. If he guessed correctly, she wasn't one to back down from a challenge.

"I guess I could use a lift," she said ungraciously, her mouth twisting. "If you're sure."

Tallulah climbed in the old Chevy and he shut the door, hurrying to the driver's side and getting out of the pouring rain.

She sat as far from him as possible, her body jammed against the door. "Does the entire timber crew live out here?" she asked with a nod toward the farmhouse.

Payton shot her a sideways glance as he shifted into Drive and pulled away. Evidently, he wasn't the only one fishing for more information. "We do. It's more convenient that way. What about you? Do you live alone?"

"Yes."

"No, *Mister* Silver?" he asked.

"Only my twin brother. No husband and no father." She faced him, direct as usual. "You married?"

"Nope." He could be as circumspect as she could.

They came to a stop sign. "Right or left?" he asked. "I need directions."

"Take a right. I live about seven miles down this road."

"Pretty long walk you took tonight," he observed. And she was willing to walk that distance alone in the rain? Just to spite him?

"I'm in excellent health," she said icily.

He surreptitiously glanced at the shirt clinging to her full breasts, the toned biceps of her arms, her long, lean legs. What he wouldn't give to see her without clothing, to explore every inch of her fit, golden body. Something about her drove him wild, made him as sex-obsessed as a teenager hyped up on testosterone.

The windshield wipers beat out a steady rhythm, emphasizing the charged silence between them. Tallulah didn't speak again for several minutes, and when she did, it was a curt instruction. "This is it. Slow down and turn on the next dirt road to your right."

The unpaved road twisted and curved for at least a quarter mile. A wooden cabin appeared, surrounded by magnolias and oaks. Small, but not too rustic.

"Nice place."

Her mouth curved into a genuine smile, the first one he'd seen. It transformed her into a radiant beauty. "Thanks. Tombi, my brother, built it. He's a carpenter."

One of her hands was already on the handle. She was ready to jump out and slip away into the dark night.

"Can I see you sometime?" he asked quickly, before Tallulah could make her escape. For all her bravery, she was on the skittish side. Somehow, he needed to earn her trust, discover if she harbored secrets, as he did.

She gave him a considering look. "It's a small town. We can't help but run in to each other again."

Ruefully, he watched as she slammed the door shut, strode purposefully to the cabin and never once looked back. So much for making headway by acting charming and gallant. At least he knew where she lived, and that was a start.

Payton turned the truck around and went back down the driveway. *You betcha I'll run in to you, Miss Tallulah Silver. We have unfinished business.*

Chapter 3

Tallulah scrambled out of her vehicle, clutching her coffee cup, and joined her brother and over a dozen of their friends—mostly fellow shadow hunters—where they gathered by the timber site.

Dawn had barely broken, but the logging crew would be arriving soon. She approached her twin. "What did you find out about this property?" she asked with no preamble.

"It belongs to Hank and Sashy Potts. Rumor is that they're hoping to sell it to developers interested in building a strip mall and a storage warehouse on the outskirts of the bayou. They're making it more attractive to them by clearing the land. And in the process, the couple are making a huge profit selling the timber."

"This is Hank's doing," she said darkly. "Always was one to sell out for a quick buck."

"You're right about that. Sashy's a decent sort of person, though." Tombi raked a hand through his long black hair. "We might make more headway putting pressure on them than harassing the timber crew. Whether we like it or not, they're just doing their job."

She sipped her coffee and gazed at the gashed landscape. "No reason we can't attack it from both ends."

"Can't be out here every day protesting," Chulah said. "We all have jobs, including you."

"There's always the weekends," she muttered.

Several vehicles pulled onto the side of the road, including a faded red Chevy truck. Payton and the other workers had arrived.

She watched as he jumped out of his truck and sauntered over their way, along with Matt, the crew supervisor. Her stomach gave an eager, betraying little lurch. If she'd hoped seeing Payton again in the broad light of day would make her come to her senses, she was dead wrong. If anything, the dawn's light shining on his ash-blond hair and the hard flint of gunmetal-gray eyes made her toes curl. None of last night's good humor or desire showed in his face today. In fact, he didn't look at all pleased to see her. Had she really kissed this foreboding man last night? Felt his desire pressing against her abdomen?

Matt spoke first. "What are you all doing here?"

"Protesting the desecration of our land," she said quickly. "I told you I'd be back with more people."

"You got a permit for this demonstration?" Matt scowled, ignoring her as he stared at Tombi.

Two natural-born leaders seemed to recognize each other on some primitive level. Must be some testosterone signals in the air.

"Don't need one," Tombi said levelly. "This strip of land we're standing on is public property. We're not on your work site."

"Make sure it stays that way," Matt said with a growl. "We don't take kindly to intruders on our property." He pinned her with a direct stare.

Tallulah's gaze flew to Payton. So he'd told Matt she'd been at the farmhouse last night.

She drew her shoulders back and regarded Matt with a level stare. "If that's a threat, you don't scare me."

"What's all this about?" Tombi asked, puzzled.

"Payton caught her skulking behind one of our vehicles at the house last night. If there's any damage to our vehicles or property, we know where to look."

"It's not your house, it belongs to Jeb Johnson," she said hotly. "And I'd never destroy—"

Tombi cut her off. "None of us are going to hurt your stuff. That's not our way."

Matt huffed. "See that you don't." He aimed another glare at Tallulah, then stalked away.

"Well, that's a fun start to the morning," she drawled, staring accusingly at Payton.

"He has a right to know what's going on."

"I'd like someone to clue *me* into what's happening," Tombi insisted.

Payton raised a brow. "And you are…?"

"Tombi Silver, Tallulah's brother."

Payton extended a hand. "Nice to meet you. Tallulah spoke of you last night."

Her twin shot her a quizzical look as he shook hands with Payton.

"We met yesterday when she stood in front of my skidder while I was doing my job," Payton continued.

His manner was calm and friendly. Damn him. "Then we ran in to each other again last night when I found her hiding behind one of our vehicles at the house."

Her cheeks flamed. He was painting her in the worst possible light.

"Is that true?" Tombi asked her. His face grew rigid, which meant he was getting riled.

"Yes, but—"

"It won't happen again," Tombi said to Payton.

"You can't speak for me," she sputtered. Her brother might be the leader of the shadow hunters, but he had no right to act so bossy.

Payton nodded. "Thanks. Much appreciated. We'll just put this unpleasantness behind us."

He faced her, his mouth upturned in one corner. She couldn't tell if he was smirking or was genuinely amused at her expense. He held out his hand and she glanced down at it like it was a snake. She was conscious of all the protestors watching the little drama. If she refused to shake Payton's hand, everyone would accuse her of being surly and unreasonable. And that meant the protests to the land destruction might cease.

Reluctantly, she placed her hand in his and then quickly tried to pull back.

Payton maintained a tight grip. "I'm still interested in that date we talked about, if your social calendar happens to be free."

Someone in the crowd snickered.

Tallulah seethed. He made it sound like they were already an item. Well, she *had* kissed him, but she hadn't agreed to a date.

Payton let go of her hand and smiled genially at

Tombi. "Maybe we could all get together for dinner sometime and talk."

"I'd like that," Tombi agreed at once. "Matter of fact, if you're free tonight, my wife and I would love to have you over to our place for supper. About seven?"

"Great, thanks." Payton gave her a triumphant wave. "Pick you up about quarter 'til the hour. I remember the way."

Tallulah rounded on her brother. "I can't believe you just did that."

"I think it's time we all took our leave," Chulah said. "I've worked on Hank's motorcycle a time or two and know him fairly well. I'll see if I can talk to him about the land. Find out for sure what's going on."

"We'll just stay a bit longer," one of the protestors said. "Make a general nuisance of ourselves and see if we can stop their cutting for the rest of the day."

"Why did you invite him to dinner?" she continued. "I don't want to see him."

Tombi raised a brow. "You sure about that? I saw the way you looked at him when he walked over to you."

A telling warmth flooded her cheeks. "Yeah, well, that doesn't have anything to do with the issue. The fact is, he's destroying our land and—"

Tombi raised a hand. "Did you or did you not go over to their farmhouse without permission?"

"Yes, but—"

"We'll talk about it at dinner tonight. Okay? I've got a busy day scheduled with work." His face softened. "Listen, sis. I think it's terrific you're interested in seeing someone again. I know how tough it's been on you with Bo's death and then that mess with Hanan.

This Payton seems like a nice enough guy. Give him a chance."

With that, he strode away and left her standing, mouth ajar. What had just happened here? The roar of a machine erupted nearby and she glanced toward the sound.

Payton raised a hand and waved at her, a grin splitting his face.

Jillian slanted Payton a long, assessing look as she stood by the stove, stirring soup made with fresh vegetables from the local market. The lone female of their pack, she kept their various residencies running smoothly and was indispensable in keeping them organized.

Inwardly, he groaned. Since she'd already seen him headed for the fridge, he continued on, brushing past her. A musky pheromone scent, a harbinger of desire, hovered close to her body like a horny aura.

He pretended not to notice as he poured a glass of iced tea and returned the pitcher to the refrigerator.

Jillian smiled tentatively. "Haven't seen much of you since we arrived in Alabama," she said.

"Been busy," he mumbled, knowing the excuse was lame.

Her smile faltered. "Are you upset with me about anything? Have I done something wrong?"

"'Course not. Been busy settling in with the new job. That's all."

Damn. How was he going to get out of this without hurting her feelings? Sure, they'd shared a few experimental kisses and more over the last couple months, but she didn't excite him. Not like Tallulah. Damn it to hell. He desperately wished he desired Jillian. After all, she was the alpha's sister. Mating with her would be acceptable within the pack. As she was the only female wolf in the group, several of the males would jump at the chance to mate with Jillian.

He was a fool.

Payton took a long swallow of tea. He needed to find a tactful way to break it off, but he wasn't sure which would be worse—Jillian's hurt or Matt's anger.

"I made that stew you like and homemade bread to go with it," she said.

"Sorry, I've got plans for supper tonight."

"Plans?" she asked, her mouth slightly downturned. "What kind of plans?"

He suppressed a sigh. "With a couple of friends." Not a lie, but not the whole story, either. It was easier to avoid a confrontation. He kept hoping she'd get the message he wasn't interested, but Jillian was persistent.

"We've only been here a week. You sure make friends fast."

Did he imagine the disapproving note in her voice? He left every conversation with her feeling vaguely guilty.

"I'm a friendly kind of guy," he mumbled.

Russell winked at him from the hallway, and Payton scowled at his best friend. Nothing funny about the situation—just pure awkwardness. With another wink, his friend strolled into the kitchen.

"We've got a couple hours free this afternoon before you have to get ready for your date," Russell offered. "Let's take a stroll and go exploring."

"Date?" Jillian asked sharply. "I thought you said it was dinner with friends."

"A date with friends," he said grimly. Payton hurried out of the kitchen, rolling his eyes at Russell, but still thankful for the diversionary tactic he'd provided. Perfect opportunity to bail out of the heavy talk with Jillian.

"A walk sounds great," he replied, trying to keep the relief out of his voice. "Later, Jillian."

They beat a hasty exit out the back door. Heat slammed into every pore of his body, and he sighed. "Thanks, man. Although you didn't have to mention the date part."

Russell chuckled. "Thought I'd give her a little wake-up call. Been in that situation before. You want her to get the message, but at the same time you have to tread easy with her feelings or risk Matt's wrath."

"Like I didn't know that," he muttered. How the hell was he supposed to manage that?

Guilt twisted his gut. He'd never meant to encourage Jillian. He hadn't discouraged her, either, if he was being honest. He'd hoped that one day his feelings would change, or that he'd want to settle down with an acceptable mate. Which was totally unfair to Jillian. A beautiful woman, and a shapeshifter like himself, shouldn't have to wait for anyone. She deserved more.

Payton followed Russell across the cotton field. His friend was more familiar with the new place since Payton hadn't had much time for exploring.

"This job is turning out to be a pain in the ass," Russell said. "For such a small town, they've had lots of people show up protesting our work."

Payton hid a grin. Tallulah had shown up that morning with almost a dozen people, peacefully protesting the tree clearing. And by *peaceful*, he didn't mean *pleasant.* It was as if the momentary closeness of last night had never happened. Tallulah had been as abrasive as at their first meeting, frowning, snapping and making a general nuisance of herself at every opportunity. Work had slowed to a snail's pace, and Matt had decided they might as well take off early. "They'll get tired of protesting after a few days," Matt had predicted.

Payton wasn't so sure. The others might tire, but he guessed Tallulah was made of sterner stuff.

"Do you ever feel bad about the work we do? I mean, we do destroy the land."

If he couldn't talk about this with his best friend, who could he talk to?

Russell shrugged. "Nah. If we don't do it, someone else will."

That reasoning didn't entirely soothe his conscience, even though he'd used that excuse as well. Plenty of wrongs had been committed throughout history with the same justification.

"What about vet school? You used to dream of being a veterinarian when we were in high school."

"Idle dreams. I didn't have the grades to cut it," Russell said. "You know me."

"Well enough to know that if you'd applied yourself to your studies, you'd have made it. Always were smart as hell."

Unlike himself. The only thing he'd ever shown aptitude for was mechanical tinkering.

"You don't have to work a skidder all your life." Russell peered at him intently. "There's room in the pack if you want to leave the lumber crew and try something you like better."

Payton bristled. "What's that supposed to mean? That I'm not needed?"

"Relax, dude. I'm saying there's enough men in the timber crew that you can branch out on your own."

Something of Payton's reluctance must have shown on his face, and Russell shook his head. "I get it. You feel like you owe Matt and the others for taking you in. But you don't. No one will think less of you for leaving the crew."

"Maybe not you. Others might."

Russell had been a true friend when Payton first entered the pack, one of the few to accept him unconditionally. His parents had died in a terrible boat accident when he was a teenager, and he'd been left alone in the world until the pack brought him in. Given his father's murderous past, Payton would always be grateful that Matt took him under his wing, and for Russell's immediate friendship.

"Doesn't matter what anyone else thinks," Russell insisted. "As long as Matt understands, that's all that counts."

"All right, already. I'll consider it one day."

They both knew it was a lie. Payton avoided anything that made it appear he'd deliberately distance himself from the pack. He would *not* be like his father.

As they hiked the small trail from the field and into the woods, Payton unwound, soothed by the unique beauty of the bayou. Thanks to the shade from a canopy of trees, the temperature cooled considerably.

"It's way different than out west, but it's pretty amazing here," Payton commented. "Has a spooky feel with all that Spanish moss and those gnarled cypress trees."

"It's different, all right. Wait 'til you see what I found close by."

Curious, Payton followed. A few twists and turns later, Russell stopped. "This is it."

Feathers and ribbons hung from low-lying branches in about a twelve-foot-wide diameter that was bordered by seashells. The sandy soil was raked clean with precisely placed crystals sparkling in the ground like unearthed treasure. In the center was a pile of rocks and timber for a fire.

Payton stepped inside the circle, feeling as if he was violating sacred land. He touched a faded ribbon and inspected the hanging artifacts. "Dream catchers," he said, remembering the miniature one Tallulah had worn.

"I know *that*," Russell scoffed. "But what are they doing out here in the middle of the woods? It's weird. And kinda creepy."

Strange, yes. But the feel of the area was peaceful, if a bit melancholy.

"Beats me what the purpose of this place could be."

He walked around the edge of the circle, examining the crystal grids and the dozens of hanging dream catchers. A bright red ribbon caught his eye. It had not yet faded like the others, and the turkey feather fastened beside the ribbon looked new. Payton held it, turning it in different directions. A small patch of beadwork on the back, only a couple of inches long, read For Bo, Love Always, Tallulah.

His breath caught. Who was Bo? His palm fisted over the beaded message. His Tallulah was in love. Jealousy, then shock, washed through him. Tallulah wasn't *his* anything. He dropped his hand to his side and looked at the area with new eyes. Was this some lovers' tryst, far from prying eyes? If so, why the secrecy? Why the elaborate decorations?

"Hey, found something," Russell called. "Come here and check out this carving."

Payton strode to where Russell stood by a massive oak, fingers tracing a primitive message—RIP Bohpoli.

Bohpoli—*Bo*?

Of course. This wasn't a secret meeting place for lovers. It was a shrine to a dead lover.

"What's a Bohpoli?" Russell asked.

"I suspect it's a person's name. That person must have died here. You know, like you see crosses by the side of roads, marking where loved ones died in a car accident."

"Makes sense. But the survivors have gone a little over the top, don't you think?"

Payton took in the meticulous care and attention, at the various states of decline in the dream catchers' ribbons and feathers. Tallulah had loved long, and loved deeply. Underneath that prickly exterior was a highly sensitive woman. One that maddened and intrigued him all at once.

"Over the top?" Payton said, aware of a loneliness he didn't know existed until that moment. "Maybe. But it would be damn nice to have someone love you like that."

"Amen, brother. Amen."

Annie served everyone salad and dinner began.

Tallulah's normally reticent brother and Payton seemed to be getting along famously, chitchatting about motorcycles and places to see while in Bayou La Siryna—which weren't many unless you were into nature sights. Tallulah didn't see how a lumberjack could possibly appreciate natural settings.

"The wildlife sanctuary is open on Saturdays," Tombi said, helping himself to more salad.

"I don't think Payton's interested in wildlife." She smiled sweetly. "Considering how he's part of a team destroying their habitat every day."

"Disturbing the snakes and skeeters and possums? 'Cause that's all I've observed down here so far."

"We have deer and gators and yellowhammers…" She stopped at the grin on his face. Yep, she'd taken his bait and run with it. She laid down her fork. "It really doesn't bother you to cut down trees for a living?"

"Tallulah," Annie admonished gently.

Tombi shot her a warning look. "Payton's a guest in our house."

"It's okay." Payton set down his glass of tea. "I'll admit it bothers me a little. But it's honest, tax-paying work and I'm not ashamed of my job."

"At least you didn't make the excuse that if you didn't do it someone else would," she muttered.

"Well, there is that."

"Chulah spoke to Hank today," Tombi interrupted, taking the heat off Payton. "Hank said if the developers offered him a good deal on the land, he would take it. Can't blame a man for doing what he needs to with his own land."

"Don't you care about our woods? This could start a bad precedent."

"Hank and Sashy have two children starting college in a few years," Annie said quietly. "There's two sides to every story."

"I still don't like it," she insisted.

Annie stood and began collecting plates. "Hope you like pot roast and potatoes," she said to Payton.

"Love it."

Tallulah stood as well and gathered up her and Payton's plates, then followed Annie into the kitchen.

"Might want to go a little easier on your date," Annie said offhandedly.

"He's not my…oh, okay. I'll give him a pass for the evening. But I'm still going to protest what they're doing."

Annie pulled the roast out of the oven and set it on the counter. "Maybe that won't be needed. I think all we have to do is send April over to sweet-talk Sashy. Chulah's wife will convince her the deal is bad."

"That's actually a great idea," Annie agreed. "Sashy can get her husband to come around. All we need to do is ask April to wield her magic."

"Magic?" Payton stood in the doorway.

Tallulah and Annie exchanged a secret smile.

"So to speak," Annie said.

"What are you doing in here?" Tallulah asked bluntly. Was he trying to sneak up on them?

"Came to see if you needed any help."

Annie handed him a pair of kitchen gloves. "You can carry in this casserole dish if you'd like."

The sight of the tall, handsome lumberjack wearing kitchen gloves made Tallulah want to giggle. No, take that back. It was adorable. Melt-your-heart kind of cute. She grabbed the basket of rolls and followed him back to the dining room.

The rest of dinner proceeded smoothly and they left the cabin after another hour or so of après-dinner drinks and talking.

The warm glow on the drive home wasn't just from partaking of Tombi's excellent whiskey. The blond giant driving beside her had much to do with her good humor. She glanced at him, suddenly shy. "Glad we could set aside our differences for the evening."

He laid a hand on her left thigh. "I have high hopes for us."

She eyed his hand suspiciously. If Payton had high hopes about sleeping with her on a first date, he could think again.

At her cabin, he hurried to open her car door and escorted her to the front door.

The awkward moment had arrived. "Would you like to come in for coffee?"

He leaned an arm against the door and stared at her, his gray eyes so dark that the glints of blue in them were the subtle hue of an oiled, polished handgun. "Better not," he said gruffly. "You're much too tempting."

"I am?" Her voice was a whisper in the breeze.

"Very much so. First dates, I don't believe in anything more physical than a kiss."

She laughed.

"I'm serious."

Tallulah cocked her head to the side and studied his face. Yes, he meant what he'd said. She found it oddly endearing. Old-fashioned, chivalrous and sexy as all get-out. She stuck out a hand. "If you'd like we can just shake hands and call it a night."

"Not on your life."

He bent down and claimed her mouth, his tongue dancing with hers until she felt weak-kneed and fevered, never wanting it to end.

He drew back and then rested his forehead on hers. "I better go, Lulu."

"Okay," she agreed, still in a haze. She inserted the key into the lock opened the door and then swiftly turned back to him. "What did you call me?

"Lulu. *Tallulah* is a mouthful."

She frowned. "I don't like it. It sounds...undignified."

"It's adorable. It suits you."

"Humph." She shut the door and went to the window, watching as Payton drove off. The man could make her go from joy to irritation in two seconds. And passion? It always seemed to shimmer between them like a promise.

He began his slow descent to a night of freedom— no small feat considering that it was under the noses of over a dozen pack members. Even sleeping, their heightened senses were sensitive to noise. Ever so slowly, he climbed out of bed and padded barefoot out of the bedroom, down the hall and stairs and through the den. At the back door he paused for several minutes, ears alert for the slightest stirring of movement.

They would never understand.

The blood thirst churned his gut and would not be sated, no matter how hard he tried.

Satisfied that the rest of the pack was still asleep, he turned the doorknob with painstaking carefulness. He briefly considered shifting and using the doggie door, but it had an annoying flap that was surprisingly noisy. Carefully, he slipped into the dark cover of night. Even then, he had to exercise extreme caution. He scurried to the hedges at the side of the house and shape-shifted. Bone and sinew twisted and transformed skin to fur.

Two legs multiplied to four and his large paws padded on the soil. Belly close to the ground, he crept to the middle of the cotton field, just in case someone had wakened and chanced to look out a window.

His heart beat more rapidly, pulsing with the conflicting emotions of excitement and revulsion. And then he was free—racing into the woods, tongue panting, senses alive with the smell and sounds of the night.

It'll be okay. I'll find some small animal again. I can control the blood hunger.

Alabama was a new start. Never again would he kill a human. It was too dangerous for him and for the whole pack. If they ever caught on to his secret, his life would be over. From here on out, he'd content his bloodlust by feasting on small animals.

And so, once more, he was on the hunt.

He sniffed and tracked a scent, only to bungle the catch, as several hares took off when he came within a few feet of them. A lone wolf on the prowl was not the natural way of the hunt. They were pack animals for a reason, working together with patience and intelligence to track prey and target the weakest animal in a group.

He'd been outside for a good while now. Every minute he was out alone, he risked the others realizing his secret. But he couldn't go back without something to ease the stomach cramps caused by a lack of blood and flesh. He continued hunting, close to the cotton field, reduced to rumbling his snout through leaves to rouse field mice.

Not how he'd imagined his future. But to admit to the pack that he'd been infected by the fever was unthinkable. They'd haul him away to that so-called rehabilitation compound in the barren desert, although—

to his knowledge—no wolf had ever been cured. It would be a fenced-in existence with constant surveillance. A werewolf prison where all were condemned to the equivalent of a life-without-parole sentence.

He'd rather die.

Like a dog with a prize buried bone, he circled around to the outdoor memorial decorated with dream catchers. The feathers and ribbons fluttered like agitated ghosts. Just as well the bitch wasn't present. His chest still smarted from the rocks she'd flung. He'd been lucky not to suffer a serious injury.

A rustling emerged at the edge of the field, to his left. His ears twitched and his belly rumbled. This sounded like a large, clumsy animal. His mouth salivated at the faint whiff of human.

Torture—like a glass of cold water waved in front of a man dying of thirst. He hesitated. No harm in going to take a look. It could be one of the other pack members had also violated the new rule of no roaming alone in the woods. He crept toward the noise and the smell.

A gray-haired man with a long beard tossed dried corn kernels from a burlap sack. A hunter illegally enticing deer.

He didn't think. He didn't plan.

One moment he was an observer, and the next, he was flying down the field and taking a running leap at the old man. Teeth ripped into flesh, tearing open the jugular vein at the man's neck. Warm blood oozed down his throat as he greedily swallowed it. He was dizzy with elation and the hunger in his belly ceased its relentless gnaw.

It was done.

He sat back on his haunches, full and content. Until

he observed the dead man, broken and bleeding, his knapsack of corn spilled into the soil like gold nuggets.

Not again. What have I done?

He whimpered and backed away. When this body was discovered, the questions and accusations would begin anew. Disgust roiled in his gut. He hated himself, hated what he had become.

He slunk back to the farmhouse and briefly considered confessing to the pack. That was one way out of this hell his life had become over the last three years.

But shame and fear overcame good intentions. He couldn't live like a caged animal.

There would be no repeat offense, he vowed. Somehow, he would learn to control the lust for human blood.

Chapter 4

Saturdays were the longest days of the week. The Native American Cultural Center, where Tallulah worked, was closed, and that meant an entire day to bide her time with nothing more pressing than housework—which she loathed.

Tallulah loaded the last of the laundry in the washer and looked out the open window. The sky was washed clear of gray clouds and the earth smelled as if cleansed by last night's storm. Too gorgeous a day to be stay stuck inside the cabin. A nice long stroll, then back home for a shower before heading to Tombi's for dinner.

She ran outside, eager as a child let out for recess, then stopped abruptly, patting the loose strands of hair plastered on her face. They'd strayed from her messy topknot and she wore an old T-shirt and shorts. Fine for housework but… Tallulah hurried back inside, changed into fresh clothes and ran a brush through her hair.

I am not *doing this in the hopes of running in to Payton.* She scowled at the mirror before swiping a tube of red lipstick across her lips. This was merely an attempt to avoid looking like a total slob. *Since when has that concerned me?*

"Oh, shut up," she mumbled at her reflection. A spritz of rose perfume and she was off again. She entered the woods, walking briskly, intent on exercise. She flung her arms in wide circles, working out the kinks from her pinched shoulders, which were stiff from scrubbing the bathroom and kitchen floors. No need to tote the heavy backpack during the day.

Unless she came upon that wolf again.

Tallulah shook her head. No borrowing trouble this morning. It was her day off, and that meant no shadow-hunting duties as well. Finishing the laundry could wait until evening. A nice day walking in the woods, dinner later with Tombi and Annie, and then she'd curl up with a good book and read until bedtime. She had her Saturday routine down pat.

So why did that deflate her spirits?

She pushed the uncomfortable feelings aside. Ever since she'd met Payton, a vague dissatisfaction with her quiet, predictable life troubled Tallulah. He meant nothing to her. Nothing. He was a damn lumberjack of all things. Part of a transient crew that could be gone anytime.

Her sneakers squished in the woods' muddy patches and her legs were speckled with mud. So much for trying to look presentable. At a fork in the path, she paused. No point in going to Bo's resting place. The storm had no doubt spoiled her handiwork and she wasn't in the mood to tidy up the site yet again.

She continued on until she reached the clearing by the farmhouse. By day it looked quiet and peaceful. No mysterious creatures hovering about. And no sign of Payton.

Not that she cared.

A smell of rotten carcass assaulted her nose. Probably a dead deer. Yet a tingle of apprehension chased down her spine and she shivered. A faint, familiar feeling also stirred her memory. Had the wolf killed the animal? If so, at least the wolf wouldn't be looking at her with those cagey, threatening eyes. Its belly should be full.

A compulsion to find the source of the foul odor gripped her mind. Tallulah tracked the scent. No special shadow-hunter ability needed for this. It grew stronger and tangier, enough to make her eyes water. She lifted her T-shirt over her nose and breathed out of her mouth as much as possible. Tallulah stopped abruptly at the edge of the field, where flies swarmed low to the ground. This was it.

She crept closer, not wanting to get too near. Only close enough to glimpse what had died.

Yellow corn kernels dotted the ground where they'd spilled from a burlap sack. A patch of blue denim, a black T-shirt and a gray beard—the body was human. Bile rose in her throat, caustic and burning. She was used to wisps, trapped souls, Ishkitini and other shadow spirits. Not this carnage of blood, flesh and bone. Did she know the victim? She edged forward for a closer view. The neck was torn open and blood stained the front of the dark T-shirt. Dried globules of red liquid speckled his gray beard. His face was as white as a cotton sheet, as if all the blood had drained out. Even though his features were contorted in pain, she recognized him.

It was Jeb Johnson, owner of the farm. Evidently, he'd been out illegally baiting deer and something or someone had caught up to him. Killed him. Brutally, at that. But *why*? Jeb mostly kept to himself—he was a quiet man who worked his land and hunted and fished. A widower, his sons were grown and they seemingly got along well with one another.

Tawny wolf eyes glittered in her mind's eye. But even that made no sense. A wolf wouldn't attack a human unless it was starving and there was no other prey available. These woods were filled with squirrels and rabbits and mice, enough to fill its belly.

She'd seen enough. Tallulah ran to the farmhouse, intent on reporting the news. Jeb was dead, but the sooner the cops arrived and observed the body, the more clues they might gather to solve the murder. She rapped sharply at the door.

A handsome, genial male opened the door, raised his brows in surprise and then grinned.

"Hello, little lady. Can I help you?"

"There's a—a…" Her breath grew more shallow and she bent at the waist, catching her breath. "There's been a murder. Call the sheriff."

The grin slipped from his face. "Who? Murder, you say?"

"Call 911."

"Of course."

He started to shut the door in her face. Damn, if only she'd brought her cell phone. She never could remember to carry the stupid thing everywhere she went.

Tallulah threw her weight on the door with her right

shoulder and slipped inside. The man was stronger than she was, but her quick maneuver had caught him unaware and she pushed past him.

At least a dozen men sat around the den, in various stages of undress. A few, apparently, had just arisen. At least half wore only shorts and sported shadows of a beard. The smells of bacon and coffee pervaded from the adjoined kitchen to the left. Payton was nowhere to be found.

The man who'd answered the door walked in front of her, blocking her view. "Bad news, guys. There's been a murder."

Tallulah stepped to his side and eyed the men.

"Shit—"

"Damn it—"

"What the—?"

One of the men rose, his forgotten breakfast plate crashing to the floor. "Not again."

Tallulah zeroed in on his clean-shaven features. Not *again*? "What's that supposed to mean?" she asked. "Has this happened before?"

Warning glances passed around the group and an unnatural silence descended.

A tall man with close-cropped black hair strode her way. She recognized him as the timber crew's supervisor.

"Who's been murdered? Where's the body?" he demanded. His blue eyes were arctic—cold and piercing.

"In the field behind your house. Call the cops."

No one moved.

Tallulah stiffened. Their reactions were off. Way off. Any other crowd this size, over half of them would have already whipped out their ever-present cell phones and called the police. Too late, she recalled the strange creature who had entered this very house. The wolf no one claimed to notice. And Jeb's bloody neck could have been the result of a bite. Chills ghosted up her spine.

"We'll take care of everything," the leader said smoothly. His eyes narrowed. "You look familiar…oh yeah, you're one of those protestors. Ms. Silver, isn't it?" He turned to the man who'd answered the door. "Eli, go upstairs and get Payton."

Eli immediately bounded up the wooden stairs. The leader gripped her forearm. "Show me where you found the body."

"After you call the cops," she insisted. Bossy men like him couldn't intimidate her.

He spoke to one of the guys, his eyes never leaving her face. "Adam, call 911. Now, Ms. Silver, I want to see the body."

"You can view it along with the sheriff," she countered, thrusting out her chin.

Shock widened his pupils. He was obviously used to being instantly obeyed. At least Adam was on the phone, reporting the murder.

He released her arm and faced the men. "Everyone go out, divide up and check the field and its perimeter."

The men scrambled to follow his orders. Two sets of footsteps clamored down the stairs. Eli and Payton emerged.

Payton's blond hair glistened, and tiny rivulets of water fell down his face. He wore jeans, but no shirt. The dark hair on his muscular chest was matted. He was sleek and lean and sexy as hell after his morning shower.

He gave her a lopsided grin. "Of course it's you,

stirring up trouble first thing in the morning. Should have guessed."

"This is no laughing matter," the leader snapped. "Another body's been found."

Another. Tallulah noticed his choice of words.

Payton's face paled underneath his tan. All traces of humor vanished. "No," he whispered, his voice strangled.

"So there's been other bodies? Other murders?" she asked.

The leader's jaw clenched. "You're the only one saying *murder.* How do you know this person didn't die from natural causes?"

She shuddered, recalling the mauled neck, the loss of blood.

Payton came to her at once. "Come, sit," he ordered. "You look like hell. Must have been a shock to find the body."

He tossed an arm over her shoulders and she leaned into his solid mass, smelling soap and shampoo. Warmth washed over her body and she allowed him to seat her on the beat-up leather sofa in the den. She stared at her hands that violently shook in her lap.

Payton closed his strong hands over her trembling ones. "Delayed reaction," he said. "I'm sure the shock is starting to catch up to you."

Somehow he understood, even if the dead body's effect on her nerves surprised even Tallulah. Death and destruction were no strangers to a shadow hunter. But she was used to dealing with animals and spirits—not coming upon a mauled, human carcass.

Poor Jeb. First, the fire last year that had destroyed

most of his cotton crop and damn near bankrupted him. And now…this.

"Eli and I are joining the others," the leader said. "Wait for the cops and keep an eye on our guest."

"I don't need anyone to watch over me," she muttered.

Payton nodded. "I will, Matt."

The door banged shut as Eli and Matt left.

"You don't have to babysit me. I'm fine."

A ripple of apprehension roiled in her stomach. Maybe they weren't concerned for her safety at all. Maybe there was something more sinister at play. They seemed in an awful hurry to find the body before the cops.

"Right. You're fine. That's why you're shaking like a deer staring at the long end of a shotgun."

He sat beside her and rubbed her shoulder. She drew a steadying breath. *Be smart.* Could be Payton was ordered to watch her for damage control. Make sure she didn't catch them hiding the body or altering the scene.

"You had a traumatic experience this morning," he said, continuing to massage her shoulders and neck. "Anyone would be shaken. Don't act like you aren't."

Tallulah inched away from his touch. She was many things, but a fool she was not. For all she knew, Payton was as untrustworthy as the rest of the timber crew. Just because his kisses curled her toes the night before was no reason to let down her guard.

"Don't patronize me," she snapped. "I'm not the swooning Southern-belle type. I can handle emergencies with logic and calm."

Payton's mouth twisted and he rose from the sofa and paced. Probably stifling the urge to throttle her.

"Go on and join the others. You know you're dying to check it out. I can take care of myself."

Tallulah glanced around the den that seethed with masculinity—a pool table, large-screen TV, a wet bar, leather furniture and not a knickknack or potted plant in sight. If Payton went outside, she could do a little exploring. There was something very strange about this group of guys, although she couldn't precisely say what. Their house had a different feel from other homes. A secretive vibe. But perhaps she judged unfairly, her view tainted by seeing the wolf enter. The one no one claimed to have seen—including Payton. Maybe she could convince him to leave so she could snoop around the place and call Sheriff Angier. Tell Payton she needed some alone time to recover from the ordeal of finding the body.

He ceased pacing and faced her abruptly. "Do you always have to act so damn defensive about everything?"

Her spine stiffened. "That's not true," she began, her voice hot and loud. She clamped her jaw shut. She'd just proved the opposite.

"It *is* true. You take offence at anything I say."

Tallulah silently counted to ten. She'd get nowhere antagonizing him. And perhaps he did have a point. Payton certainly wouldn't be the first to say that her personality had become a tad bitter over the past couple of years.

"I apologize. You're right. Seeing Jeb's mauled body did bother me and I took it out on you."

Payton's anger instantly abated. "It's okay."

"I think I interrupted your morning shower. Why don't you go ahead and finish?"

He hesitated. "Are you sure? Can I get you anything first?"

"I wouldn't mind a cup of coffee," she said sweetly. "Might calm my nerves."

"Sure. Sugar or cream?"

"Both."

"Done. Then I'm going back upstairs to finish dressing so I'll be decent when the cops bombard the place."

"Had experience with this sort of thing before?" she asked, unable to help herself. "With cops, that is."

His eyes shuttered. "Hmm."

Without explaining, he disappeared in the kitchen. She kept her ears tuned as he rumbled about for a cup, poured and stirred. She picked up a cell phone that was on the coffee table.

Damn. This one required a password to make a call. She reached and tried another abandoned phone on the end table. Oh, yes, this one was password-free. It would do nicely.

At the sound of footsteps, she stuffed the phone under the sofa cushion.

"One coffee coming up," Payton announced.

He held out a steaming, earthenware mug and she clasped both hands around the smooth pottery. Despite the appalling circumstances, the warmth in her palms spread up her arms and into her heart. There were few caring gestures in her life. Not since Bo…well, no point thinking of him now. He'd left her behind and she was alone again. Most of the time, she'd learn to accept she was on her own. Until an act of kindness, however small, undid her.

Oh, hell, not tears. Quickly, Tallulah hung her head, allowing her long hair to drape her profile on either side.

She sipped the coffee and discreetely swiped the wetness from her cheeks.

"Hey, are you crying?" Payton sat beside her on the sofa.

"Of course not." She carefully set the mug on an end table and faked a little cough. "Swallowed the wrong way. Go ahead and get dressed."

He looked doubtful, but she shooed him along with a wave of her hand. "A few minutes alone will do me good."

"If you say so."

With one last pat on her shoulder, Payton rose and tromped up the stairs. Tallulah unearthed the phone from beneath the cushion and punched in a familiar number.

"Yes, hello," she said, careful to keep her voice low. "I need to speak with Sheriff Angier. It's an emergency."

It was happening all over again, Payton thought.

He tried to make excuses as he shrugged into a T-shirt and pulled on socks and sneakers—a dead body didn't necessarily mean murder. There could be a natural cause. The bayou was teeming with rattlesnakes and water moccasins. Maybe even alligators? He wasn't sure if they were far south enough for gators; he'd have to ask Tallulah about that.

Yes, but the body had been found on *their* property. It was Montana all over again. Questions whirled through his brain in a storm of dread. He'd been so concerned over Tallulah; he hadn't asked for details. Now he desperately needed to know everything, needed to come up with a rational explanation for what had happened. An explanation that had nothing to do with one of their own.

Satisfied he was presentable, Payton returned downstairs.

Tallulah was a blur of motion. A hand swept down her side as she stood and faced him. Had she dropped something? She ran a hand through her hair and gave an uncertain smile.

"That was quick."

He strode forward. "Did the coffee help?"

"Yes, yes. I told you, I'm fine."

"Good. Because I have a few questions." He sat in a chair across from the sofa and motioned her to sit back down. A cell phone lay on the cushion beside her.

"Call anybody?" he asked.

"What makes you think this is my phone?" The old Tallulah was back in control, abrasive and defensive.

"Is it?"

"No. So what did you want to ask me?"

"Tell me about the body you found. Did you know the person?"

She swallowed hard. "It was Jeb Johnson, your landlord."

"I never met him. Just one of his sons, forgot the name."

"That would be Tommy or Ainsley. Jeb didn't get out much in the last year or so, wasn't feeling well," she said. She picked up the coffee mug and took a long draw.

Hope loosened the tightness in his chest. The man was old. Perhaps he'd gone for an early morning walk and his heart gave up the ghost.

"A possible heart attack?"

"I wish. No." She pursed her lips a moment. "His

neck was cut open. Or—" her eyes narrowed a fraction "—he was bitten."

"Bitten?" he asked, fighting to keep his voice mild, his expression neutral. Holy hell. The nightmare continued. "Bitten by what? A wild dog? A bear?"

She set the mug on the table. "No bears in these parts. Not for decades. No wild dogs, either, that I'm aware of."

Easy, Payton. Easy. Keep your eyes and face like Switzerland.

Silence weighted the space between them.

"I can't help thinking of that creature I saw near here," Tallulah said at last. "The wolf that entered the house."

Payton smiled sardonically. "If a wolf had walked in here, I promise one of us would have noticed."

"I know what I saw."

"What you *think* you saw," he amended.

"Something strange is going on around here. Is there something you want to tell me? While we're alone?"

A pang of longing shot through his heart. How nice it would be to confide in someone instead of keeping the secret locked inside. *Never. Don't even consider such a dangerous notion.* His loyalty was to the pack. To his own kind. And they were in deep, deep trouble.

"There's nothing to tell," he replied dully. "We're here to do a job and then we'll be on our way in a few months."

"You're lying," she said flatly.

Payton pursed his lips, biting back a sharp retort. Bad enough he was forced to live a lie, but he wasn't a hypocrite. He did what he must in order to protect himself and the pack. If the wrong people knew they

were shapeshifters, it would result in a witch hunt—
the likes of which would make Salem appear tame by
comparison.

He shifted the inquisition. "Who did you call?"

"I don't know what you're talking about."

"When I was upstairs, you called someone. Who?
And why?"

Her face was as calm and stoic as a piece of polished
amber. "Nobody."

"Now who's lying?"

Siren wails intruded upon their impasse, signaling
the rapid-approaching arm of the law. Footsteps lum-
bered up the back porch steps as several members of
the pack returned.

It was going to be a bitch of a day.

Chapter 5

"I understand you're the one who found the body."

Sheriff Angier casually maneuvered her to the side.

A young Bayou La Siryna cop frowned, clearly irritated. "I can take her statement."

"Relax, rookie. We all want the same thing—to discover what happened to Mr. Johnson. Now go talk to some of the others."

The rookie flushed, but left them alone, grumbling under his breath.

"Tell me why you wanted to speak to me personally," the sheriff said. "Do you have some suspicions you're afraid to voice in front of anyone else?"

"I trust you. Your dad and my dad went a long way back."

"I remember," Angier said.

"So hear me out. What I'm about to tell you is a little weird."

He gave her a sideways glance. "I'm plenty used to weird in Bayou La Siryna."

Tallulah knew that. Annie claimed Angier's wife was "different" and perhaps otherworldly. Her sister-in-law, Annie, was the granddaughter of the local hoodoo queen, Tia Henrietta, and had the ability to hear auras. Tallulah didn't believe it at first, but she'd learned that Annie did indeed have powers. She'd seen her do it many times, especially during a crisis.

"Around Shelly Angier I hear the ocean," Annie had said. "It's especially clear when I'm near her cousins, Jet and Lily. With Jet, the ocean sounds powerful and releases a ferocious beauty of pounding waves. And with Lily…" Annie's eyes grew dreamy and she sighed. "I can't do justice to describing her aura. It's a beautiful voice that sounds like an angel, except the notes are carried out over the sea in waves—rippling and melodic."

She'd laughed. "Are you saying Angier is married to a mermaid?"

Annie hadn't laughed. "Anything's possible in Bayou La Siryna."

Tallulah tried to gauge the enigmatic sheriff's reaction to her probe. Her image reflected off his polarized sunglasses. Did law enforcement wear those to deliberately keep people from guessing their thoughts? 'Cause she could read no emotion on Angier's stern, rugged face.

What the hell. She had to tell him what she'd seen. If he laughed and brushed her off, so be it.

"Go on," he urged.

"Jeb's neck… I've never seen anything like it. Could it have been a wild animal? A stray dog?"

"The forensic expert will make that call."

Hah. He was stonewalling her. "I asked what *you* think?"

"I think you know something," he countered. "What is it?"

"I've seen a wolf roaming this area."

A heartbeat passed.

"Never seen one in this bayou. That's all you got?" Angier asked.

"The wolf is menacing. Its behavior is odd. One moment feral and dangerous, and the next it's—it's—"

"Spit it out."

She glared at the sheriff and then pointed to the farmhouse. "I saw it walk up those back porch stairs and then enter this house. And no one said a word after it happened."

"Anything else?"

"Awful strange that something like this happens just as the new renters come to town." There, she'd said it.

"Could be you have a bias against them. Considering how much you love this land and have protested their timber clearing."

"That's not true," she said, immediately on the defensive. She'd never insinuate a person had committed a crime based on a personal grudge. "It's not fair. I—"

"Hey, come look at this!" one of the cops cried from behind the tree line. A buzz of excitement broke out and everyone swarmed under a magnolia, trying to get a glimpse.

She and Sheriff Angier hurried over. The aggressive rookie policeman held up an object and Tallulah stopped dead at the sight.

Feathers and beads dangled in the breeze from a wooden, hooped dream catcher.

Her dream catcher.

She couldn't breathe, couldn't move. She was paralyzed with shock. How had it gotten there? Her memorial to Bo was too far away for the wind to have carried it all the way to Jeb's. Tallulah wet her dry lips and scanned the crowd. Was she being set up? Maybe by one of the new renters in Bayou La Siryna?

"What the hell is that thing?" one of the onlookers asked.

Sheriff Angier shot her a questioning look, one brow raised. He recognized a Native American relic when he saw one. The Choctaw presence was strong in the area.

"Good thing I'm not one to jump to conclusions," he commented.

"But—but—"

"Maybe you should explain to the sheriff why you continue to trespass on our property."

Tallulah whirled around, coming face-to-face with Payton. A very angry Payton.

"You always appear to be snooping around at the most interesting times," Payton continued. His gray eyes lacked any warmth. All trace of the nice guy had vanished. Now she'd done it. After today, he'd want nothing to do with her. Fine. She was used to being alone.

Matt marched over to them, clearly infuriated. "And *you* were the one who found the body."

His loud, firm voice carried and everyone momentarily paused to look their way. Even the tech people loading Jeb's body into a vehicle and the other cops, who were taking pictures of the scene and scouting the immediate area.

Tallulah's face flamed. This is what you got for

trying to be a good citizen. She focused her gaze on Angier. "If you want to ask me more questions, you know where I live."

The sheriff nodded. "I'll be in touch."

I'll bet. But she had no answers. No explanation as to why her dream catcher was located near Jeb's body. She straightened her shoulders and headed to the street, conscious of Payton's eyes on her. Walking on the road added significant distance to the journey home, but she didn't care to be alone in the woods after the sight of Jeb's bloody neck with its jagged skin.

Her legs grew heavy; the whole event had wearied her more than she'd realized. The emotional turmoil had sapped her energy. It would be a long, lonely walk back to her cabin.

And this time, there would be no offer of a ride home from Payton.

The pack crowded into the living room, awaiting word from their alpha, Matt. The mood was as solemn as the night they'd decided to leave Montana after confronting the unfair accusations of other wolf packs.

Only now it appeared the accusations weren't false.

Someone among them was infected with the lycanthropic fever. A cold-hearted killer who would stop at nothing to fulfill his cravings for human blood. The fever had been widespread out west. No one knew how it started, only that it spread from one wolf to another through biting. Those infected by the fever were ordered to live at a secured, medical compound until an antidote was developed.

Absolute compliance to this law was strictly enforced. Werewolves had evolved over the years, learned to shape-shift and satisfy their animal nature without posing harm to humans and without exposing their secret nature. But the lycanthropic fever threatened their gains. A series of unexplained human murder victims, all bitten in the neck, all drained of blood, had aroused the attention of the law enforcement and the fear of the community. For now, the murders were theorized as being committed by an unknown serial killer. But if this spread across the country, if word leaked on the hidden world of shapeshifters, their existence would be threatened. It would be a return to the days of wolf and witch trials. A bloodbath that might end their kind forever.

"We're in a tough position," Matt began, standing in front of the fireplace. "By tomorrow morning, the law enforcement people in this town will most likely see the connection of the victim's body here as identical to other victims out west." He took a deep breath and intently regarded each of them. "One of you is infected. I can't deny it any longer."

But who?

Payton's gaze swept the room, studying the guarded faces of his friends, his family. Each one appeared shellshocked. Eyes reflected varying degrees of dread and many had slumped shoulders, an aura of defeat. Jillian appeared to take the news the worst. Her eyes were bloodshot and her hands trembled in her lap.

"But maybe it wasn't one of us." Adam, their youngest member, spoke up. "There was that Native American thing found by the body. Maybe whoever left it was the real killer."

Russell caught his eye. Payton shook his head a fraction, signaling not to speak. His friend frowned, but kept quiet.

As quick as Tallulah had been to judge all of them, he wasn't ready to attach blame. The dream catcher at the scene, combined with the fact that she was the person to discover the body, looked bad. He didn't know Tallulah well enough to determine her character, but the ripped flesh on Jeb's neck and the loss of blood was an ironclad indictment against one of them.

"It was one of us," Matt insisted. "But that Tallulah Silver concerns me. She suspects something and she snoops about the place too much."

Matt stared straight at him. "Didn't you have dinner with the other evening? How well do you know her?"

Jillian stopped sniffling and cast alert eyes on him.

"Evidently, not well as well as I thought."

"Then get closer to her," Matt commanded. "Find out what she knows and then throw her off our trail."

"She's freely told the sheriff what she's seen. As far as throwing us off our trail, I don't see how I'm supposed to do that."

"Distract her. Use your charms. Maybe even move in with her to keep an eye on her movements."

"Hell, Matt. You want me to be a damn gigolo?"

Snickers erupted from the group, relieving a bit of the tension. At his expense.

"I don't see why that's necessary," Jillian blurted. "That woman doesn't know the first thing about us. About our werewolf nature."

Matt raised a brow. "Are you questioning the wisdom of my idea?"

She flushed and pursed her lips, unwilling to argue with the alpha, even if it was her brother.

"So the question remains. Which of us is infected?" Matt continued.

No one spoke.

"Has anyone observed another pack member breaking the rules by leaving the house alone?"

Still no answer.

"Okay. Has anyone observed any suspicious behavior or witnessed another member exhibiting symptoms of excessive sweating or shaking?"

Still no answer.

"There must be something," he urged.

"Maybe we should be looking at Payton," Eli suggested. "After all, look at what his father did. Murdered another man, a fellow pack member."

Payton jumped to his feet, anger scalding every nerve in his body. "Leave my father out of this discussion. It has nothing to do with me or this situation."

"You have the same quick temper." James, an elder and generally regarded as Matt's beta, studied him.

"Same could be said for at least half of us," Payton pointed out, struggling to keep his voice controlled.

Jillian came to his side and clutched his arm.

"No way it's Payton," she insisted.

His neck heated with embarrassment at her unwanted defense. Her outburst made them appear like a couple, a team, intimates. He sat back down on the couch and tugged the sleeve of her T-shirt to have Jillian do the same.

"Let's all keep our eyes and ears open," Matt said. "Report to me at once if you observe anything suspicious. As far as the guilty one…" He again scrutinized them each individually. "Meet with me in private. Today. Before any further damage can be done. I promise, I'll see that you get treatment. I will personally drive you to the compound in Montana for reconditioning."

As if the person suffering from the L-fever could be reasoned with. The fever slowly destroyed their humanity until the blood lust for humans consumed them day and night.

"Should we consider moving again?" Lincoln asked quietly. The much picked-on omega of the pack apparently wanted to retreat, his usual response to danger. "At least out west there are more of our kind and the killer might be caught by another pack on the prowl. And we'd be closer to the holding compound when we do catch the killer."

Matt shook his head. "It would serve no purpose except make us appear even more guilty. We'll find the culprit ourselves and have him removed." He clapped his hands. "Now we should break into groups and get to work. We'll set up a system where we alternate night duty to catch anyone sneaking out. Payton, time for you to visit Tallulah Silver."

Terrific. He suppressed the resentment. Matt was their leader, looking out for everyone's safety. Still, it chafed to take orders on his personal affairs. It didn't matter that Tallulah intrigued him and that he'd planned on visiting her anyway to discover why she continued to intrude on their privacy.

He rose and headed for the door, Jillian close behind. Outside, the sun was beginning to set over the cotton field, casting coral and purple rays. Payton faced her reluctantly. "What is it, Jillian?"

"My brother thinks he's so smart. But this idea is stupid. You don't have to make a move on that woman."

He scratched his head. "I'd really rather not talk about it with you," he said at last. If he bad-mouthed Matt, she might let it slip to him. Blood was thicker than water, as the saying went. With others in the pack dredging up his father's past, he didn't need Matt's good opinion of him to waver.

Jillian thrust her face next to his, her eyes round and tearful. "Tell Matt you tried, but that Tallulah isn't interested in you."

Which was probably the truth.

"I'll do my duty," he said. "I have no choice. You know that."

Her mouth planted onto his, strong and demanding. Just as suddenly, Jillian stepped back. "Don't forget me," she insisted. "We're two of a kind. I could be a good mate."

When this was over, he'd have to firmly break the news to Jillian that he didn't share her strong feelings. She seemed incapable of taking a hint.

"You know I won't forget you," he said, appeasing her. "You're my friend."

He quickly bounded down the steps to avoid seeing her reaction. Hard enough dealing with his own emotions without throwing hers in the mix.

Payton drove the short distance to Tallulah's cabin. With any luck, she wouldn't be home. But as soon as he pulled in her driveway, he saw a light shining from the front room. The truck's tires rattled over dirt and rocks. Tallulah's face appeared at the window and she frowned as she recognized his truck.

With a sigh, he shut off the engine and approached her home. His fist stopped in midair, as she whisked the door open before he could knock.

"Why are you here?" she asked.

She wore shorts and a red tank top, looking sexier than hell. It threw him off his game, made him think like a sex-obsessed teenager. He drew a deep breath, gathering his thoughts. "We should talk."

"I wasn't sure you'd ever want to talk to me again after I called the sheriff."

"You sure like to get right to the point," he said wryly. "As for the sheriff, someone would have called the man soon enough."

To his surprise, she left the door open, turning her back on him as she went and sat on a sofa. He entered, observing the inside of her cabin with curiosity. It was pristine and minimalistic, yet managed to convey a sense of comfort. On the coffee table was a large bowl of fresh fruit. The cushion on the high-backed leather chair held a colorful ball of yarn and needles.

"You knit?" It seemed incongruent with her assertive personality.

She shrugged, moved the bundle of needlework to an end table and sat down. "Crochet. Have a seat."

He sprawled on the sofa and stared at a display of dream catchers on the opposite wall, anything to keep from staring at her legs and cleavage like an idiot.

"So you enjoy craft stuff," he remarked. "I thought that was for grannies."

"Lots of women crochet now to relax. It passes the time."

Might as well get right down to business, same as Tallulah. "I was upset earlier because you found the body and always appear to be snooping around. Was that your dream catcher the cops found by the body?"

"It was."

"How do you suppose it got there?"

Tallulah set down the yarn and crossed her arms. "I have no clue."

"Okay, then answer this. What were you doing on our property again?"

Her cheeks subtly reddened. "I'd gone for a walk and smelled something. So I went to investigate."

He frowned. "I couldn't smell anything until I came within a dozen yards of the victim. And I have an excellent nose."

"I have a strong sense of smell."

Hah. No way it was as strong as his. What wasn't she telling him? He had his own extraordinary nose, but only in wolf form.

"You're spying on us, aren't you?" he accused.

"If you don't have anything to hide, it shouldn't bother you."

She tucked her long, bare legs underneath her. He had a sudden vision of those legs wrapped around his ass and back, drawing him closer... He bit the inside of his mouth. *Focus.*

"So you don't deny it. People have a right to their privacy, you know."

"Not if they're dangerous," she countered.

"We aren't," he said. "You think you saw an animal come in our house one night and you've blown that one incident all out of proportion. Truth is, you resent us clearing the land and are looking for a reason to turn the community against us."

"You sound like Sheriff Angier." Tallulah rose to her feet and paced the small room. "You're right about one thing. I do resent you and the rest of your crew. You don't belong here. I've made my feelings plain about your job."

"That's no grounds for what you did, trying to throw us under the bus with that sheriff."

Her fingers curled into her palm. "I was telling the truth."

"Look at a couple of other truths—you found the body, and your dream catcher was found on the scene."

She sucked in a breath and glared at him. "I'm no murderer."

He rose and stood face-to-face with Tallulah. "Neither am I."

Her breasts rose and fell. The air crackled with anger and tension and…something else. Something more elemental and primitive. Tallulah's copper-brown eyes darkened and her gaze dropped to his mouth.

This was crazy. Utterly absurd. She infuriated him and turned him on all at the same time. Payton cursed under his breath.

"Wh—?" she began.

His mouth crushed down against hers. It was better between them when Tallulah *wasn't* talking. Her lips were pliant and willing. And her body was soft and yielding, even if her temperament was the opposite.

The kiss deepened and all he could do was drink in the sensations of this woman that intrigued him like no other. She was fierce and gentle, abrasive and yet oh, so sweet.

Tallulah pulled away first. "I think you should go now."

Was he pushing for too much too soon? Or was she still hung up on her dead lover? Payton brushed a finger against her slightly swollen lips. "I'll be back," he promised. "Soon."

Keeping an eye on her for the wolf pack would be no chore.

Chapter 6

Was somebody framing her for murder? Tallulah wondered as she circled the area surrounding Bo's memorial, her agitation increasing. No. She had no enemies, save for the shadow spirits. And this was definitely not their modus operandi. But who?

Tallulah snatched up a dream catcher that she spotted in the brambles. Good thing she found it before the cops scoured the area—if they came this far out. Her temples throbbed. There could be more. She'd comb every inch of these grounds.

An hour later, she'd collected five more discarded dream catchers, each close by an animal carcass. This had to stop. She hurried back to her sanctuary.

"I'm sorry, Bo. These have to come down."

With trembling fingers, she untied all of the dream catchers from the tree branches, stuffing them into her

backpack, crushing them to make them fit. Instead of
feeling better, the act made her more desperate, more
panicked. Her labored breathing sounded like the roar
of a hurricane to her sensitive ears.

She had to stop. *Think*. Tallulah sat on a stump and
took a long swallow of water from her canteen. That was
better. She surveyed the area. It looked bare and deso-
late. Except for the ring of shells and crystals. With a
sigh, she stood and tossed the shells from the inner circle
into the woods. Shells were everywhere—they wouldn't
lead anyone to her. But the crystals were a problem.

Tallulah gathered the crystals and dropped them into
her overloaded backpack. When she returned home this
evening, she'd place them around her favorite framed
photo of Bo.

Shadows lengthened in the late afternoon sun, pro-
viding a bit of relief from the stifling humidity. Clumps
of wet hair, which had escaped her ponytail, stuck to
her face and neck. Tallulah gathered the loose strands
and retied the elastic headband.

Had she found all her dream catchers? She'd have to
return again in the morning and widen her search area,
but she'd done the best she could for now.

And tomorrow was the start of the full-moon week.
She'd tell Tombi and the other shadow hunters what had
happened and alert them to be on the lookout for any
more missing dream catchers. Between them, she could
be assured there were none left unaccounted.

The heavy dread in her stomach eased. Action usually overcame fear. Satisfied, she stepped onto the trail
to return home. Time to think of pleasant things.

She smiled broadly, remembering Payton's kiss last
night. He'd wanted to take it further this time, but she'd

stopped his advances. It was still way too soon for her. After Hanan's betrayal two years ago, she'd vowed to never be duped again. Not that she'd been in love with Hanan. He'd been convenient, had made her feel like a desirable woman again. And how she'd paid for their brief fling. Because of Hanan, she'd placed all of the hunters in jeopardy. What horrible judgment on her part. How could she ever trust her instincts about a man again?

Stop. Pleasant thoughts, remember? She touched her fingers to her lips, recalling the press of Payton's lips against her own. The immediate, all-consuming desire that had erupted through her body. Even the memory—

A twig snapped. A low growl vibrated in the air—the wolf had returned.

With a practice born of years of experience. Tallulah swiftly and silently loaded her slingshot and drew back the band. Another growl erupted and she aimed the slingshot toward the sound. Her eyes strained to observe patterns in the dim twilight, to locate the slightest shift of movement.

An explosion of crackles and snapped vines emerged from the underbrush. The brown-haired wolf charged, its primal eyes pinning her with deadly intention.

Tallulah let loose the band, aiming the stone at its heart. The wolf dipped its head and body in one swift movement and the stone harmlessly hurtled past it.

Damn. Unusual to miss at this close range. The animal was more cunning than she'd guessed. It leaped in the air, determined and fast.

"Get out of here!" she screamed as loud as she could, hoping the noise would scare it away. The wolf never slowed and she drew her dagger. Another lunging leap, and it was close enough to touch. A metallic, pungent scent of blood and fur flew at her. The wolf bared its teeth. Bubbling drool spilled down the corners of its powerful jaws.

Was it mad?

She thrust her right hand forward. If it jumped on top of her, the dagger would do damage to its soft underbelly.

Solid animal muscle pounced, throwing her to the ground with the impact. She plunged her dagger into the wolf's belly, felt the rip as the weapon shredded through fur and skin to guts. It let out a howling yelp, as if she had delivered a mortal wound.

She prayed it was.

It rolled off her body and glared at her. The hate and intelligence in its eyes were undeniable. Was it so territorial that just the notion of sharing space with a human made it murderous and reckless with rage?

She held the bloody dagger in her hand, returning its stare. Wolves were foreign; she knew nothing of their nature. Not the way she did with native animals like deer and foxes and the occasional wild boar.

Her eyes dropped down its torso to where her dagger had pierced, leaving a small incision around its abdomen. Small, but deep. Blood gushed from the wound. Surely now it would tuck tail and leave.

It didn't.

Unblinking yellow eyes stared into her own with an intelligence she'd never encountered in a wild animal. It hobbled up onto its four legs and turned its tail to her, preparing to retreat. *Finally.*

Yet she didn't dare move. A nagging instinct warned her the wolf had not truly submitted to her dominance.

The bloody dagger clenched in her right hand was warm and wet.

The wolf suddenly turned and ran behind her prostrate body. She scrambled to her knees, but she felt pain burst into her right shoulder.

The damn wolf had bitten her. Its teeth ripped her flesh, its jaw tightened and her stabbing arm was immobilized, a useless appendage. The more she tried to jerk herself free, the tighter its bite became. Her slingshot was lost somewhere, knocked loose from her hands when the wolf had jumped her the first time. Tallulah screamed—a volley of angry curses.

The wolf released its grip.

Tallulah rose on unsteady feet and regarded her foe. Its ears were pinned back, as if it heard something that she couldn't. The wolf turned tail on her again, this time hobbling past the tree line and out of sight.

Loud ringing flooded her ears. Tallulah took a deep breath. Just a bite. *I can make it home.* She turned her neck, observed her torn, bloody flesh. At least it hadn't bitten her neck. She'd live.

A vision of its drool flashed in her mind. Yeah, she'd live. If the thing didn't have rabies.

She gathered her backpack and retrieved her weapons. Got to…go…

Blackness trickled into her awareness until it coated her vision, her mind. Her body responded last, dropping to the earth. She braced herself for the impact that never came.

Payton bent low to the ground, scowling. A dead squirrel—and beside it a sparkling rock that was too pretty to be natural. He picked it up and ran his fingers across the smooth, tumbled crystal of yellow citrine. Where could this have come from?

He'd barely framed the question when he recalled Tallulah's special place. There had been crystals there. Lots of them. Scattered in mosaics with seashells in some kind of tribute to her dead lover.

First, a human body with Tallulah's dream catcher and now a dead animal with another one of her relics. His fist tightened over the citrine. Were these the sick trophies of a demented killer?

He didn't believe in coincidences.

He stuffed the crystal into his pants pocket, unwilling to leave the incriminating evidence behind. Not until he had a chance to ask Tallulah for an explanation.

Payton closed his eyes, pictured her dark eyes deepening darker still with desire when they'd kissed last night. He couldn't reconcile that image with one of a murderer. Just as he couldn't reconcile the fierce woman as a secret knitter by night.

So who and what was the real Tallulah?

He'd find out. Whatever it took.

A howl pierced through the silent twilight. Payton stilled. That was a wolf howl. No doubt about it. He hadn't heard of any approved outings. Matt had warned them all not to shape-shift, not even as a group. It was too dangerous. Cops kept surveillance on the crime scene, hoping the killer would return.

Payton rushed toward where he'd heard the sound. If he was quick enough, perhaps he could catch the infected wolf. The sooner the identification was made, the sooner the entire pack could resume their lives and stop living with fear.

Heedless of the cuts and scratches from bramble and

low-lying limbs, Payton ran unerringly to where the howl had originated. *You could get there faster in wolf form.* The thought tempted him, but he'd sworn obedience to his alpha. The rules were in place for everyone's greater good and protection.

There were no more sounds. Did the rogue wolf know he was being pursued?

Payton stilled, straining to hear the sound of the wolf running through the woods. A shuffling, grunting noise emerged nearby. He continued on, a little slower to mask the sounds of his own movement.

Payton caught sight of a small, circular clearing that he recognized as Tallulah's sacred place. All the dream catchers were gone from the trees, but there was no mistaking the topography. He ran harder, longing to glimpse her tall body walking around the circle.

At the edge of the circle he burst through the vines and brambles.

Blood littered the sandy soil, almost directly at the circle's center—like some sort of sacrificial offering. His mind whirled in panic. Where was Tallulah? Where was the wolf?

Footprints and paw indentations led to another trail into the woods. He followed it. Not twenty yards in, he found Tallulah.

Her right shoulder had been chewed and blood oozed from the torn fabric of her T-shirt. Her body was crumpled onto one side. She didn't move.

Payton rushed to her side and pushed the hair from her face. Her eyes remained closed.

"Tallulah? Wake up. It's me—Payton. Can you hear me?"

She moaned and her eyes fluttered.

Not dead. Relief made him almost dizzy.

"Open your eyes, baby. Please."

She licked her lips and her eyes slitted open a fraction. "Wh-what happened?"

"You've been hurt. You're bleeding."

Tallulah's eyes popped open and she glanced to her left and right.

"Who hurt you?" he asked, anxious to keep her talking.

She faced him. "Wolf," she whispered.

Anger and guilt and fear slammed into him like a sucker punch to the gut. What would happen to her now? He'd never heard of a case where an infected wolf had bitten a human without killing them.

"It's okay," he assured Tallulah. "I'm going to get help." He whipped out his cell phone to dial 911.

No signal. Terrific.

He stuffed the useless phone back in his pocket. "Going to have to carry you then." Gently he tried to pick her up without touching her wound.

"Hurts," she moaned.

"Sorry, darling."

Payton lifted her and she drew in a sharp breath. "Put me down," she ordered. "I can walk, just let me lean on you a bit."

"Still trying to boss me around," he teased, secretly relieved she felt good enough to argue. He walked, still carrying her in his arms. "I'll take that as a good sign."

"You never listen to me." In spite of the complaint, she rested her head against his chest.

"Maybe sometimes I actually know what's best."

"Impossible," she muttered, but a smile ghosted over her pale face.

He trudged onward, adrenaline boosting his strength. "How far from here 'til we get to your cabin?"

"About a quarter mile. The trail empties into a clearing that backs up to my place. You getting tired? I can walk, you know."

"Oh, shut up," he said cheerfully.

"I don't think a man's ever told me to shut up before. If I wasn't injured, I'd make you pay for that remark."

"Exactly. I took advantage of your weakened condition."

The banter helped loosen the terror clawing his gut. How would the lycanthropic fever spread and affect her? At least she had a chance. He picked up his pace to a light jog.

"Ouch," she complained.

"Shh—"

"Don't you dare…" She licked her lips. "Don't."

He glanced at her in alarm. Her face and chest had broken into a sweat. Her eyes held the glaze of fever.

Payton ran, almost as fast as the nights he ran in wolf form.

"It hurts when you run. Stop it."

Bossing and complaining as usual. Payton tried to take heart at that. At last, they reached the clearing. He raced up the porch steps and opened the screen door.

"You shouldn't leave your doors unlocked."

"Shut up," she murmured.

He smiled and carried her to the couch.

"Where are your car keys?"

"Don't need them."

"You're going to the hospital. Looks like you might need stitches." And who knows what kind of infection was spreading through her blood with each beat of her heart.

"No hospital," she insisted.

"For once, will you stop being difficult?" he asked, exasperated. He walked to the kitchen counter and eyed the area, looking for the keys.

"Listen to me." She paused. "Please."

He returned to her side at once.

"I can't go," she whispered.

"Why not?"

"If I told you 'none of your business,' would you honor my wish?"

"No."

She licked her lips. "The thing is, I have a problem."

"Go on."

"If they have to run tests," she said, swallowing hard, "I might—they might—find something unusual. I can't have that happen."

"Unusual?" The word slipped past his choked lungs. Tallulah couldn't know it, but she expressed his own inner fears of doctors and hospitals. The lycanthropic blood that ran through him was bound to catch notice in standard tests.

"I can't—no, *won't*—explain it to you. So don't ask."

He sat beside her. "I won't," he said gently. "I understand."

"You do?" Her eyes widened in surprise.

He threw her own words back at her. "Don't ask because I won't tell you why."

"Fair enough."

"But if this gets infected, I'll have to take you in," he said firmly. "Got it?"

Tallulah shifted her gaze to the ceiling. "Mmm."

He'd fight that battle when or if it became necessary. "But in the meantime, you have a nasty bite that needs to be cleaned."

"Call Annie. She'll do it. She's a healer."

He raised a brow. "Like a nurse or something?"

"Or something. Get my phone, it's on the nightstand in my bedroom."

"Yes, ma'am." He gave a mock salute that earned him another faint smile.

He returned with the phone and she awkwardly scrolled through the screens with her good left hand and punched a button.

"Annie? Come over right away. I've been bitten by a wolf."

"You wha-a-at?"

Even he could hear the shriek.

"You heard me. Drop everything and come at once."

He snorted and Tallulah bit her lip. "Please," she added. She tossed the phone on the coffee table. "See? I can be nice."

Was he imagining it, or was she turning pale beneath the golden bronze complexion? "Let's get you out of that shirt and take a look."

"No. Annie will be here in a few minutes. Let her do it."

"Don't be a baby. I'll be gentle. Shouldn't hurt but a moment."

She frowned. "I'm not afraid."

Ah, she was rising to the bait. "Prove it."

Without preamble, Payton lifted up her T-shirt and she sat forward, allowing him to slip it from her shoulders. Some of the blood had dried and as he raised the

shirt above her shoulders, the wound bled fresh. Tallulah bit her lip, but didn't utter a single moan.

The bite mark was imprinted in her tender flesh.
The puncture wounds bled freely and the skin was jagged where she'd struggled to get away. If it had bitten
her neck and penetrated her jugular—no, he wouldn't
think on it now.

Her practical white bra contrasted with the cinnamon
glow of her skin. To his relief, she didn't try to cover
herself with a blanket or act modest.

"I'm going to get some towels and clean it up while
we wait for your sister-in-law."

"Um, not necessary—" she began.

He left, not waiting to hear her protests. Returning
with clean, dampened towels, he gingerly cleaned
around the bite and then as gently as possibly directly
placed a washcloth on the wound itself.

Tallulah sucked in her breath, but said nothing.

"Damn." It did appear as if a few red streaks were
beginning to form, a sure sign of blood poisoning—an
abnormally fast onset of infection. This did not bode
well.

"What is it?" Tallulah craned her neck, trying to observe the damage for herself.

"I'm worried about infection. How can Annie help
you? Does she have any nursing or medical back-
ground?"

"No." Tallulah waited a heartbeat. "I might as well
tell you, you'll find out soon enough when she arrives."
Her face brightened. "Unless you need to go home?"

"I'm not going anywhere."

"Oh." The hopeful expectancy dimmed. "You should

go." Tallulah warmed to her subject. "This is my cabin and I'm telling you to leave."

He folded his arms. "I'm not going anywhere."

"I'm too tired to argue." She sighed and reclined back on the sofa.

Well, this was a first. But instead of taking satisfaction at her submission, Payton was flooded with concern. She was hurt more than she let on.

"If Annie isn't here in five minutes, I'm driving you to the ER."

"She'll be here any minute. Their cabin isn't far from mine."

Tallulah closed her eyes and the sight chilled him to the bone. He had to keep her talking, had to know she wasn't succumbing to a coma or worse.

"Tell me about Annie's healing. What does she do?"

Tallulah answered, keeping her eyes closed. "Hard to explain, but she practices hoodoo. Insists she isn't a witch, but judge for yourself. She'll mutter lots of mumbo jumbo and then probably will apply a salve and make me drink some horrible herbal concoction."

"I don't find this reassuring," he replied drily.

Tallulah opened her eyes. "I know how it sounds, but it works. Tombi was once badly injured and she cured him. I've seen her do it many times since with someone ill. If she thinks they need to see a doctor, she'll say so."

"Will you listen to her if she recommends you see one?"

She gave a reluctant nod. "I'm starting to feel dizzy and the burn feels deeper, larger. Like it's spreading."

His unease grew to fear. *Don't let her know.* He sought words of encouragement. "The shock is probably wearing off and that makes you feel the injury more."

She nodded, accepting his theory. "Could be."

The question that burned his heart and mind had to be asked. "Are you sure it was a wolf that bit you? Could it have been a wild dog perhaps?"

"A wolf." She pinned him with a fierce gaze. "The same one that entered your farmhouse several nights ago."

"Describe this wolf."

"It had yellow eyes and grayish brown fur."

He stifled a sigh. She could be describing almost any one of them.

"No distinctive marks?"

Her face scrunched and she tilted her head to the side. "By the time it was close enough to be seen, my only thought was to injure it or escape."

His hopes collapsed.

"There was one thing, though. It had a tuft of black hair that started an inch above its eyes and broadened as it stretched above its ears."

Holy crap. It couldn't be.

Tallulah's eyes narrowed. "Why do you ask?"

"We'll need to find it in the wild. See if it has rabies," he lied.

Her dark, sharp eyes missed nothing. "You're keeping something from me. Something to do with this wolf."

"No." His denial was immediate and total. He would say nothing to jeopardize the pack. Without them, he was nothing. A freak. An outsider. This was a matter for the pack. He'd go home and confront the killer. The pack would seek treatment for him.

"Yes," she insisted. "You've got a secret."

"As do you."

Disquieting silence created a void between them. One that seemed impossible to bridge.

The crunch of tires on gravel sounded from outside and he stood, glad for the distraction. He hurried to the door and flung it open.

Tombi and Annie scurried out of their pickup truck. Annie looked especially slender and petite walking with her tall and commanding husband.

Annie brushed past him carrying a black leather bag. Tombi came to a stop less than a foot away.

"What happened? Were you with her?"

The man could be every bit as fierce as Tallulah. His long black hair emphasized his high cheekbones and the sharp angles of his face. It was a different side of Tombi from the one he'd shown at the dinner party.

"I wasn't. I was out in the woods and heard her scream. I carried her here. She insisted on calling Annie and not a doctor."

"Never heard of a wolf attack in these parts."

He didn't accuse, but Payton felt the sting nonetheless.

Wordlessly, he stepped to the side and Tombi strode into the cabin, Payton following.

Annie was bent over Tallulah, studying the injury. "There is an infection of some sort," she pronounced, pulling packets of herbs and vials from her satchel. "Tombi, set a kettle of water to boil."

Tombi obeyed at once, his face grim and foreboding.

"Shouldn't she go to the ER?" Payton asked. He feared doctors as much as Tallulah seemed to. What would the tests show? The results could be dangerous not only for his pack, but also for all werewolves. But if Tallulah needed it, the consequences must be faced.

"Let me try first," Annie said. She pulled a couple of candles from her tote and set them on the coffee table, along with a picture of a saint, or an angel with wings—he wasn't sure which.

Candles and saints and herbs? It would be no match against the strength of the lycanthropic fever.

Annie lit the candles and a stick of incense and the roomed filled with a pungent odor. "I beseech thee, Blackhawk and all the saints. Be with us to heal Tallulah."

She unstopped one of the vials and anointed Tallulah's forehead, then rubbed the mixture on her forehead and chest.

For once, Tallulah was silent. A shrill whistle from the kitchen interrupted the quiet procedure.

"Dampen several towels with the boiling water," Annie called out.

Tombi walked in carrying the steaming cloths. Annie placed one on the open wound. Tallulah moaned and bucked. The sound wrenched his heart.

"Are you okay?" He edged between the women and held Tallulah's hand. She gripped it silently. "I'll stay with you, Lulu," he whispered in her ear.

She gave a faint nod, not even wincing at the nickname. "Thank you."

Annie held her other hand and spoke more of her mumbo jumbo. Tallulah's face and chest grew clammy, the red streaks of infection worsening.

"It's not working," he groaned. "She needs a doctor."

"Don't interrupt." Tombi glared at him. "Give it a chance. You're not helping."

"The infection and fever will worsen temporarily as I draw out the poison," Annie said in her quiet, calm way. "Perhaps it would be best if you both stepped outside until the ritual is finished."

"I'm not leaving Tallulah," he declared.

"Go," Tallulah ordered. "I'll be fine."

"No." He squeezed her hand. "I can't leave you like this."

Tombi laid a hand on his shoulder. "We need to talk anyway."

Tallulah withdrew her hand. With a sigh, Payton rose to his feet.

Tombi motioned to the porch. "We can talk out there."

"Call me if you need me." Payton bent down and kissed her fevered brow before following Tombi outside.

Even though it was late afternoon, the humidity was stifling. He swiped a hand over his face. But this was nothing compared to what Tallulah must be experiencing with the fever.

Tombi leaned against the porch railing. "Just how close are you and Tallulah?"

"Maybe you should ask her. From my end, I'm, um, very attracted to your sister. But you saw for yourself that she has issues about me and my job." Payton shifted on his feet, uncomfortable talking about his feelings. Interrogation by someone's family member was new territory. He was never involved long enough with one woman for such entanglements.

"How did this attack happen?" Tombi said, moving on from emotional issues. "What do you know about it?"

"Like I told you before, I didn't see the attack."

"She finally told me about the wolf entering your house. The one you and the others claimed not to observe."

He drew up stiffly. Much as he liked Tombi and was attracted to Tallulah, his loyalty to the pack came before everything else. "I have no explanation for that."

"I think you do," Tombi said quietly.

Payton stared out into the bayou woods. "I'll speak to the others when I get back to the farmhouse. Get to the bottom of things."

"See that you do. I respect a man's privacy, but Jeb was killed and now my sister's been attacked. I won't have it. This is my land, my family. We protect our own."

"Understood."

There would be no more attacks. He'd make damn sure of that.

A scream rent the air and Payton's fists tightened by his sides. "Annie is hurting her."

"My wife knows what she's doing. She's cured many of us from far worse."

Ah, but the lycanthropic fever was an unknown quantity. They had no idea of the danger. "What if the wolf had rabies?" he argued, to give Tombi a notion of how serious this injury could be.

"If Annie is unsuccessful, we'll get Tallulah medical attention at once."

Another scream. To hell with staying outside. Payton barged through the door.

Annie didn't look his way, but held up hand. "The worst has passed."

It was true, Payton saw when he got to Tallulah's side. Tallulah's flushed face had returned to its natural color. Damp hair plastered her scalp and cheeks, but her eyes were open and clear.

"Told you Annie could heal me," she said, a self-satisfied gleam in her eyes.

He smiled. Even after an ordeal like this, she kept a fighting spirit. "You win this round."

Tombi nodded at him. "I believe you have some business to take care of."

Payton glanced uneasily at Tallulah. He was desperate to confront the attacker, but loathe to leave her side.

"We'll stay with her until you return," Annie assured him.

"I'll be back tonight," he promised Tallulah. "There's something important I need to handle first."

He'd never dreaded anything more.

Chapter 7

Tallulah took a sip of the herbal tea and scowled. "What is this? Boiled grass?"

"Feverfew, chamomile and a special blend from my Grandma Tia. Now drink up," Annie ordered.

"Witch," Tallulah joked.

Theirs had not been an easy relationship at first meet, but she'd grown to love Annie as her very own sister. She had a gentle heart and was a perfect mate for Tombi. Her brother was the stern leader of the shadow hunters, but Annie brought out a tenderness in her twin that astounded Tallulah.

"Go on, drink," Annie insisted.

A gentle tyrant. Best to down it all at once and be done with the vile drink. Tallulah tipped the mug and washed it down. It wanted to come back up. She took deep breaths to quell the nausea. If she vomited, Annie would make another cup and force it on her.

"There. Done." Tallulah set the mug on the coffee table. "Now all I need is a hot bath."

"Not so fast." Annie drew a needle and thread from her satchel and expertly threaded it.

"Hell no." Tallulah stood. "No stitches."

Tombi laughed. "I've seen you face evil spirits and sustain many an injury with no complaint. But you've always been a baby about needles."

No sense denying it. "Fine. I'm a baby. Now let me go get my bath."

"You have to get stitches," Annie insisted. "It will close the skin tears and prevent infection."

"I'll take my chances."

Tombi pressed an amber-colored drink in her hand. "Drink up."

"Whiskey?"

"It'll do the trick," he promised. "Make the inevitable less painful."

Tallulah downed the alcohol and gasped at the burning that spread down her throat and to her stomach. "More," she demanded.

Tombi dutifully poured another couple of ounces and she drank. Abruptly, she retook her seat on the sofa. "Get it over with."

"I'll be quick," Annie said.

Tallulah closed her eyes, like she did for any shot. It was a tad better not to see the needle going in.

A sharp prick on the already tender skin and she screamed.

"Good thing Payton's gone," Tombi quipped. "He'd be climbing the walls."

"What are you talking about?"

"When we were outside and you screamed, you'd have thought he was the one hurt."

"Really?" Her stomach did a little happy dance. She wished he were still here, holding her hand. She focused on remembering his handsome face, the way he had run through the woods holding her, the concern in his pewter-gray eyes. Her gentle giant with the golden hair.

The needle slid in and out, but it was bearable.

"What kind of business was he in a rush to take care of?" Annie asked.

"I'm not exactly sure," Tombi said. "But he promised there would be no more attacks."

Tallulah's eyes flew open. "How can he make such a promise?"

"We need to find out," Tombi said. "How well do you really know this man?"

Good question. One she wasn't sure how to answer. "Evidently, not well enough. But I thought you liked him?"

"You can hardly blame me for a doubt creeping in after what happened to you."

"Give it time. If he's trustworthy, and I believe he is, then all will be revealed in due course." Annie knotted the thread and snipped it off with scissors. "All done."

Tallulah heaved a sigh of relief. A sudden thought struck her. "What do you think of him, Annie? Did you hear his aura?"

Her sister-in-law wasn't a shadow hunter, but she possessed her own unique gift. She could hear music around other people, could intuit something of their hidden natures.

Annie blew out the candles and began packing up

her supplies. "His was unlike any others I've ever heard." She hesitated.

"Go on," Tallulah urged. "What did Payton sound like?"

"Like the howling of a wolf."

Chills sent a tremor down her spine. "What does that mean?"

"Is he Tallulah's attacker?" Tombi was on his feet, anger sparking his copper eyes.

"No, I don't think so." She tapped her lips with a finger. "It wasn't an angry growl or a howl of an animal on the hunt. It was more…more of a lonely cry. I sensed a consuming loneliness in his soul."

"Lonely, my ass." Tombi strode to the door. "The man has some explaining to do."

"Wait." Tallulah rubbed her temples. "Are we really considering that Payton can shape-shift to an animal form? Like a werewolf?"

"I intend to find out."

"I can handle this on my own," Tallulah said sharply.

Annie intervened, ever the peacemaker. "A woman has her own ways, more effective ways, of unearthing the truth."

Tallulah snorted. "Are you seriously suggesting what I think you are? Seduce Payton to learn his secrets?"

"For what it's worth, I sensed no evil in Payton. I think he's a good man with hidden secrets."

Tallulah pondered werewolf tales she'd heard. Maybe he turned into a werewolf and either couldn't remember or couldn't stop his violent nature in wolf form. And maybe… "Oh, hell."

She sat back down on the couch, her head spinning. "If I've been bitten by a werewolf, does that mean I'll become one?"

Payton entered the farmhouse. Eli, Matt and a few others were watching a Braves baseball game on TV.

"Where've you been all day?" Eli asked.

"Busy. Where is everybody?"

"Adam, Riley, Jason and a few others went out for groceries and other supplies, Russell's in the kitchen cooking supper, and Logan and Ben are sleeping."

Matt pinned him with a hard stare. "Anything wrong?"

"Nothing," he answered, a queasy rumbling in his gut. He'd never lied to his alpha before. Never. "I'll go help Russell with supper."

In the kitchen, Russell's back was to him. The stove top sizzled as he flipped steaks, and the scent of baking bread in the oven permeated the air. It smelled of home and comfort. He turned and walked to the fridge.

"Oh, hi, Payton," he said with a familiar grin. "How long have you been standing there? Give me a hand, will ya?"

Payton went to the stove and turned off the burners and the oven.

"What are you doing?" Russell asked. "Those steaks need a few more minutes."

"We have to talk."

"Sure. What's up?"

"Outside. I don't want anyone else overhearing."

His friend's face only registered mild curiosity. Payton went out the back door and down the back porch steps. He kept walking.

"Where are we going?" At last, a vague alarm crossed his features.

"Farther out, where no one can hear."

"Dude, what the hell?"

Payton didn't speak until they were over a hundred yards from the house. Turning abruptly, he faced him. "Where have you been today, Russell?"

"Mostly hanging out around the house. Although I did go into town for a couple of hours. Why?"

"Tallulah was attacked by a wolf today." He scrutinized his best friend's face, studying it for any trace of guilt.

"The hell?" Russell gave a low whistle. "Have you reported it to Matt yet?"

"No. I wanted to give you a chance to explain before the others find out."

Russell paled. "Explain what?"

"Admit you attacked Tallulah."

He threw up his hands and snickered. "You're kidding me, right? I haven't attacked anybody."

"She described you, Russell. Right down to the streak of black hair on your scalp. You're the only one in the pack with that streak. No way it could be anyone else."

His jaw tightened. "I don't know what you're talking about."

"It's you. It's been you all along. You're the one with the fever. The killer in our midst."

Stunned silence greeted his pronouncement. Tension crackled between them.

"You can't believe that," Russell finally said. "You've just met the woman. You're going to believe her over me? I've been your best friend since you joined the pack as a teenager."

Pain sliced through Payton, white-hot and burning. "That's what makes this so hard. It's why I wanted to confront you away from the pack."

Anger distorted Russell's face, twisted his features into an unrecognizable version of his old friend.

"You can't tell the others." His voice was hard, uncompromising. "I won't go to that hellhole of a place they call a treatment center. It's a jail. A place of no hope and no freedom. I won't live caged like a damn dog."

"Maybe the center can eventually cure the fever. I can understand you're ashamed to face the pack," he said softly. "You've been infected. You can't help what you've become. But you should have told us, told me. Let us help you."

The anger vanished, leaving in its place a broken man. "Please. I'm begging you. Just let me go. I promise I won't hurt anyone else."

"Where would you go?"

"Back out west. I'll live alone in the desert. Survive off the land—miles from other humans."

"Impossible. The craving will overcome your intentions. You know this."

Despite everything, despite the fact that this man had killed, had placed their pack and all other werewolves in danger, despite his attack on Tallulah, Payton hurt for Russell. He couldn't help the murderous impulses that now drove him. Russell had been the one who'd first offered friendship within the pack. Had been a loyal friend through all the turmoil and dark days.

Payton laid a hand on his shoulder. "If you can't

confess to the others, I'll tell them myself. Pack your bags and I'll drive you myself to the treatment center. I've heard they are making strides, that a cure may—"

"No!" Russell's eyes turned wild. "Keep your mouth shut or I'll tell them it's you that's infected. Who do you think they'll believe? I'm not the son of wolf killer. *You* are."

All sympathy fled. "Give it up, Russell. There are witnesses. Tallulah identified you. It's over."

Russell lunged at him, hands gripping his neck in a death vise. Payton dropped to the ground and rolled, managing to get on top of Russell. *Don't let him bite you. He'll infect you and take you down to hell with him.* Payton kneed him in the groin. Russell's hold on his neck loosened and Payton inhaled deeply.

Russell scrambled to his feet, but he was still doubled over in pain. Yet he charged again.

This time Payton was ready and delivered a right hook to his jaw. Russell fell on his ass and stayed down.

"Son of a bitch," he yelled.

Payton stared at his savage eyes and mottled face. His friend was dead to him. "Be a fucking man and get your ass back in the farmhouse."

"Never." He spit, blood dribbling out with saliva. "Come make me." He bared his teeth. "I'll get one good bite in if you try. I promise you that."

He stared at the stranger before him. The fever had burned away most of his humanity. He was no longer a member of the pack. He'd made his choice, and now Payton's decision was easy.

Payton turned away. He'd get Matt and the others. They'd hog-tie Russell's sorry ass and drive him to Montana at once.

Russell clutched his arm and Payton faced him. The fever was taking over Russell. The combined forces of anger and stress made it impossible for any infected wolf to restrain the burning disease inside. Sweat rolled off his forehead and his lips began to curl.

"Give it up, buddy," he said, trying to calm Russell. Slowly, Payton took a few steps back toward the farm-house and scanned the ground for a possible weapon. "We can work this out," he continued, hoping his level voice would get through to his old friend.

But it was too late. Russell's humanity was partially— if not totally—destroyed by the fever. The part of him that had been his best friend, the one he'd watched ball games with and had hunted with, and who had shown him the ropes in the pack's social functioning—that Rus-sell was dead.

His face distorted into a rapid scowl and his skin transformed to a thick coating of gray fur. The damn-ing streak of black fur formed on the top of his head, where tufted ears now appeared. His nose elongated to a snout, and green eyes morphed to yellow. Soon, two legs would become four.

The beast was almost completely primed for attack.

A low growl rent the air. Soon, very soon, Russell would pounce.

Run! Get to the house. Payton fought the instinct. He'd be dead before he made ten feet. Why hadn't he brought along a weapon? His eyes skittered to the ground, finally locating a two-by-four piece that had fallen from the old fence at the edge of the property line. He despaired it would be rotten, but it was worth a shot.

Another step backward, this time angling toward the bit of broken plank.

Russell growled again, louder. The transformation had completed. He lunged, an explosive leap in the air that was so fast, Payton narrowly missed being taken down. He rolled to the ground and grabbed the two-by-four. As the wolf was in midflight over his body, Payton jabbed the weapon at its chest and sent Russell flying to the opposite side of the fence.

I need help. Fast. Payton ran toward the farmhouse, still clutching the two-by-four. "Hey, get out here!" he yelled.

The wolf was in front of him, blocking the path. Payton held up his weapon and it charged. He swung, connecting with the wolf's head.

It barely fazed Russell, who swiped at him again. Pain seared Payton's right leg and blood oozed from torn flesh. The vicious clawing sent a wave of fear and anger through him with a predictable result—bones crunched, and muscles and flesh twisted and morphed him into a wolf. One thought consumed Payton. *Don't let him bite you.*

Unrelenting, Russell charged again.

His best bet was to run. Even if he could beat him in a fair fight, chances were good that Russell could get in a bite. That's all he needed to do, and Payton's life would be ruined.

He ran, all four legs beneath him pumping faster than they'd ever been required. Russell's breath and the pounding of paws was close behind. Gaining on him. Where the hell were his friends?

The chase continued. Payton swerved and darted, narrowly escaping the nips at his heels. He barely registered the creak of the door opening and human voices.

His entire concentration was focused on avoiding the chance of infected saliva burrowing into him.

Men ran toward Payton and Russell slowed, obviously hesitant to engage with more than one adversary at a time. Payton dropped at the alpha's feet, willing his body to transform back to human as Russell turned tail and disappeared into the woods. Damn it, they needed to go after him.

Matt's face thrust near Payton's, concern radiating from his gray eyes. "What happened? Why were you two fighting?"

Payton fought to speak, but the change from wolf to human wasn't instantaneous. He yipped and then cleared his throat as his lips and lungs fully formed. "Russell's the one infected," he panted, exhausted from the chase. His chest heaved up and down as he gathered energy. "He attacked Tallulah today and she can identify him."

Matt scowled. "How could she know which wolf attacked?"

"She described the tuft of black fur on his head. I confronted him and he admitted the truth."

A strange silence descended and Payton glanced around, stumbling to his feet. Eli and Adam had followed Matt out to the yard.

The two men exchanged a glance. "How do we know it's not you?" Eli asked bluntly. "Could be you've concocted a story to throw us off the trail."

Heat flooded his face. "And how do you explain Russell's running away? I'm still here."

"Maybe Russell feared we'd believe your claim," Adam suggested.

He stared at them, appalled. Payton knew suspicion

of his loyalty and character ran deep because of his father's unprecedented act of killing a fellow pack member. After all these years, the sins of the father hadn't dimmed the memory and mistrust of his pack. He'd suspected that was the case and now his fear was confirmed.

"Stop it," Matt said. "I'm inclined to believe Payton."

Inclined? That was still an insult. Anger rendered him speechless.

"We'll search the woods and find him. Hear his side of the story." Matt was taking control. "Eli, get back to the house and gather everyone. We'll spread in different directions."

The alpha fixed him with a domineering stance—hands on hips, teeth bared. "Return to the house with Eli and stay with him while we search."

Payton found his tongue. "You're putting me under some kind of house arrest?"

"It's only temporary. With any luck, we'll get this resolved tonight."

"To hell with this bullshit. He attacked my girlfriend."

Girlfriend? The word had slipped out, catching him by surprise.

"The same girlfriend who's been snooping around and spreading stories to the sheriff?" Eli said with a snarl.

"Something weird about that one," Adam chimed in. "No way she should have seen one of us enter the house in wolf form."

"Enough bickering," Matt snapped. "Eli and Payton to the house. Now."

Payton turned from them, taking large, loping strides

to the farmhouse. The more they talked and strategized, the better chance Russell had for escape. Eli caught up to him.

"Stay in my sight," he warned.

Payton didn't even look at him. "Fuck off."

A hand gripped his shoulder.

"I've never trusted you," Eli said, his face red with anger and exertion. "You ingratiated yourself in this pack when you had no business being one of us. For all his rough ways, Matt can be too soft."

"Go to hell. I'm returning to the house on Matt's orders. Not yours. So leave me alone, asshole."

Payton mounted the porch steps and entered the house, Eli close on his heels.

"Everyone join Matt and Adam outside," Eli commanded. "He's calling a search for Russell."

The men lounging by the TV sprang up and rushed toward the door, not even taking time to ask questions. The alpha's commands were absolute.

Payton watched the screen door bang shut and then stood by the window. Matt and Adam had already shifted to wolf form. In the twilight, their yellow eyes glowed in the shadow of the magnolias and oaks at the edge of the woods. His inner wolf howled to join them, to be one with the pack as they searched for the traitor. It had been weeks since he'd shape-shifted and his wolf craved release. His loneliness was absolute. They had excluded him.

Eli joined him by the window. He felt it, too.

"I'd rather be out hunting than stuck with you," Eli complained bitterly.

"Ditto."

At least in this, they were one.

Payton paced the room, trying to burn off his hurt and anger. The last fifteen years of his life had been a farce. He'd given all his heart and mind to the pack only to discover they had never considered him one of their own.

It was almost enough to make him entirely sympathetic to his father's rash act of murder.

After a while, shadows changed from a whisper of night to an inky darkness, but the others still hadn't returned from the hunt. Russell had slipped away. The next hunt for the rogue might be too late for an unsuspecting human wanderer. The longer he lived in the wild with nothing to feed on except the blood of animals, the more dangerous the lycanthropic fever grew. Even if he was captured later, the chance to reclaim his human nature might be forever lost. Payton suspected that time might have passed anyway. If the craving had been so consuming as to attack a human in the middle of the day, it had indeed taken root in what was left of Russell's soul.

As his anger receded, Payton grew more concerned for Tallulah. What if she had taken an unexpected turn for the worse? He'd promised to return to her tonight, but if the pack didn't come back…where did his loyalty now belong?

"I see them," Eli said, jumping up from his chair.

Payton hurried to the window, eyes straining to pierce the night. His vision was much keener than a normal human's, but not near as good as it was in wolf form. He studied the black tableau through the pane of glass. Ah, there. Over a dozen yellow eyes and moving shadows headed to the farmhouse. Too early to tell which was which. Had they captured Russell? The specks of yellow wolf eyes disappeared and the shadows shifted to vertical columns. They'd already shapeshifted to human form.

Matt walked at the head of the hunters, his mouth a grim slash of frustration.

No Russell.

His alpha was as frustrated as he was. He'd been so close to capturing Russell.

They filed into the house, silent and seething.

Matt cast him the briefest of looks before striding to the fireplace and resting his right arm on the mantel, a familiar pose. Time for a lecture, a strategy session or both.

No one else glanced his way as they took their seats, as surely as if each spot had been marked by an unsaid teacher's assignment.

"What happened?" he blurted. "Did you find any signs?"

Matt gave a terse nod. "We found paw prints. But they looped and circled until we finally lost the thread of their direction in the swamp water. This terrain is the perfect place for a man—or wolf—to disappear."

"We need to find him," Adam said. "Get his side of the story."

He couldn't hold back his anger. "There is no other side. Russell has the fever and I confronted him. He attacked me first, refused to listen to reason—"

"You had no right to confront him." Matt clasped his hands behind his back in an obvious attempt to rein in his own temper. "I was here in the house, even asked you if anything was wrong, and you walked right past me and tried to talk to Russell on your own. Why?"

"I wanted to assure him he'd get treatment, that I'd

stand beside him when he confessed to the rest of you that he was infected. He was my friend."

"And I am your alpha. That takes precedent over anything else. It's the law of the pack."

He should feel shame. In the past, this type of rebuke would have lanced his soul. But tonight? His heart was longing to be near Tallulah.

"Maybe Russell would have been found if you all had believed me to start with. Instead, you each questioned my integrity and forced two members of the pack to house arrest while a search was organized."

"Hey, don't lump me in with you," Eli blustered, ruddy face aflame. "I was ordered here to keep watch on you."

Knuckleheads. "I didn't need watching because I've done nothing wrong."

"A killer's on the loose and it's your fault," Eli accused.

"That's not true!"

But even as he formed the denial, Payton's conscience convicted him. If he had the chance to do it over, he wouldn't have faced Russell. He should have foreseen this happening. Stupid, stupid, stupid to handle it on his own. Would a true pack member have tried to salvage a friendship, as he had? No, they always considered the pack's welfare above all else.

To hell with that.

Matt held up a hand for silence and faced Payton. "You said Tallulah identified Russell as the attacker."

Payton nodded.

"I want you to find out what's going on with her. She seems to be at the core of all our problems. Sheriff Angier was around this morning. Acted like he was just taking a casual stroll—but the wily old man senses something. If he's already made the connection to similar murders in Montana, he didn't let on. Thanks to Tallulah, he's predisposed to think the worst of us."

"He didn't need Tallulah's help to think the worst," he argued. "Trouble has followed us because of Russell, not her."

"She's seen things no human should be able to see and she's always around. I want to know why."

So did he. But not for the same reasons. She fascinated him, intrigued him. "What are you suggesting?" he asked Matt.

"Get her to confide in you and tell us her secrets."

A few of the men snickered. "Gigolo," one of them muttered under his breath.

For the second time this evening, unfamiliar rebellion roiled in his gut. He wouldn't do it.

Matt frowned, as if reading his thoughts. "You got a problem with that?"

He drew himself up, glancing at all the faces of the pack members regarding their exchange.

"I will not." Three simple words that could cost him everything.

A heavy, absolute silence hung in the air. Outside, the sudden screech of an owl broke the spell—an angry cacophony of doom.

Matt lowered his voice, but his harsh whisper echoed through the den. "I brought you in as one of ours when no other pack would take you. Guided you into our ways and provided you a home, a shelter. You want to throw it all away on a piece of ass you've only known a short time?"

His temper flared, the flames licking and eroding his normal reserve.

"That's not what she is. Her life was in danger today but she survived and helped me find the killer." He looked over Matt's shoulder at the men he'd regarded as friends. Brothers, even, bonded through their rare lycanthropic blood. Part creatures of the night that roamed the land together and reveled in their wild, animalistic yearnings.

"But instead of relief at ending the taint on our names, our very lives, you all turned against me. I've never been one of you. Not really. You hold my past against me. I can't help what my father did. He broke a cardinal rule, yes. But I am not my father."

Matt strode past him, beckoning him to follow. "Let's discuss this on the porch."

Outside, Payton drew in the fresh air, finding some comfort in the open space.

Matt stepped off the porch and into the yard. He heaved a sigh and faced Payton. "Perhaps we were a bit harsh earlier."

A bit? But even this small concession wasn't easy for the alpha. He kept his silence.

"On further reflection, I realized you told the truth. Russell is infected. Tallulah has no reason to lie and Russell was your friend. If you falsely accused anyone, it would be Eli. The two of you have always clashed."

"Thank you," he replied stiffly, still unappeased. The halfhearted apology would have been more generous if Matt had spoken it in front of the others. But no, as alpha he sought to save face at all times.

"Russell is dead to us," Matt said abruptly. "I don't want to lose you as well."

"Why should I stay? The pack has shown their true feelings about me today."

Matt waved a dismissive hand. "That's just Eli bull-dozing everyone with his paranoid personality. Adam is young, looks up to Eli like a father figure. He just parrots Eli's opinions."

And yet, his alpha had done little to defend him against the unjust accusations. Matt cared more about pride and power than fighting for truth. Sometimes Payton even wondered... "Do you even care about Jeb and the other people Russell has killed over the past year? Or are you more worried about the cops and possible arrests."

"It's my job to look after the pack's own interests." Matt lifted his chin a fraction. "Russell can't help what he's become. I want to find him before the cops, see he gets help. I see nothing wrong with that."

"I can't argue with your logic. I don't want him in jail, either."

"Good, we're on the same page on that issue. Now about Tallulah, I don't see the harm in uncovering how she spotted Russell in wolf form, in the dark no less."

We all have secrets, Tombi had said. *I don't want them to discover my unusual nature*, Tallulah had admitted. Yes, his curiosity was definitely aroused.

Matt interrupted his thoughts. "We need to know how she does it to avoid detection in the future. That's all."

Again, he couldn't fault the man's logic. Yet the idea of spying on Tallulah offended him. There must be a way to learn her supernatural senses without having to reveal all of it to his alpha.

It was all too much to ponder tonight. For now, he

wanted nothing more than to be with Tallulah. He'd
figure it out later, in his own time and his own way.

"I'm going to visit her tonight," he said, avoiding
an outright commitment to the alpha's order. Let Matt
draw his own conclusions.

Chapter 8

Where was he?

Tallulah stared out the window, sipping a shot glass of whiskey to ease the pain gnawing at her shoulder. It had taken hours to persuade Tombi and Annie to leave, but she'd finally convinced them after promising to drink the herbal concoction Annie had left behind. That, and another promise to call if Payton never came. It was after midnight. The man was definitely looking like a no-show. Had he gone after the wolf who'd attacked her?

She didn't know whether to be worried for his welfare or curse an empty promise. Worse, she realized she didn't even have his cell phone number to call and check in.

Elliptical beams of light flowed into the driveway. She stepped away from the open curtains and peeked out the side of the drapes. A long, lean man scrambled out of the truck and reached over the seat, retrieving an overnight bag from the passenger side.

Moonbeams shone down on sun-streaked, golden hair. Payton, at last.

Equal parts relief and anger washed through her. Relief he was okay, anger that she'd been forced to wait and worry for hours. Tallulah hustled from view as he climbed the porch steps and knocked at the door. She paused a suitable amount of time, then opened the door, blinking, as if she'd been woken from a deep sleep instead of pacing the floors worrying.

Never admit you care, never admit vulnerability. Her mantra since losing Bo and acting the fool over the traitorous Hanan. For all she knew, Payton might have a dark underside he had yet to display.

Tallulah stretched her arms over her head and made a show of yawning. "What time is it? Didn't expect you back tonight."

"I said I'd return."

She stepped away from the doorway and ushered him inside. "You didn't have to come. I'm perfectly fine. What's with the bag?"

Payton's lips curled slightly. "That's your automatic reaction to everything."

"What is?"

"Saying you're *fine*. Even when you obviously aren't."

"I've managed to get by on my own for a long time." She pointed at the gym bag.

Payton shrugged. "Thought I'd stay over in case you needed protection, or if the fever returned. I promised Tombi that I would."

Irritation buzzed along her nerves. How like her twin

to butt into her business. "Like I said, I'm…" Tallulah broke off at the amused gleam in his eyes.

"Fine?" he prompted.

"Doing well," she insisted.

He followed her into the den, where she settled into her rocking chair. Payton dropped his gym bag by the end of the couch and sat down, patting the soft suede material. "I can sleep on this."

"Suit yourself."

"Glad to be so wanted." He gave his customary grin, but it didn't reach his eyes.

"What's wrong? Wh—" She narrowed her eyes, taking in the two red welts on his neck. Alarm tripped her heart. "You've been attacked."

He casually lifted a shoulder. "Yeah."

She picked up the shot glass of whiskey on the end table and carried it to him. "Drink this," she ordered, settling by his side.

He dutifully downed what was left in one long swallow, coughing a bit, as if his throat were raw.

"Want another?"

Payton shook his head. "Nah. This will do me."

"Tell me what happened. Did you go after the wolf that attacked me?"

"I did." He set down the glass carefully, avoiding her eyes.

"Well? Did you kill it?"

He breathed out a deep sigh. "No. It escaped."

"So how did this happen?" She lightly ran her fingers down the side of his neck. "These are not bite marks."

"Those are courtesy of my former best friend, who tried to kill me tonight."

He said it so calmly, so matter-of-factly, his voice

hollow. Something more than a physical injury had drained him.

"But why were—"

"Shhh." He placed a finger on her lips. He dropped his hand lower, pushing aside the opening of her loose T-shirt. "I've been worried about you." His breath drew in at the sight of the stitches. "Did Annie sew this?"

"After I'd downed a few shots of whiskey. Still hurts like hell."

"Poor baby."

Warm lips touched her forehead like a benediction of grace. Tallulah closed her eyes, allowed the safe, gentle feeling to spread over her ruffled nerves. His breath was hot against her face, sweet as honeyed whiskey.

She rested her head rested against his chest...and picked up a faint trace of something metallic. The same scent that had been on the wolf, tangy beneath the fur odor. She jerked up her head, all cozy warmth evaporating.

"You smell like *him*," she accused, her pulse quickening. Could he be the one—? No, he would never do that. At his blank stare, she continued. "Like the attacker."

"That's because he's the man I fought."

Her brow puckered in confusion. "You said your best friend did this to you."

He stood. "Correct. I'm going to shower, if you don't mind."

"But..." She shook her head. This made no sense. Some might claim a dog or other house pet as a friend, but a wolf? "Your best friend is a wolf?" she asked.

"Not now, if you don't mind. Later."

She stood and eyed Payton under the overhead light.

He looked like hell. Red streaks of clay dirt lined his T-shirt and jeans. Besides the red marks on his neck, there were dark shadows under his eyes. And the eyes themselves were storm pools of pain and misery. She'd give him a break for now.

"Definitely later. You have lots of explaining to do. This way." She led him to the bathroom connected to her bedroom and motioned at the door. "It's all yours."

He suddenly pulled her against his hard, lean body and kissed her. His mouth and tongue were hard, full of need and promise. Just as suddenly, Payton released her and her body missed his body pressed intimately to her own. Without a word, he went to the bathroom, leaving the door ajar.

Tallulah scurried from the open doorway. There was the unmistakable sound of a belt unbuckling, a zipper being undone and then the heavy thud of his jeans as they hit the tiled floor. The water spray started and she pictured him, naked, walking into the shower stall. Tallulah stared at her face in the mirror and swept an unsteady hand through her sheen of black hair.

Did he find her attractive? He must. They'd certainly had their share of stolen kisses. Tallulah lifted the loose white T-shirt and drew in her breath at the sight of the black puckered stitches on her shoulder and the angry red skin where she'd been bitten.

She looked hideous. Quickly she lowered the T-shirt back over head. It flowed down to about an inch below her ass. It was practical and clean, but not the look she was going for tonight. She could do better.

Tallulah went to her dresser and searched until she found a nude-colored satin shift that Annie had bought for her last Christmas. It wasn't supersexy, but it showed some cleavage and a lot of leg. Payton would approve.

Her eyes lit on a photo of her and Bo together on horseback. A happy day, only two months before the shadow spirit Nalusa Falaya had fatally bitten her lover. Tallulah laid it facedown on the dresser. She also took off the engagement ring he'd given her and that she wore on her right hand. Slowly, she stored it away in her jewelry box. "Sorry, Bo," she whispered, knowing it was illogical. He'd want her to continue on, to find love and happiness. Too bad that the only time she'd had physical relations after Bo had been with Hanan.

Memories threatened to sour the night, but she wouldn't let them. She was a fighter—in all things. Carefully, her shoulder still aching, Tallulah changed into the satin gown and returned to the dresser mirror. She picked up a bottle of cologne and sprayed her neck and chest. A bit of the cologne's alcohol base accidentally landed on her stitches, stinging like a swarm of bees.

"Damn it," she cried out.

The shower spray stopped and Payton walked out, a towel wrapped around his lean hips. "What's wrong? Are you hurt?"

Her mouth went dry. "It was nothing," she stammered, feeling like an idiot.

"I heard you cry out." He scanned her body, eyes full of concern.

"I, um, forgot about my injury when I changed into my pajamas."

His eyes dropped, raking in the swell of her breasts, and down her long legs, where her bare toes curled against the oak flooring. He repeated the process from the ground up until his eyes met hers once again.

"Beautiful," he said hoarsely. "Did you change for me?"

"No," she lied. "I spilled something on the T-shirt and grabbed the first old thing I pulled out of my dresser drawer."

"Is that right?" A slow, sexy grin spread across his strong, masculine face. "Must be my lucky day."

He saw right through her. She turned away from him, facing the mirror. "Go back and finish your shower."

"I'd rather be here with you." Payton walked up behind her and splayed his large, calloused hands against the soft fabric draping her abdomen. The rough texture through silk made her thighs and core clench with longing. His eyes burned into her own in the mirror's reflection. He kept his eyes focused on hers as his hands slipped up and cupped her breasts.

Tallulah inhaled sharply and arched into his palms, her nipples hard and straining under his touch. She closed her eyes, savoring the delicious feel. It had been too long—way, way too long.

"Open your eyes," he commanded, voice rough with need.

She did, obeying his orders without thought. His fingers tweaked and pulled at the round, rosy nubs, teasing her into a frenzy of desire.

"Look how sexy you are," he whispered harshly, his breath fanning against her ear.

She pressed against his hips and the towel fell to the floor. His manhood bulged and pulsed against her ass.

What the hell was she doing? It was too fast. Too much too soon. Her mind argued as her body continued to hum and tingle. Logic was losing the battle. Yet she stiffened, brown eyes full of confusion and doubt.

"What's wrong, baby?"

She shook her head, shielding her face with her hair. She felt so…bare. Raw.

Payton stepped back and placed his hands on either side of her hips, turning her around to face him.

She dropped her eyes to his chest, where dark blond curls were matted against his muscular torso. "I—I'm not sure I'm ready," she admitted.

"Is it Bo?" he asked gently, lifting her chin.

She was shocked and dismayed to feel tears spill over and run down her cheeks. "No. Yes. I don't know. It's just—you're only here temporarily. And then I'll be alone again."

There. She'd admitted it. Probably sounding like every other needy woman who'd had a fling with the handsome lumberjack who had drifted through their town. "Forget it," she growled. "Must be the pain and the whiskey talking."

He picked up the towel and redraped it over his hips, but not before she caught sight of his swollen manhood. Her pulse raced at the sight.

"I understand," he assured her. "I'll finish my shower—with cold water." He gave a wry grin and headed back to the bathroom.

Tallulah sank to the edge of the bed and covered her face with her hands. What was wrong with her? She was no virgin and certainly not one to tease a man in a vain attempt to satisfy her ego. They were two consenting adults who were attracted to each other. She could have a night of passion as long as she guarded her heart from wanting more.

Take what affection you can while he's here. You want Payton. When he leaves, don't be filled with regret, thinking of the nights you could have been with him. Enjoying him. Life was too unpredictable. Bo's death had taught her that.

Full of resolve, Tallulah wiped her eyes and set about turning down the bedspread and cotton sheets. Setting the lamplight to low, she climbed in bed and pulled off the gown, tossing it to the floor. Even though she tried not to move her injured shoulder, pain radiated down her arm and she hissed, stifling a cry of pain. Naked, she sat up in bed, settling against the pillows and rested. Better. The whiskey from earlier was beginning to numb the pain to a dull ache.

What the hell would Payton think when he saw her open invitation? Her moment of fear and doubt had probably turned him off her for good. What if he walked out that bathroom door and continued on, never giving her more than a second glance? Nervously, she settled her long hair over her shoulders, covering her wound and the peaks of her breasts. She hated this vulnerable feeling, hated showing him her need. Maybe she should forget the whole thing. Before she could act on the sudden case of nervousness, light spilled from the bathroom and Payton exited, clad only in jeans. His muscled chest, with the curly matted hair, glistened with moisture. He started to walk past the bed, then did a double take.

She patted the space beside her on the mattress.

He hesitated, but settled on the opposite side of the bed, eyeing her warily.

Tallulah slid down into the sheets and held out both arms to him.

"Are you sure?" he asked. "We don't have to do anything. I'm okay with sleeping on the couch. Or leaving, if that's what you want."

"I want you," she admitted, her voice strong and steady. "I'm as sure as I've ever been of anything in my life."

Let tomorrow be its own worry. If it was the madness of the new moon, she'd accept responsibility in the light of day. Tonight, she craved Payton's arms and passion.

Swiftly, he shed his jeans and underwear and slid in beside her.

"I'll be careful of your injury," he promised.

"I trust you."

It was as simple and complicated as that. No matter their individual secrets, what was important now was the need to make love and explore the mystery of their bodies.

A hand slid down the curve of her hip. Her naked flesh tingled under his large, calloused palm. He brushed a lock of her hair from her breasts, exposing the rose-red peaks that hardened from his intense gaze.

"So beautiful," he murmured.

She carefully ran a hand through the tuft of hair on his broad, powerful chest. "Payton," she whispered. He was really here with her, desired her as much as she did him. She kissed the red welts at his neck, skimmed a finger across the dark shadows under his eyes and showered butterfly kisses along his left jaw, where a bruise was beginning to form.

Payton kissed her, claiming her lips. As exciting as his other kisses had been, there was no comparison to this one as they lay naked beside each other. She opened her mouth, felt the velvet warmth of his tongue as it skillfully swirled and danced with her own. She could kiss him forever.

He was careful to keep his weight on one arm as he tenderly explored her breasts. He sank down, planting his mouth on one of the hard buds, suckling and flicking his tongue over the sensitive areola. Fire exploded, a hot wire of nerves traveled like lightning to her core and her inner muscles tightened. A moan escaped her lips.

"Did I hurt you?" he asked huskily.

She shook her head and traced her fingers up and down the hard ridges of his back. His muscles tensed and rippled beneath her fingertips. Her hand shifted lower, caressing the toned muscles of his ass.

He moved out of her grasp, his long body sliding down her length, kissing the smooth plane of her abdomen. And then, lower still. His hot breath fanned her mound and caressed her womanly folds. Excitement pulsed in her core. By the time his mouth kissed her there, Tallulah gripped the bedsheets with clenched fists for mooring against her turbulent emotions. She was free-falling, racing for fulfillment, out of control. His tongue stroked the slick wet heat of her, undoing the little reserve that remained.

"Payton," she breathed, loving the sound of his name on her lips. For now, she was all his. Damn the morning.

She ached to pleasure him as well. She tugged at his hair, signaling him to stop.

He didn't.

Payton continued his ministrations and she arched and groaned, fully surrendering to the wild pleasure. Euphoria slammed into every pore of her body as she climaxed.

"Lulu." Her name on his lips reverberated inside her

body, a soothing emotional caress that said he was there with her, holding her as she broke apart in his arms. He rose up, hovering inches from her body, and kissed the swell of her breasts. She could feel the need and tension in his body. She parted her legs, urging him to enter.

Payton flipped onto his back, placing her so that she straddled his hips. "Your shoulder," he explained, voice gravelly and taut with desire. "I don't want to accidentally hurt you."

Even in this, he sought to protect her, placed her needs above his own. She put her hand on his erection and guided it into her slick core. He drew in a sharp breath.

She raised and lowered on his hardness, watching his face grow tight with tension. He placed his hands on her hips, encouraging her to go faster, deeper. Her excitement built, the same passion matching Payton's need. Their pace was frenzied until she burst once again. Payton drove into her twice more, long deep thrusts as he spilled into her hot, womanly core.

Tallulah rolled to the side, careful to land on her uninjured shoulder, and cuddled into his strong, muscled body. He stroked her hair, planted kisses on the top of her scalp. His rapid heartbeat drummed beneath her ear.

"That was amazing," he breathed, pausing a moment. "For you, too?"

The odd vulnerability in his voice touched Tallulah. "Amazing," she agreed, hastening to reassure him. "Any more amazing and I wouldn't have survived it."

He chuckled and squeezed her close. "Now that's what I like to hear."

Tallulah kissed his hair-roughened chest, inhaling the soapy, masculine scent and tasting the salty tang of his skin. A peaceful lethargy settled in her mind and body. Yawning, she stretched and wiggled her toes. "You *are* spending the night in my bed, right?"

"You couldn't kick me out with a team of field mules."

She giggled. "Now that's what I like to hear," she said, mimicking his earlier words.

His stomach roiled and his tongue was thick and coated from his last meal of possum. The raw repast disgusted him in the dawn's light.

Russell rubbed his sore jaw, still aching from Payton's blow the previous evening. His legs were useless appendages of jelly, exhausted from the midnight running. Several times, Matt had caught his scent, and capture had been a near thing. As much as Russell despised the heat and swampy conditions, the water had saved his ass as he'd run in circles and backtracked through the slimy morass.

Now what was he supposed to do?

At least it was a Monday—the pack would be on the timber-clearing site. But if they were smart—and they were—one or two would have been left behind to guard the farmhouse. He would have to lie in wait and look for an opportunity to sneak in, grab some clothes and find his truck keys. He wouldn't feel safe again until there were a few miles between him and them.

As of today, the boundaries were clearly drawn between his former life and his homeless future without the pack. He'd been close enough to hear Matt and Payton discussing him last night. Close enough that they should have smelled his scent. But their high emotions had blocked them from using their wolf abilities to their fullest.

His ploy to play off Payton as the infected wolf hadn't worked. Not that there had been much hope of deflecting suspicion. The evidence against him was overwhelming.

Damn them all to hell. Especially Payton and that bitch Tallulah. They would all pay, every last one. He'd been one of them—they had no right to kick him out of the pack. Not his fault he'd been bitten by another wolf in Montana and contracted the fever. And if they thought they could hole him away in that treatment prison, they could think again. He'd never go. Would rather die than have his freedom constricted to a sterile building of concrete and steel. Hell, no.

Already the sun baked his skin through his ripped T-shirt and jeans. Vomit and blood coated his clothes and he recoiled at the putrid scent. He raised an arm and sniffed. Fur and sweat assaulted his nostrils and made his eyes water.

Was this his life from now on? Reduced to an animal? Fighting for his next meal and constantly on the defensive for predators? Speaking of which... Russell's gaze swept the ground, fully expecting to find a coiled rattlesnake. A miracle he hadn't been bitten while on the run last night.

Again, his gut bubbled, protesting against the possum that he'd never fully digested as he fled his pursuers. He vomited again, mostly dry heaves. He spit out the vile aftertaste. His tongue was gritty and throat parched.

Water.

Thirst consumed him. Russell eyed the green, algae-infested swamp water and licked his lips. Disgusting as the water appeared, it tempted him, teased him with the promise of *wet*. No doubt it teemed with parasites and bacterial hazards. A cauldron of intestinal disaster.

Turning away, he stumbled toward the clearing by the farmhouse. His jellied legs tripped over an oak root and he fell to the ground.

"Son of a bitch," he cursed. "Mother—"

He stopped. How stupid to scream. If someone was near, he would have to run again, a race he was sure to lose in this weakened condition. Russell leaned against a tree, gathering his strength should he need to take off. His pulse raced and his breathing was rushed, as loud and labored as a brisk breeze.

He listened intently for the even the smallest disturbance of sound—a snapped twig, the brushing of a boot against pine needles. His fingers twitched and his teeth ground together. At the prolonged silence, Russell shoved off and continued on his journey. Near the clearing, he dropped to the ground and rubbed his temples, where engorged blood pounded his veins. The first warning sign of dehydration. If an opportunity didn't soon present itself for sneaking into the house, he'd have to force his way in and kill.

Rage and fury corded the muscles of his neck and he wiped away the sweat stinging his eyes. "I'll get you. Every last one of you. This is your fault, not mine."

The pack should have protected him from the lycanthropic fever outbreak. He'd done them a favor by not infecting them. All the nights he'd sneaked out, he could easily have entered their rooms, bitten them in their sleep.

A pounding roared in his ears as he watched the

house. Russell grabbed a pinecone and dug his palms into the rough shell, the pain a distraction from the headache. In the driveway, there was only one vehicle. Adam's. The luck of the damned was finally with him. The youngest of the pack was the weakest. He'd bet anything the guy was taking the opportunity to sleep in while everyone else toiled in the hot sun.

And if Adam were awake…too bad. Russell felt the tight smile stretch the skin on his dirty face. Because whatever it took, he was getting something to drink, and grabbing a fresh change of clothes, a wallet and truck keys.

The next time he entered the farmhouse after today, he wouldn't be sneaking around for a few necessities. Next time it would be for revenge.

Chapter 9

Payton swiped at the sweat on his brow and watched Matt approach across the scarred, flat earth where they'd cleared timber. The exposed red clay looked like bloody gashes, the work site an assault on Mother Nature. Payton stopped the skidder and set the brake. A few of the men looked up from their work, but immediately returned to it. His reception today had been on the cool side, but not hostile. No doubt Matt had smoothed things over with the others after he'd stormed out.

Unlike his exit from Tallulah's this morning. What a screwed-up morning after a glorious night. He needed to speak to Matt about all this and warn the pack not to search for Russell tonight—or risk getting shot. Even more than that worry was the shock when he'd made love to Tallulah. The moment of his climax, he'd realized the truth. A sucker punch to his gut that had him reeling.

Tallulah Silver was his fated mate.

His. She should be his forever. The knowledge had slammed into him, stunned him into an astonished reverie that had quickly turned to bitter irony.

His destined mate was a woman who hunted wolves at night.

Matt climbed into the cab beside him now and handed him a cold bottle of water from their cooler. "Glad you showed up today."

"Wouldn't trust anyone else with this baby." He patted the dashboard and accepted the drink, running the iced container over the back of his neck before unscrewing the top and sating his thirst. "Heard anything from the cops?"

"Nope. But they're still hanging around. Matter of time before they connect the dots. I'm thinking the day may come when we'll have to pick up and leave in the dead of night."

"That's the worst thing you could do," Payton blurted.

Matt raised a brow in surprise.

"In my opinion," Payton muttered. He wasn't usually so outspoken with the alpha. It was like he was channeling Tallulah. Remembering her, his mate, he shifted uncomfortably. Sure as hell wasn't sharing that tidbit of info with Matt or anyone else.

"I need to warn you that Tallulah and several others plan to hunt down the wolf that attacked her."

"Damn it." Matt threw his hands in the air. "Like I don't have enough to handle. When do they plan on it—this weekend?"

"Tonight."

"What the hell?"

"I know it sounds crazy. I'll talk to her after work and try to figure out what's going on."

"Stop them," Matt ordered.

"Easy for you to say. You've met her, remember? The woman that's slowed down our operation for hours with her organized protests."

"Lie to her then. Tell her the situation is under control."

"That's not going to go over well if another dead body shows up in the bayou," he pointed out.

"Russell's probably hundreds of miles from here."

Payton wasn't so sure. Russell's anger and hate had been intense. The fever had warped his mind so completely that he'd been brazen enough to attack Tallulah by day.

Matt cut through his thoughts. "You coming home tonight or moving in with Tallulah?"

"Not sure." He took another long swig of water. "I'm playing it by ear."

Matt nodded. "Whatever it takes, keep her and her friends from the hunt." He opened the door and started to climb down, then paused, as if a sudden thought struck him. "It goes without saying that we expect your undying loyalty when it comes to the pack. You can't tell her about us."

Payton's jaw clenched and his hands gripped the steering wheel, his knuckles going white. "Of course I won't." Some of the bitterness leaked into his words. "That goes without saying."

Matt nodded. "I expected no less from you." He scrambled out of the skidder, shutting the door behind him.

Payton turned the ignition key and the loud engine

roared to life. For once, he took a savage satisfaction in felling the timber, as if he were knocking down the obstacles to his peace of mind.

Stop Tallulah? He snorted. The best option might be to go along with the hunters and deflect them from discovering anything incriminating about the pack. Surely, she and her friends were harmless—no match against his wily wolf pack.

Unbidden, he felt his lips curl in amusement. Tallulah was anything but harmless—a sharp-tongued warrior guarding a vulnerable heart. His mate. When he left Bayou La Siryna, left Tallulah behind, he'd be leaving the one woman fate decreed should be joined to him forever.

Fate, once again, proved a cruel bitch. Much as he admired and desired Tallulah, the selection of her as his mate couldn't have been worse.

He wasn't happy about it. Not a bit.

"You can't be serious." Tombi scowled at her and carefully set the historic Native American flute back on the countertop.

Tallulah returned the artifact to the glass-encased shelving, glad she'd picked this location for announcing the news. She'd been right to ask Tombi to drop by the Native American Cultural Center, where she worked. The trickle of visitors kept her fiery twin from going into full ballistic mode.

"Hard to hide my true nature from Payton."

"Try," he said harshly. "The man will be gone in a few months anyway."

Tombi's words pinched her heart, but she kept her features stoic. Ever since the attack, her brother had grown more and more distrustful of Payton. "I'm going to tell him about my true nature. I don't need your permission, but wanted you to know."

"He's a stranger. How can you possibly trust him?"

"And he'll stay a stranger if I'm not honest. Besides, look how quickly you and Chulah confided everything to your girlfriends."

"Who later became our wives." His voice rose. "You really see a future with this dude?"

Tallulah cocked her head, indicating that he'd drawn the attention of an elderly couple that had been eyeing a woven Choctaw blanket.

Tombi nodded and leaned in. "Well?" he muttered. "Do you?"

She shrugged. "Maybe."

Hope was a foreign emotion but it had seeped into her armored heart last night.

"*Maybe* isn't good enough. The last man you fell for tried to kill us."

Anger, pain and shame rumbled in her gut. She rushed to a defensive stance, squelching the little niggle of doubt about her judgment of men. "That's not fair. Hanan was your friend, too."

"You're right." He held up a hand. "Sorry."

"That was different anyway—"

"How?"

With Hanan, it had purely been a sexual affair, a friends-with-benefits deal. Not that she would admit that to her brother. *Ewww.*

"It just was. Let it go."

Tombi's eyes narrowed, as if he'd guessed her thoughts. She glanced at the clock—almost closing time. She couldn't help it; a little bubble of joy rose in her throat. Payton had promised to come by for dinner.

"I see you've made up your mind so I won't bother arguing with you." He lightly rapped his knuckles on the countertop. "But I don't agree with your decision."

He didn't trust her judgment. Not that she could blame him. Her own confidence in matters of the heart had been shattered by Hanan's absolute betrayal.

Tallulah lifted her chin, determined to prove her twin wrong about Payton. "Understood."

"Excuse me, miss. I'd like to buy this blanket." The gray-haired man placed the colorful woven blanket on the counter.

Tombi eased away. "See you tonight."

Tallulah rang up the purchase, her mind on Payton. What would he think of her shadow hunting? Would he even believe her? Maybe she should invite him to the hunt, show him what she was capable of, share her secret world.

She was still pondering the questions when she arrived home. Payton's beat-up Chevy was already parked out front. Before she reached the end of the driveway, he emerged from the truck, a huge pizza box in hand. When was the last time she'd arrived home to a handsome man with dinner waiting?

Years, actually.

She climbed out of her car, grinning.

"Figured you'd like pizza," Payton said. "Who doesn't? Pepperoni with extra cheese, okay?"

"Perfect."

"Hell, if I'd known all it took was a box of pizza to make you happy, I'd have ordered one before now," he joked.

"I'm not cheap, but I can be had. Pizza's my weakness."

"Good to know for future reference. Whenever I tick you off, I'll remember to order pizza instead of roses."

"Cheapskate."

He chuckled and followed her up the porch steps, with the tantalizing scent of melted cheese and spicy pepperoni wafting toward her. She threw her purse on the coffee table. "Let's just eat in the den. I'll get some paper plates and soda from the kitchen."

Despite the heavy weight of unburdening her secret, the coziness of Payton in her home lifted Tallulah's spirits.

Uh-oh. Don't get used to this.

Tallulah kicked off her shoes. What the hell. Enjoy it while it lasted. She sat down on the sofa.

Payton nodded approvingly. "Good idea." He shrugged out of his work boots, placing them in the entryway. He sat beside her on the sofa, threw an arm over her shoulder and they dug in, their socked feet propped on the coffee table and playing footsie.

Tallulah inwardly grinned in wry amusement. Footsie? Who the hell would have thought she'd enjoy that? As much as she wanted the moment to last, the clock ticked. Tombi and the other hunters would be here within the half hour.

"About the hunt—"

"Tell me about—"

They both spoke at once, then stopped.

"Yes, go on—the hunt," Payton said.

She set her empty plate on the table and rose, sitting in the chair opposite Payton. The distance gave her courage. "How open are you to believing in the supernatural? That there are secret worlds others are blind to?"

"Totally open," he said at once.

"Because…wait. You are?" His quick answer caught her off guard.

"Let me make this a bit easier for you. The first day we met, you saw a wolf, in total darkness, cross the field and enter our farmhouse. You've also said the darkness is no problem in seeing to hunt." His gray eyes hardened like steel. So something weird was definitely up. "I want to know how all this is possible."

"As far as my sight, I can see almost as well as the owls and bobcats at night." She clenched her hands in her lap. This was the first time she'd tried to explain the shadow world to an outsider. "Bayou La Siryna has been home to my people forever. Through the ages, a select group of us inherit special abilities to protect the bayou from evil shadow spirits that roam in darkness. The shadow beings seek power over men and feed on human suffering."

Payton leaned forward, drinking in every word. "Go on."

"We are called shadow hunters. Like our ancestors, we seek and destroy the spirits, especially during nights of the full moon."

"How do you kill them?"

Her face heated. They carried a bag of stones, a slingshot, a compass and the weight of the dark shadows that constantly threatened their people. Payton needed to observe them in action to see their effectiveness.

"This will sound primitive, but we use the same weapons that have always been used. You'll see tonight."

His eyes widened. "I will?"

"Well, the other hunters may balk at first when I tell them, but they'll come around."

He settled back against the sofa and drew one leg up over his knee. "That was easy. I was prepared to argue with you. I need to be with you on this hunt."

Her breath caught, stifling the flow of oxygen. *Not again.* This had been the one issue between her and Bo that had caused friction.

"I don't need a protector. I can take care of myself. I only invited you because if we're going to see each other, this is a huge part of my life, one that would be almost impossible to hide."

He held up a hand. "Whoa. I saw what happened with the wolf attack and—"

She rose to her feet, incensed. "An isolated incident. I won't let it happen again. So if you think—"

Payton reached a hand across the distance between them and tugged at her shirt. "Sit down and let me finish my sentences."

Startled, she plopped back down.

"What I'm trying to say is that you survived the attack. I'm not sure that I, or anyone else, could have done so. You're the strongest woman I've ever met."

Tallulah swallowed past the dry lump in her throat. "I expected you to get all macho and forbid me to hunt alone."

His grey eyes softened from steel to smoke. "Like anyone could forbid you from your will."

"Oh, believe me, they've tried." She couldn't help the bitter laugh that escaped her lips.

Bo had been at her side at all times in the woods, refusing to let her hunt alone. It had irritated her and chafed at her spirit, even though she knew he did it out of a desire to protect. Hanan had also been stifling—but for a different reason. As it turned out, Hanan had always wanted her in sight so he could manipulate and control her every move.

"I trust you to do what you must. We all follow our own instincts."

"Thank you," she breathed. Unexpected tears formed. Embarrassed, Tallulah stood and paced the small den. "Now then, anything about you I should know?" she asked brusquely.

Payton stilled, eyes wary. "No."

Her tender feelings fled and her eyes dried at once. "I don't believe you. Tell me about the wolf. You said it was your friend."

He shifted in his seat. "A figure of speech. I'd seen it around. Fed it a bit."

Payton was lying.

"I opened up to you," she complained. "Why can't you do the same?"

He rubbed his face with his hands and then ran both hands through his blond hair. A trapped look of sadness haunted his eyes and the turned-down corners of his mouth. "It's complicated. If it was just me…"

A loud rap at the door, and Tombi entered with his best friend, Chulah, and half a dozen other shadow hunters, each carrying backpacks loaded with rocks and slingshots.

Tallulah scowled at the relief that swept Payton's face. One way or another, she'd learn his secret.

Chapter 10

Twilight whispered in the rustling of pines and the long tendrils of Spanish moss that waved in the bayou breeze.

Without even encountering one, Payton was already half inclined to believe in the ancient spirits.

He ignored the curious and vaguely mistrustful stares of the men. If someone had dared intrude on his wolf pack's outing, the results would be bloody.

"This way," Tallulah called.

He followed her lithe figure as she unerringly strode through the woods in the gathering darkness. In human form, his eyesight was no match for hers. Not unless he shifted to wolf, then his vision would prove superior. For now, he stumbled along behind her as best he could.

She cast him a quick glance over her shoulder. "I'll walk slower," she whispered. "I'm used to a brisker pace with the other hunters."

Talk about injured male pride. "Where are we heading?" he huffed grumpily.

Tallulah placed an index finger on her lips. "A little farther south."

A bend in the path, and Payton caught his bearings. He'd only explored these woods a couple of times in wolf form, but that was enough. The play of branches and brambles, the feel of the soil beneath, a certain odor of wild onion, and he guessed where they were.

Sure enough, they entered the circular clearing. A very bare clearing. Tallulah kept walking, not sparing a sentimental glance at her shrine. He tapped her uninjured shoulder.

"What happened to everything?" he blurted. "All your dream catchers and stuff?"

"What do you know of this?"

Even though she kept her voice low, the fierce hiss of her words was unmistakable. Too late, he realized his blunder.

"I stumbled on them one day out walking." Which was close to the truth. Russell had found the shrine by pure accident.

"This is where I first noticed the wolf watching me. It stalked me with an intelligent hate. As if I were an intruder in its territory. Our best chance of catching it is here. The other hunters are circling this same area."

"They are?" He hadn't heard a sound.

She motioned to an overturned tree and they sat on the rough bark.

"Now what?" he asked.

"We watch and wait."

It was as if their bodies absorbed the darkness and they become one with the woods. Squirrels and possums darted about on the ground, cicadas and mosquitoes buzzed and the air was thick with humidity.

"Tell me more about Bohpoli."

She stiffened beside him. "So you found my memorial to Bo."

"We didn't mean to intrude. We were curious and—"

"We?" Copper flecks glowed in her brown eyes.

"I was with a friend."

A thin line of white rimmed her tightened lips.

"I'm sorry. If I'd known we were intruding on something so private, I'd have left at—"

"He was my boyfriend. My first love. We had planned to marry." She turned her face, staring into the darkness.

"He died out here, didn't he?"

She nodded. "Bit by Nalusa Falaya."

She'd explained the basics of the shadow world as they'd headed out for the hunt. The will-o'-the-wisps that trapped men's souls and the Ishkitini—birds of the night that served an evil spirit by the name of Hoklonote. But the ultimate evil spirit, Nalusa Falaya, ruled over everything and had the ability to shape-shift to a snake. Thankfully, the great evil one was under containment, courtesy of the shadow hunters who battled against his quest for power and dominion over all the bayou and beyond.

They didn't speak. Payton placed a hand on her thigh and squeezed. Tallulah kept her profile faced away from him, but one of her small hands clasped his and squeezed back.

"So what happened to the dream catchers that hung from the trees here?" he finally asked.

"Gone. I burned everything that could be destroyed and what I couldn't burn, I tossed in the swamp."

"But…why?"

"Because my work kept showing up beside the carcasses of dead animals."

Understanding flashed. Her mementos were planted just like they were with Jeb's body, and just as they were with the squirrel he'd found. But no need to tell her that and fuel her resolve to arrest Russell.

Why did Russell frame her? Had he viewed Tallulah as a threat? Perhaps in wolf form Russell instinctively recognized that she was an unusual human. If that were the case, he'd have done what he could to deflect attention to his crimes.

"That," she continued, "is why I took everything down in the woods."

So she knew…and had pieced everything together. A tinge of disappointment blackened his mood. He'd hoped she'd gotten rid of the artifacts as a symbolic act—to demonstrate that she was finished grieving for Bo.

"It was time anyway," she said quietly, as if reading his mind. "Bo would approve and want me to move on."

"Good." His anger and disappointment melted at her softening. Instead, his fury was directed at Russell.

Bastard.

Payton hoped Matt was right, that Russell was long gone from Bayou La Siryna. He could excuse Russell's bloodlust; it was an unfortunate side effect of the lycanthropic fever. But this clever, calculating attempt to frame Tallulah was unforgiveable.

A whisper of movement—Tallulah withdrew her hand, silently opening her backpack and withdrawing several rocks and a slingshot. Had she heard a noise? Wordlessly, she slipped him a slingshot and he grabbed a handful of the rocks, smooth and heavy and cool in his palms.

Payton looked around but saw and heard nothing. His hands fisted in his lap. So frustrating to be outside in the wild darkness and unable to shift. His inner wolf howled for release, longing to roam and explore. An owl hooted from far off and Tallulah tensed.

"What is it?" he whispered.

"Ishkitini."

He rose, remembering her earlier warnings. "And where the Ishkitini fly—"

"The wisps will surely follow."

She rose as well, loading the slingshot with a rock. *Swish*.

The beating of a hundred wings roared in his ears, loud as hurricane. Yellow and red eyes glowed in the dark as the nocturnal beasts descended from above. So Tallulah had spoken the truth. Bayou La Siryna was a haven for dangerous beings of the night.

Small wonder his alpha had been drawn to pick this location for their next worksite. As wolves, they were true creatures of the night as well and the remote swamp had seemed like the perfect hideaway.

Like attracted like.

"We're outnumbered." No use keeping his voice down, they'd been spotted.

"They'll sweep through en masse and then leave as quickly as they arrived," Tallulah said, never moving her eyes from the approaching Ishkitini. "And don't forget the others are with us. We aren't alone."

He fitted a rock in the slingshot pouch and drew back the band, ready to strike.

"Not yet," she cautioned, readying her weapon. "Let them fly a bit nearer."

"Nearer?" he sputtered. His wolf clamored for release. Already, Payton fought to contain its snarl and its desire to bare teeth.

At last she faced him, brows drawn together.

"Okay, okay," he growled. Damn. That guttural rumbling had slipped past his control. He needed to pounce, to attack. But this wasn't Tallulah's first battle; he'd have to trust she knew the best strategy for success.

She raised her arm, drawing back the band. He followed suit, straining not to release the rock. His skin prickled all over, every pore quivering to release the wolf fur chafing underneath flesh. The Ishkitini was so close that Payton feared its large talons were in striking distance. It looked like a cross between an owl and an eagle. Its wingspan was huge, terrifying. But the eyes and beak were unmistakably owl. Or, rather, some kind of owl mutation. Payton's eyes watered from the pungent scent, unlike anything his wolf nose had encountered. A scent he imagined that stunk as bad as buzzard excrement would smell. His biceps shook under the strain of waiting.

"Now!" she commanded.

He let loose the taut band, aiming at the nearest Ishkitini's heart. It thudded against the bird, which released an unholy screech before dropping to the ground at his feet. Payton loaded another rock, then another, vaguely aware of the whirring of rock missiles from all directions. The experienced hunters let loose a stream of volleys twice as fast as what he could manage.

The Ishkitini screeches were deafening, setting up a frenzy that set his teeth on edge.

And then, just as suddenly as it had begun, the attack was over. About two thirds of the birds flew off at some invisible signal, leaving behind their fallen soldiers in combat. En masse, they flew skyward, disappearing who knew where to strike again who knew when.

Silence reigned once more, although Payton could swear the echo of their cries vibrated in invisible sound waves. His ears twitched involuntarily, itching to elongate to a point.

"Payton? Are you all right?"

Tallulah thrust her face inches from his own, and sucked in a sharp breath. "Your eyes. They've turned... yellow."

She took a step back. "Who are you? *What* are you?"

Muscle and bone crunched, twisting and contorting to wolf. Ripped clothing fell in shreds by his feet. He was past all control. Worse, he couldn't run away. He'd waited too late for that, had been too intent on helping fend off the Ishkitini. His body was paralyzed, at the mercy of his wolf, who would no longer be denied. All he could do was watch and wait for the opportunity to escape.

And all the while, his eyes stayed locked with Tallulah's. Helpless to speak, to explain what was happening.

The accusation blazing on her face gutted Payton. She had opened up to him, let him enter her world, and this is how he repaid her trust. For all Tallulah knew, he was the enemy. Some new manifestation of evil birthed by Nalusa Falaya. She might even think *he* was the wolf who had attacked and tried to kill her.

Four paws anchored him to the ground. The transformation was complete.

A blue-and-green vapor lit the air behind Tallulah, framing her body like a demonic aura. His wolf ears laid flat at its toxic miasma.

"Wisps!"

Tallulah whipped around and loaded her slingshot in a fluid movement born of years of experience and training. She cast a troubled eye at him, then maneuvered her body sideways against both threats.

She believed he meant her harm.

Payton charged, swiftly moving past Tallulah and running to the light. Pain burst on his left hindquarters as she nailed him with a rock.

The light coalesced into orbs—at least a dozen of them. Blue on the edges with green hearts beating inside the wisp's core. These must be the trapped souls Tallulah had described earlier. She'd said the only way to free the soul was to penetrate the wisp's body. The shadow hunters did this by a stone's throw, unable to draw to close to the wisp because of its ability to drown them in waves of misery that resulted in despair. From this place of wretchedness, a hunter would give up the fight and become trapped. A lamb to the slaughter.

He was no lamb.

Another rock peppered his ass from behind and he bit back an undignified yelp of pain. The eerie light became blindingly strong. A colorful wet mist from the wisp clamped onto his blond fur, coating it and weighing down his movement. He wouldn't be deterred. Payton bared his teeth, snarling…salivating. He crouched on all fours and then attacked, leaping through the blue-

and-green wisp as if it were no more substantial than a ghost. It deflated like a punctured balloon.

He must kill them all at once. He leaped into the nearest wisp form, a rock grazing the side of his snout. A narrow miss, but he didn't care. His frenzy to protect Tallulah drove him to keep going.

Peripheral movement caught his attention. Tallulah had shifted her focus and was aiming for other wisps other than the ones he'd killed. At last, the blue and green lights faded. In their place, tiny white lights spiraled to the heavens. Tallulah claimed it meant that the trapped souls were now free to ascend to the After Life.

He slowly turned and faced her.

The wolf—Payton—was all blond fur that glittered with blue and green sparkles, a leftover reminder from the wisps he'd killed, and that temporarily clung to his body.

Tallulah stared into his yellow eyes. A tinge of pewter-gray radiated in a sunburst pattern from the iris, a reminder that Payton was one with the animal. Incredible. Shock doused her, sending alternate waves of hot and cold through her body. She'd known he was hiding a secret—but *this*?

Animal guides and spirit communication were areas she understood and had experience with. But shapeshifting from a human body to a wolf? No, she hadn't seen that one coming.

"Tallulah!" Tombi's voice rang out in the woods. "What's going on? Are you okay?"

Payton…the wolf—she hardly knew which to call it—gave her an indecipherable stare. A plea for understanding and silence, if she had to guess its meaning.

Suddenly, he took off, running in the opposite direction of Tombi's voice. His light-colored, glittering fur disappeared into the underbrush. Even with her excellent eyesight, he managed to hide. Some animal instinct drove him undercover. Familiar with animal behavior, Tallulah guessed he would wallow in the dirt in an attempt to cover his conspicuous form.

She didn't speak, unwilling to draw the others nearby until Payton had a chance to get away.

Other hunters' voices called out in the night as they closed in where she stood. *Run, Payton. Hurry.* The need to cover for him was strong and immediate, even though he'd kept the truth from her. Quickly, she gathered up the ripped clothing left behind and stuffed it in her backpack.

Chulah Rivers was the first to break through the clearing. "I saw the wisps gather at your position. Have you been injured?" he asked, assessing her from head to toe.

Dear Chulah. She'd hurt her childhood friend deeply last year when she'd turned down his offer of marriage. Not that he'd been heartsick for long. April Meadows, now his wife, had come into his life and flipped his world upside-down. All for the best as it had turned out. Through it all, they'd managed to stay friends.

"I'm okay."

Chulah did a 360-degree turn. "I counted at least eight souls released. How did you do it? It happened so fast, too."

She shrugged. "You must have miscounted."

Tombi, Marcus and several others emerged from the woods.

"What's happened? Where's Payton?" her brother

asked. Her twin always did get straight to the heart of a matter.

"He had to leave."

"Leave?" Tombi snorted. "What kind of a coward is this dude?"

"He's not—"

"The guy couldn't just up and leave," Marcus interrupted. "A human couldn't see the path to get out."

Her mind scrambled. "I let him borrow a flashlight that I had stored in my backpack."

Tombi narrowed his eyes at her. "You're my twin, I can tell when you're lying. If he's a coward, we're bound to find—"

"I'm no coward."

Payton stepped forward into the middle of the fray and crossed his arms below his chest. He stood resolute, as if challenging anyone to question his honor. Tallulah noted the change of clothes—new jeans and a different T-shirt. He must have had them stored in his own backpack. How inconvenient the shifting must be for him. A giggle bubbled in her throat that she quickly suppressed. She must be semihysterical to consider tonight's freak show as a mere *inconvenience*.

"Then where did you go?" Tombi asked.

Payton raised a blond brow. "Call of nature?"

Chulah lifted his chin and inhaled deeply. "There's a foreign scent in the air. Smells like...fur."

"It's just the dead Ishkitini smelling funky," Tallulah lied. "Let's head home. We've done enough work for the night."

Tombi didn't move. As leader of the shadow hunters, the others followed his lead and remained standing where they were.

"Could have sworn you had on a brown T-shirt when we left the cabin," Tombi noted.

Tallulah laughed and walked away. "Goes to show you can't be right all the time, little brother." Her fraternal twin had been born a mere minute after her, but she liked to remind him of the technicality. If he could tell when she was lying, she knew just how to irritate him.

"Ready to go, Payton?" she asked sweetly. As if she wasn't furious and confused about what she'd witnessed.

He followed her down the path without a word. From behind, the murmur of her brother and the other hunters buzzed. They knew something was off, but no way would they ever guess that Payton was a werewolf.

Werewolf.

Chills inched up her spine. She really had been bitten by a werewolf. She'd asked Annie and Tombi earlier if that meant she would become one herself. They had no answer. But Payton would. She whirled around. "Am I going to turn into a werewolf like you?"

His mouth twisted in a grimace and he pointed to the almost-full moon. "Yep. Couple more nights and you'll wake up covered with fur and howling at the moon like a bitch."

"Not funny. If anyone has the right to be angry and hurt, it's me. Why didn't you tell me you were a wolf?"

"Would you have believed it possible?" he asked quietly.

"You'll never know, will you? Because you didn't give me a chance. I spilled my guts to you and you kept your lips locked."

He nodded. "I'm sorry, Tallulah. If it were just my secret, I'd have told you."

If it were just him... Bells rang in her head, like an
alarm exploding in a brain fog of sleep. The answer to
the wolf puzzle had always been there, if she'd been able
to connect the clues. "I get it. All of you in that farmhouse, you're all...wolves? Like a pack?"

His lips pursed.

"Even now you say nothing?" she snapped. More
warnings detonated inside her brain. "The wolf that
attacked me, you said he was your best friend. Which
one is he?"

Payton hesitated, then let out a long sigh. "His name
was Russell."

"Not sure I remember him."

"It doesn't matter."

"Maybe not to you, but it certainly does to me. He's
going to pay for killing Jeb."

"Too late, he's gone. Fled. We don't know where, but
Matt thinks he's headed back out west."

"Matt...the timber supervisor, right?"

"And our alpha, the pack leader."

"Yeah, not surprised. He's kind of an ass."

"He's not that bad," Payton argued.

So that's where his loyalties lay. His automatic defense of Matt bothered Tallulah. "Is he like your king
or something? You have to obey his orders?"

"He expects obedience."

She snorted. "Sounds to me like you're all his lap-
dogs."

"You go too far." Payton's words were clipped and
his nostrils flared. "You don't understand anything
about my wolf nature or how a pack operates."

"You're right. But I *do* know you as a man, or I

thought I did. A man takes responsibilities for his own actions. Makes his own decisions."

"Of course."

"Then speak the truth. Did Matt order you not to tell me that you're part wolf?"

"It's an understood law of the pack," he hedged.

"That's what I thought." She turned on her heel and viciously swiped at the branches around her face, practically running down the trail toward her home—the opposite of their cautious entrance as she'd led him to the thick of the shadow world. Payton could take care of himself and transform to wolf if he had difficulty seeing or got lost. He didn't need her.

"Wait up."

She walked faster, uncaring of low branches whipping her face and chest.

A strong hand landed on her shoulder, pulling at the tender, stitched skin. "Ouch!" She spun around and glared at Payton. "Don't touch me."

He held up both hands. "Sorry. Forgot about your injury."

"Courtesy of your best friend," she complained bitterly.

"*Former* best friend."

"So you say. For all I know, y'all have him harbored in that farmhouse. Protecting a fellow pack member."

A muscle on the side of Payton's jaw rippled. "Russell's gone. We can't find him."

"Oh? Are you telling the truth *now*?"

"I am."

"I should call Sheriff Angier. Have him shake down the farmhouse just to make sure."

"Leave him out of this."

She folded her arms under her chest. "I've known Tillman Angier since we were kids and trust him as well as I can trust anyone outside of the shadow hunters. He's a damn good investigator. If Russell's around, he'll find him."

"And what are you going to say? That Russell attacks people when he turns into a werewolf? Nobody will believe that. He'll think you're crazy."

"He doesn't have to know about the wolf thing."

"No. We can't risk it. Exposure threatens all of us."

"Frankly, my dear, I don't give a damn."

Tallulah smirked at her private joke. Not being a southerner, Payton wouldn't recognize the quote from *Gone with the Wind.*

"I've seen *Gone with the Wind,*" Payton said drily. "And you, my dear, are no fragile Southern belle. You don't need to run to the cops for help. I'll protect you until Russell's caught."

"I don't want your protection. I can take care of myself."

He glanced pointedly at her injured shoulder.

"I'm fine." She bit her lip, remembering Payton had pointed out that this was her familiar refrain. "Well, it's true," she mumbled.

"Give us at least a couple of weeks to handle this ourselves. Deal?"

"No deal. I'm calling Sheriff Angier. Russell killed Jeb." She drew a sharp breath. "And I bet he's the one who framed *me* for the murder." Son of a bitch. Tallulah started walking again. The sooner Russell was arrested, the safer she and everyone else in Bayou La Siryna would be.

"At least it made you get rid of all your shrine stuff. That wasn't healthy."

"It's wasn't a shrine," she snapped.

"What would you call it then? Looks to me like an obsessive need to immortalize your dead boyfriend."

It felt like a vise tightened, compressing her heart and lungs in its grip. She could hardly breathe.

Payton ran a hand through his hair. "Oh, hell. I'm sorry, baby. I shouldn't have said—"

"Damn right you shouldn't have said that. You wanted to get back at me for calling you a lapdog? Congratulations. You win."

She ran from Payton. Salty, unshed tears turned the harsh landscape to a blurry watercolor of gray and black sludge.

He had no right to say that. He didn't understand. No one did. If she wanted to spend all her free time for the rest of her life making dream catchers for Bo and sitting out in the woods, alone, where he'd died—that was her business. Matter of fact, she'd replace every damn dream catcher that she'd destroyed. Soon as Russell was out of the picture, she could hang them on the trees again and everything could return to normal.

At last the trail led to the backyard of her cabin.

"Lulu?" he called from behind. She ignored him and his stupid nickname calling. Running faster, her heart jackhammered a ripping beat that felt like a hole drilling into her chest. Her right foot caught under an exposed tree root and she hurtled forward, free-falling. The side of her left cheek slammed into the hard ground a second before the rest of her body.

"Oomph." It felt like a belly flop from a hundred feet in the air. A full body smack.

Payton was beside her on the ground, gathering her into his strong arms. She pushed at him, but he held on tighter, rolled her body on top of his own.

"Sorry, baby." He brushed the hair out of her face and gently tucked it behind her ears. "You okay, darlin'? Tell me you're okay."

"I'm fine. Oh, geez. There I go with those words again."

She laughed, but it mutated into a sob. The dam broke loose and her whole body shook with wracking sobs. Damn it to hell. *Stop. Stop it right this instant*, she commanded her traitorous body, but it wouldn't obey. If anything, she cried harder.

Payton twisted, tucking her into the side of his body, stroking her hair, her back. She curled into him, head resting against his chest, soaking his T-shirt with her tears.

"Shhh, shhh," he whispered. "Everything's okay, Lulu."

She wanted to believe him.

Chapter 11

Tallulah was right. He was an ass.

Every sob wrenched his gut. He continued stroking her back and the soft silk of her black tresses, willing her to forgive him. Her hair was a dark stream that bent and shimmered with mysterious currents of light and he wanted to wrap himself in its healing warmth.

Her body stopped shaking and he planted a kiss on her forehead.

She laughed shakily. "How embarrassing. Haven't had a meltdown like that in ages."

"More embarrassing than shifting into an animal in front of your new girl?"

Her lashes dropped and her full lips curved as she traced the edge of his chin with her fingertips. "Is that what I am? Your girl?"

What was he doing? In a few months he'd be back on

the road. It was the way of his pack and she didn't fit in. This could never be more than a physical relationship.

He didn't respond, instead kissed her lips in a sad desperation. If only...

Payton pushed aside all thought of the future, intent on the moment. Tallulah placed her hands on either side of his face, kissing him passionately. Her hips wriggled against his manhood and he moaned his need.

Baritone voices emerged from the trail, penetrating the haze of his passion. Immediately, Payton rolled off Tallulah and stood, offering her a hand.

A bemused expression swept her lovely face as she grasped his hand and stood. Pure, male pride at his effect on Tallulah made him lighthearted.

"I'd rather not explain to your brother why we were lying in the field."

"It's none of his business," she said. Yet, she hastily smoothed her hair and swiped at her face. "I'm a mess. I'd rather not let them catch up to us."

They resumed their walk, this time holding hands.

"Do the hunters usually meet at your cabin after a hunt?"

"Normally, we're out 'til dawn and then I fix breakfast for everyone. But tonight's been..." She hesitated. "Unusual."

He squeezed her hand. "I don't think I made a very good impression on Tombi and your friends."

"It doesn't matter." She cast him a pointed look. "Tombi's our leader, not our dictator—unlike Matt."

"Is our truce over already?"

"We haven't even begun to finish our discussion."

"I was afraid of that." They got along so much better when they weren't talking.

Payton hesitated as they approached the lit cabin. Did she want him to sleep over again? Not only had he insulted her with the comment about Bo, but they also hadn't addressed the wolf in the room. She'd been angry at his lies, but he hadn't a clue what Tallulah thought about his shape-shifting.

It was a strange, unsettling night.

He followed her into the cabin and ran a hand through his hair. "Guess I'll be packing my bag and heading back home."

"Suit yourself," Tallulah said, plopping down on the couch and laying across its suede surface. She put a pillow beneath her head and yawned. "I'm exhausted."

A crimson stain spotted one shoulder of her pink T-shirt.

"You're bleeding. Must have busted your stitches in the fight. You got any hydrogen peroxide to clean it with?"

"I'm f—" She swallowed the word. "Underneath the bathroom sink."

He quickly found it and returned. The rumble of truck engines sounded and headlight beams flashed by the window as the hunters took their leave. Good. They were alone.

"Take off your shirt."

Tallulah eased out of it, flinching slightly as she raised the injured shoulder.

He poured a little peroxide on a washcloth and, kneeling beside her, gently cleansed the wound. The skin had pulled away a bit from the suture, but the stitches were intact. Even better, there was no sign of infection.

She inhaled sharply, but didn't complain.

"I'll get you a clean shirt," he offered. "Do you want some ibuprofen for pain?" Wrong approach—she didn't admit to pain. "Besides, it will help the inflammation," he added for good measure.

"I guess."

Again he left her, returning this time with the medicine, a bottle of water and another warm washcloth. Tallulah downed the medicine and sank back on the sofa. "What's with the washcloth? My stitches are clean, or so the stinging burning peroxide tells me."

"It's for your face."

She closed her eyes and he placed the washcloth over her eyes and carefully mopped up her forehead, then drew it down her tearstained cheeks and neck. Noting a speck of mud by her ear, Payton gently lifted her hair and wiped the delicate earlobe. Damn, every inch of Tallulah turned him on.

"You're beautiful," he whispered in her ear.

Her eyes flew open and she regarded him soberly. "As are you. In every way, shape and form."

His ears rang. Did she mean that…?

"As a man and as a wolf," she said softly. "Even though I was shocked and angry when you shifted, I can't deny you took my breath away. You stood out in the darkness with your blond fur coated with blue and green sparkles from the wisps. And the way you looked at me with those golden gray-tinged eyes… You were a sight."

The woman was full of surprises. He'd never shared his secret with any female, much less shifted in front of them. "You weren't repulsed?"

"No. If I were, I'd tell you."

Payton chuckled. Tallulah was direct, and for the

first time he fully appreciated her frankness. He cleared his throat. "I think I should stay the night. Take care of you if you need anything."

"Works for me," she whispered. For the second time this evening, he glimpsed the vulnerability in her eyes, a sweet, soft side that she mostly hid from others.

He scooped her in his arms and carried her into the bedroom. When the pack moved on, this woman was going to be hard to leave behind.

"Got back the forensics report on Jeb Johnson yet?"

Sheriff Angier leaned back in his chair, crossed his arms and studied her face. "Why are you so interested?" he countered.

Tallulah shrugged. "I found his body. I feel a certain responsibility."

"Mmm-hmm. We got it." As usual, Angier was circumspect.

"Well? Can you at least tell me if it was an animal or human attack?" she asked impatiently.

"Animal."

Impatience prickled her spine. "Do you know what kind of animal?"

He rubbed his chin, as if considering how much to disclose. "From the bite marks, the coroner thinks it was a large dog or wolf."

"So this isn't a murder case."

"I didn't say that."

Well, wasn't he full of surprises. She hardly knew if she felt relieved or dismayed. She didn't want trouble for Payton, but wanted to see Russell brought to justice. Tallulah tilted her head, debating Angier's meaning. "I see what you mean. Someone could have a trained fight-

ing dog that they deliberately unleashed on Jeb. That's
at least manslaughter, if not murder. Right?"

Angier abruptly planted his feet on the floor and
leaned across his desk. "How well do you know this
Payton Rodgers? Word is you've been seeing a lot of
the man."

"Why do you ask?" She donned her best poker face.

He rapped his fingers on the green metal desk, hedging.
"We've known each other a long time."

"All our lives," she agreed.

"And we both know there's a lot of weirdness that
goes on down here in Bayou La Siryna."

She fought the automatic temptation to deny it. But
if the sheriff had something to confide about the case,
she needed to cooperate. "That's true."

He slowly stood and walked to the window, his
brown uniform crisp and the pants ironed into perfect creases. Even his damn black shoes were polished
to a high shine. Angier looked every bit the typical
conservative law enforcement officer. What kind of secrets had he and his father, who had served before him,
encountered over the years? Several years ago, Angier
had arrested a serial killer in a high-profile case. There
had been rumors of mysteries and mermaids and unexplained events surrounding the arrest. Tallulah had
dismissed the whispered gossip as mere local legends—
now she wasn't so sure.

Angier faced her. "I think everyone in that new
timber crew is dangerous. At the very least, I believe
they're harboring a murderer."

He'd nailed it somehow. "What led you to that con-
clusion?" she asked cautiously. "Cop instinct?"

"Hell, no. Nothing that flimsy." He returned to his

desk and let out a huge sigh. "I shouldn't be telling you this, but you need to be aware of the danger."

Chills tingled her scalp. "What danger?"

"When we entered the incident report in our computer database, we found there have been a series of similar deaths in Montana. Over two dozen as a matter of fact—all unsolved." He paused a heartbeat. "And that's where this crew lived until recently."

It had to be Russell. And he was on the loose. He had to be caught—fast.

"You know anything about this?" Angier asked.

"The Montana deaths are news to me," she said truthfully.

The sheriff frowned. "If you have knowledge that would help solve this case, or if you even have any suspicions, now would be the time to tell me."

Angier could find Russell. He had resources that Payton and the pack didn't have access to. And Tallulah had faith Angier would make Russell pay for his crimes—something she couldn't say for the wolf pack.

"You need to find and question a man named Russell. He's your man. Sorry, I never heard his last name mentioned."

Angier's body stilled unnaturally and his eyes glittered with intensity. "He's on that crew here in Bayou La Siryna?"

"Yes. I've met him." Had she ever. She had the stitches to prove it. "He's tall with dark brown hair that is darker at the top, almost a black color."

"Why do you think Russell's to blame? Does he have an attack dog or something?"

"Or something," she agreed. Not that she was divulging the rest.

He tapped a pencil on the desk. "I see."

A long silence enveloped the room. From down the hall came the clatter of men's voices and the clang of steel doors opening and closing from the county jail that was housed behind the Englazia County sheriff's office.

"Am I correct in guessing the other men feel protective of this man, to the point they would hide his whereabouts?"

"Not Payton," she said at once. To hell if the others got in trouble.

"And the others?"

"Possibly. They say Russell's split. I'm not so sure I believe it. You'll want to question Matt, the guy who's the timber crew supervisor."

"I'll get on it at once," Angier vowed. "If there's anything else you want to confide, I'll keep it under my hat."

She stood at once and settled her purse strap across the shoulder. Ouch. She kept forgetting the bite mark was still tender.

"What's wrong with your arm?" Angier asked.

The man noticed every little thing. She'd best remember that fact.

"Nothing. If I hear any news of Russell, I'll call you at once." Quickly, she made her way to the door.

"Tallulah."

She turned and faced him.

"Be careful."

The sun beat down relentlessly. Payton popped open a water bottle and downed half its contents in one gulp. The poor schmucks working on the ground with chain saws had it even worse than he did.

A silver-and-blue sedan with patrol lights parked at the edge of the work site. Even though the lights were unlit, apprehension burrowed into his chest. A tall, familiar form ambled out of the vehicle. Sheriff Angier was a shadowy figure that seemed to be ever-present at the farmhouse. The fact that he sought them out in the middle of the day could not be good news. Two deputies exited the car with him, eyes hidden beneath dark sunglasses.

The sheriff made his way to Matt. Payton switched off the skidder's key and every man stopped working. None of them could hear anything from this distance, but they could observe their alpha's face. The deputy sheriffs stood several feet away, legs spread and arms straight at their sides, faces forward—as if they were standing at military parade rest.

Matt's lips pressed together and his eyebrows drew together in a scowl. No doubt about it, something was seriously wrong. Matt took a step back from the sheriff and waved his arm in a long arc, signaling them to gather at his side.

What the hell? Payton locked down the brake and scrambled out of the skidder's cab. He was the last of the pack to join the men standing with Matt and the sheriff, but the group was silent, evidently waiting for everyone present to begin…whatever this was.

Matt cocked his head at Angier. "The sheriff wants a few words with us as a group and then will speak to each of you individually. Your full cooperation is expected, of course."

Angier paced in front of them, searching their faces, not saying a word. It was unnerving. Payton speculated that if this was some cop trick of intimidation, it worked surprisingly well.

"My staff has been doing a little digging in the wake of Jeb Johnson's death. The coroner ruled that he died from an animal attack. I was prepared to accept that until this morning. And I'm betting that most of you can already guess what I'm about to say."

None of the men so much as blinked an eye.

"The way Jeb died is identical to a series of vicious animal attacks in Montana and other western states that have never been solved. Not only did people share the same kind of bite mark, but later lab tests revealed they were infected by some unknown virus. Possibly some type of rabies mutation is the current theory."

Payton had been expecting this news, but the determined expression on Angier's face made his blood chill. This sheriff would stop at nothing to solve the case.

"Imagine my surprise when I found out that this crew transferred to Bayou La Siryna after completing a job in Fayette, Montana." He paused and took off his sunglasses. "Where the latest victim in these strings of attack was found mere days before you arrived down here."

Still, no one spoke. No one moved an inch.

"Coincidence?" Angier asked, skepticism in his gruff voice.

"It's also come to my attention that one of your crew members has gone AWOL." He turned to Matt. "Russell...? What is his last name?"

"Hull." Matt's one-syllable reply was robotic and flat.

How did Angier find that out? Payton's lips went numb and he swallowed past the hard lump in his throat.

Tallulah. Had to be. She'd even talked about going to the police. He'd just assumed after their night together that she'd drop the matter. Anger whipped through him. Russell needed treatment, not punishment.

"Where is Mr. Hull?" Angier asked.

Matt shrugged. "I don't know. Haven't seen him since he left one night without a word to us, taking his old truck with him. No one's heard from him since. Guess the heat down here wasn't his thing."

"I see. Did Mr. Hull own an attack dog?"

"No," Matt said curtly.

"You sure of that?"

"Very."

Angier turned abruptly from their alpha. "Each of you, pull out your driver's license. Right now."

Payton dug his wallet out of his back pocket, as did the rest of the men. Had any of them guessed Tallulah had brought this on them? No one looked his way.

Angier spoke again. "I'm going to speak with each of you individually in the patrol car. My deputies will stay here with the group until everyone has been questioned. There will be no talking amongst yourselves. Is that understood?"

"Couldn't you have waited until the end of the shift?" Adam complained. "Even better, you could have waited until we returned to the farmhouse to question us. It's hot as hell out here."

Matt frowned at the youngest wolf, but the damage had been done.

A cold smile tightened Angier's face. "Oh? Have I inconvenienced y'all? On behalf of Jeb Johnson's sons, who have been grieving for their father, my sincerest apologies." He walked within a foot of Adam. "It's only

May, summer hasn't even begun. I can promise you, though, *the heat* is on. And it will be unrelenting."

Angier's meaning was clear. He'd be hot on their tails until he broke the case. He wasn't buying the coroner's report.

"Let's begin with you." He snatched the license from Adam's hand. "Adam Bentley."

Adam scowled but kept his mouth shut as he followed Angier to the waiting patrol car.

Men shuffled impatiently, a few wiped their brows. None uttered a word, but several shot him surreptitious glances. Oh, they blamed him for this all right. The divide between him and his brothers widened another fraction. One day, it might be too big a gap to bridge.

And then where would he be?

Payton stared straight ahead at Matt. The alpha's eyes locked on his. Once he finished his turn with Angier, Matt would have his own interrogation later. His cool blue eyes held that promise.

A deputy answered his cell, nodded and disconnected the call. "Payton Rodgers, you're up."

Conscious of all eyes on his back, Payton picked his way through the mounds of limbs and stumps. Cool air smacked him as he entered the passenger side of the air-conditioned vehicle, chilling the layer of perspiration on his skin. By contrast, Angier appeared crisp and in command.

"The man I most wanted to see," Angier began.

Then Tallulah *had* been to see the sheriff. "I can guess why."

"Don't worry. She was adamant in her defense of you. It's the others she's not too sure about."

"We haven't done anything wrong."

"Even Russell?" he countered.

"Can't tell you that."

"Can't or won't?"

Payton hedged. "I don't know where the man is."

Angier stared him down. "Did Russell kill Jeb Johnson?"

"I couldn't say for sure." It was sort of the truth. Not like he had actually witnessed a murder—he'd only assumed that Russell killed their neighbor because of the fever. Still, the technicality didn't ease the guilt that weighted him down.

"You're no different than anyone else on the crew," Angier said with a sigh. He handed over a business card with his phone number. "If you decide you want to talk, call me. I can help find Russell if you have any leads. I don't want to see anyone else killed."

Payton slid the sheriff's card in his wallet.

"I especially don't want to see Tallulah Silver hurt again—mentally or physically." The warning in his eyes was unmistakable.

"Message received," Payton said curtly. "You done with me?"

"Get outta here. And don't leave town."

Payton hustled out, resisting the temptation to slam the door. He made his way back to the pack and waited with them until the last man had been questioned and the sheriff and his deputies drove off.

"What prompted that visit?" Matt asked the group. He waited for a response in the hot sun, the work site unnaturally quiet.

"Payton?"

Everyone turned and stared.

For the second time in the space of an hour, Pay-

ton was led away for a talking-to. And he was damn
sick of it.

At least Matt had the courtesy to pull him away from
the curious stares of the pack. He'd ordered everyone to
return to work and the buzz of chain saws again filled
the bayou.

"Did that woman go to the sheriff again? I'm sure we
have her to thank for this fiasco," Matt said.

"Appears that way."

"Can't you control that female?"

As if. Payton snorted. "Are you kidding me?"

"What did she tell them?"

"I have no clue. Didn't know she was going to the
cops."

"I sense you're hiding information. As your alpha,
I'm commanding you tell me the entire truth. Now."

His gut twisted. No way to sugarcoat the devastating
news. "She saw me shift last night," he admitted.

Matt sucked in his breath.

"Tallulah guessed the rest—about the pack, that is.
She also knows Russell's a killer and wants him brought
to justice."

"Son of a bitch." Matt's face was as dark as thunder.
"You've violated the number one rule of the pack—
secrecy and loyalty above all."

"It was an involuntary shift." Payton's spine stiffened. "I was under tremendous pressure."

"That's no excuse. You should have run away at the
first sign you were shifting. Who else saw you?"

"No one." At least there was that.

"Spill it," Matt said, words dropping like hard peb-
bles. "How did it happen?"

"I went on a night hunt with Tallulah and others like

her. They're called shadow hunters. Turns out, they have unusual abilities of their own. Not shifters, but they can sense ancient, evil creatures that live deep in the bayou woods."

Matt raised a brow. "Evil creatures?"

"Strange shadow beings. The way she explained it, there's always been a remnant of the Choctaw that exist to keep the shadow world contained. These hunters keep the power of light and dark in balance. Anyway, as a hunter, they have heightened hearing, sight and smell, especially at night."

Some of the anger diffused from Matt's stern expression. "Incredible. No wonder she saw Russell in wolf form that night."

"So, see? Tallulah and her people have their secrets, same as us. It's not like she freaked out and is going to run and blab this to everyone in town."

"You're still not off the hook for losing control and shifting. Explain yourself."

Payton chafed under Matt's brusque questioning, but refusing to answer his demands was unthinkable. "We were under attack by the shadow beings. I was afraid Tallulah would be hurt, and my protective instincts overrode all logic."

Matt let out a deep sigh. "I hate this, but I can see how it happened." He narrowed his eyes. "But don't let it happen again. You found out how Tallulah sees what other humans can't. Come back to the farmhouse now and distance yourself from that female."

That female? Resentment flushed his face. "C'mon, Matt. You've gone too far."

"You still trust Tallulah after she's gone to the cops on us? And this is the second time she's done it."

"It's not like she lied to me." Angry as he was that she'd gone to Angier, he couldn't say she'd betrayed a trust.

Matt ran a hand through his dark hair and sighed. "I suppose it's better to keep an eye on her up close. Are you sure no one else saw you shift to wolf?"

"Only Tallulah."

"Let's keep it that way. No more hunting. Got it?"

"Got it," he grumbled, thoroughly annoyed.

"Sorry." Matt laid a hand on his shoulder. "We can't chance any more exposure. Tell Tallulah not to let the others know."

"I can tell her, but I promise nothing."

Chapter 12

"Maybe it's time I got a spare key," Payton suggested.

Tallulah shifted the bag of groceries in her arm and unlocked the front door. She casually accepted his comment, as if it were no big deal. "Works for me."

"I'll get that." He took the bag out of her arms and they entered the cabin. "Got a visit today from your friend Sheriff Angier."

She cut him a sly glance. "Oh, yeah? What did he have to say?"

He set the bag on the kitchen counter and began unpacking groceries. "Pretty much let me know that if I hurt you in any way I'm dead meat."

"You've been warned," she said drily. "Everyone in Bayou La Siryna looks out for each other."

"Why did you have to go to him, Tallulah?"

She opened the fridge and set a carton of milk inside.

"Like I told you last night, the sheriff can find Russell better than y'all can."

"Can't you just trust us—trust *me*—that we'll find Russell and deal with him in our own way?"

"Trusting you has nothing to do with the facts. A man is missing. The cops can put out an APB. If he's headed out west, like you suspect, the cops will get him."

"The problem is what the cops will do to Russell."

Tallulah shrugged. "They'll arrest him and bring him to justice. Pretty clear cut to me." She went to the den, kicked off her dress shoes and settled on the sofa. "Case closed."

"You've no idea what you've done," he insisted. "If he gets arrested and placed in a jail cell, what do you think will happen if he shape-shifts to wolf form? We can't have people knowing we live among them. They'll ferret us out and hunt us down like wild animals—until every last one of us has been extinguished."

She blanched. "You can't control it?"

"You saw what happened last night. When we get in a highly emotional state we can't always suppress our wolf nature."

"Well, we can't just let him get away with murder!" Her brown eyes flashed like lightning. "What's your pack planning to do if you find Russell?"

"Send him to a treatment center out west. He can't help these attacks. Russell's infected with a lycanthropic fever that affects his behavior. It slowly makes him lose all humanity until he'll stop at nothing to satisfy his blood cravings. He needs our professional assistance, not your criminal punishment."

"Don't expect me to feel sorry for him. He killed my neighbor. Then the bastard not only attacked me, but he also tried to frame me for Jeb's murder by putting one of my dream catchers by the body. Remember?"

"I haven't forgotten."

He sat beside her on the sofa and reached for her hand. It was so small and soft in his own, yet he knew it held skill and power. He caressed her smooth palm and the long, artistic fingers that were unadorned. Her right ring finger had a compressed, smooth band of white flesh encircling it. "Missing a ring?" he asked curiously.

"After he died, I used to wear Bo's engagement ring there."

Damn, she'd been through so much. "When did you stop wearing his ring?"

"The first night we made love."

She gazed at him with dark, steamy eyes and he gulped, remembering that first time. It had been a milestone for each of them—he'd realized she was his mate, and she'd taken a symbolic break with the past.

Tallulah was a heady combination of femininity and warrior woman—a real Diana, goddess-of-the-moon kind of lady. Payton looked up and caught her tremulous smile.

It was almost his undoing. *No.* He still needed to get a few things straight between them. "You can't tell anyone about me or the pack. Promise me."

"But, what if—"

"Promise me."

She pulled her hand from his and crossed her arms. "No. We can help you. If Russell's still around, who better to find him than me and the shadow hunters? It's possible he's lying low in the woods somewhere."

"His truck is gone."

"Doesn't mean he won't return. From what I gather, the pack is like a family?"

"Yeah. A dysfunctional one." But he couldn't deny she had a point. There was a bond between them that went beyond friendship. It was a primitive need to belong, to be a part of a community. "Russell wouldn't be welcome in other packs. They'd be suspicious if he approached them. Maybe you're onto something."

"We can search for him. The shadow beings are mostly active on the full moon. In a few days, the full moon phase will pass, and we can concentrate on tracking Russell. If he's near, in either form, we'll pick up clues."

"No. Absolutely not. Don't tell them about me or the pack." His chest constricted at a sudden thought. "You haven't already told anyone have you?"

"Not yet. But I don't—"

"You can't."

"The other hunters won't breathe a word outside our group."

"We can't risk it."

"The biggest risk here is doing nothing."

"You don't understand." Payton's jaw clenched. "I've been ordered to not let this go any further. When Matt found out you'd seen me shift, he was livid."

Tallulah rolled her eyes. "I'm mighty sick of Matt and his orders."

"Easy for you to say. You aren't part of a pack."

"True. But I'm in a special group, too. Remember? We're all extremely close and work as a team."

"It's not the same."

She threw up her hands. "It doesn't have to be this way. You're a man. You have free will, don't you?"

"Don't be ridiculous. Of course I do." Or did he?

He stood and paced the room, uncomfortable with her probing.

"Doesn't sound like it to me," she insisted.

The woman was relentless. He had to make her understand. "You don't know my history. I'm lucky they accepted me. Without them, I'd have floundered in the foster system. When I was a teenager, my parents died in a freak boating accident. Because of my dad's past, I didn't think any pack would take me in."

Her brows rose. "What did your dad do that was so bad?"

Damn, he hated talking about it. "He killed another pack member in a fight. Dad said the guy was making passes at my mom. He warned the guy to leave my mom alone, but he kept on. The two men got in an argument one night and both shape-shifted." He spoke quickly, eager to get the story over and done. Losing control like his father had done was sinful, a disgrace to all wolves. They had evolved past such primitive wildness; it was what allowed them to exist undetected in the modern world.

Until the lycanthropic fever had erupted and set them back hundreds of years.

"That's awful. I'm so sorry."

Payton avoided her eyes, determined to spill it all out. "Dad was kicked out of the pack four years before he died. He broke a cardinal rule of the brotherhood and was never forgiven."

"And they held his act against *you*? That's not fair."

"Agreed. But that's the way it is. Matt took me in when no one else would have me. I owe him. I owe the pack."

"He did the right thing. I commend him, truly. But your life is your own. Surely Matt doesn't expect you to follow him from town to town the rest of your life, working a job where you destroy the land in your wake. That's no way to live."

Tallulah hit the sore place in his soul, where he'd been wrestling with the same thoughts of late. He lashed out, immediately defensive. "I have a perfectly respectable job and just because you've lived in the same small town all your life doesn't mean that's what everyone else wants, too."

She quietly folded her hands in her lap. "What do *you* want, Payton?" she asked softly.

No one had ever asked him that before. He dropped back onto the sofa beside her and rubbed his chin. What did he want? She had hit on some truths. The constant traveling had gotten old. And the way the pack turned on him with suspicion after the Russell incident still gnawed at him. As far as the job…it did kind of suck. He loved working outdoors and using his hands, but felling timber didn't sit well with his conscience.

"I'm not sure," he answered truthfully.

"Think about it. Where do you want to be ten years from now? Still moving around and living under Matt's thumb?"

Payton closed his eyes. If he were free to do anything he wanted… How strange he'd never allowed himself to dream. If he had imagined a future at all, it was with a vague hope that he'd fall in love with Jillian. As an acceptable mate, the pack would approve the marriage and they'd have children. A home of sorts. Instead, he'd discovered his true mate in the bed of the last woman on earth he'd thought to share a life with.

Tallulah's hand touched his knee and his eyes flew open.

"Well?" she asked.

"I'll think about it."

She gave an impatient sigh. "You—"

He held up a hand. "You make one more remark about acting like a man and standing up for myself, I'm out of here."

"Sorry. I didn't mean it like that. Don't be so touchy."

"What about you? How free are you? You say you've been called to fight the shadow beings, that it's part of your genetic inheritance. Ever stop to wonder if you're truly free?"

Her eyes widened. "But…I love hunting. And I love Bayou La Siryna."

"You sure about that? Or is that your biology talking?"

"Never thought about it like that," she admitted. "Wow."

Neither spoke for long moments.

"The difference between us is that I'm happy where I live and with what I do," she said at last.

"Are you really? Most of the time you seem…angry."

She scowled. "I'm not angry."

"Glad we got that clear." He laughed, and to his surprise, so did Tallulah.

"I do fight being bitter," she admitted. "I lost my parents in Hurricane Katrina and then later, I lost Bo."

At least she had loved. He'd never allowed himself that luxury. His lifestyle was too transient, his biology too weird.

"There's something else you should know. I'd rather you heard it from me."

Now what? He braced himself. "Shoot."

"I did something really foolish last year. I had a fling with Hanan, another shadow hunter. It was never serious, more of a mutual arrangement of convenience. I was lonely and trying to forget Bo."

Jealousy ripped through his gut.

Tallulah's cheeks were tinged with pink and she cleared her throat. "At any rate, Hanan betrayed us all, actually joined forces with Nalusa Falaya and set a trap to defeat us."

He pictured Russell's fury when he'd tried to talk him into treatment. "The worst traitors are the people within our own inner circle. Why did Hanan turn against you?"

"Power. Nalusa promised him the moon."

"Where is Hanan now?" He wished him far, far away.

"Dead. I, uh, killed him."

He thought he'd braced himself for everything, but this left him dumbfounded.

"I had to," she said quickly. "We were in a battle and he was choking Annie, would have killed her if I hadn't stopped him. If there were any other way, I wouldn't have done—"

"Stop. You don't have to justify your actions to me. I believe you."

"You do?"

Payton pulled her against him and she curled into him like a kitten. He kissed the top of her head, inhaling a flowery shampoo scent. "Sometimes you talk too damn much."

She opened her mouth, no doubt to argue. Swiftly, he kissed her lips, effectively stopping the words. Her mouth opened beneath his, warm and intoxicating. *This* was what he needed after a crappy day.

This. Their tongues melded, dancing with passion. His hand splayed over her lower back and then the soft curve of her hip. Tallulah's fingers threaded through his hair, drawing him closer.

And this. He slid a hand upward, brushing her rib cage and then cupping her breast. Boldly, she cupped his erection through his jeans. White-hot need jolted through him, eclipsing all else. It was made all the more powerful because she was his chosen mate—even if she didn't know it yet.

Chapter 13

A diminutive redhead entered the cultural center near closing time. Tallulah idly glanced over as the woman elegantly strolled through the exhibits. Hard to miss her—she glittered like an exotic jewel with auburn hair and pale, pale skin.

Tallulah turned her attention back to the computer. Only three more invoice receipts to enter and then she could close shop and go home to Payton.

Home to Payton. The past six weeks had been almost idyllic. If only she could stop the niggling worry of how long it could possibly last. With a mental shrug, Tallulah pushed aside her concerns for the moment.

"Excuse me, aren't you Tallulah Silver?" Green eyes nailed her with a glistening intensity.

Tallulah jumped. The woman had actually managed to sneak up on her. How unusual. She must have been more focused on the numbers than normal. "Yes?"

"My name's Jillian."

Was that supposed to mean something special? "Okay. Have we met before?"

"Payton hasn't mentioned me?" She fingered the diamond necklace at her throat.

Tallulah stared at the woman's long, bloodred fingernails, which contrasted with her alabaster skin. Something about the lady vaguely creeped her out. A scent of old-fashioned violets enveloped her, but underneath the flowery scent was an earthier aroma—faintly dark and disturbing.

"Um, no."

"Well, everyone in the pack sure knows who *you* are." Her voice was a dulcet velvet and her Cupid's bow lips smiled, but Tallulah's hackles rose.

"He mentioned there was a female in the group, but no names."

Jillian's smile dimmed. "Odd. We're so close. Guess he didn't want to upset you."

"Why would I get upset?"

"Because Payton and I have had a 'thing' over the years. He has his occasional fling, but he always comes back to me."

She felt the blood drain from her face and her lips went numb. "N-not this time."

Jillian elegantly lifted a shoulder. "You're only another piece of ass in a long line of casual affairs."

Crazy bitch. But Jillian had shown a weakness, and Tallulah drilled in on her obvious insecurity. "If you believe that, then what are you doing here? I should be no threat."

"I eventually grow tired of his dalliances when they

last more than a few weeks. So I'd say your time is about up."

"Then maybe you should talk to Payton. Obviously, he prefers living with me to living with you."

"This situation is…unusual. But he'll tire of you soon enough. No way he would ever stay with you for long. I'm his forever woman."

"I don't believe anything you say."

Jillian laughed with no trace of mirth. "Ask him. Then ask yourself why a werewolf would ever mate outside of his pack."

"Mate?"

"Let me put it in terms you'll understand. Among werewolves, we have a primitive, instinctive need to find one mate. We don't have elaborate courtship rituals. When we meet our mate, it's something that we feel in our gut. A feeling that won't ever die, even if we wanted it to. Humans may marry, have kids, raise a family within their community. Our mating is deeper than all that. It's meeting each other on a soul level. And *that's* what I have with Payton. We're meant to be together. He knows it, too."

"I still don't believe you." She couldn't be so wholly deceived. Not again. Hanan's image burst in her mind's eye—the hatred in his eyes when he was finally exposed as a betrayer. Yes, she could be one-hundred-percent deceived. It had happened before.

"Payton needs us. If you know him at all, you realize how deeply committed he is to his pack."

The weight of truth pressed in on Tallulah's chest.

"Living with you the past six weeks has been hell on him. I don't know if he can last until the crew finishes this job."

Tallulah's spine stiffened. "What do you mean by that? He seems perfectly happy to me."

"He's not. Matt ordered Payton to keep an eye on you, discover how you sneaked up on Russell while he was in wolf form. How you seem to know so much about our business."

"Liar," she whispered past dead lips.

"Am I?" Jillian leaned in. "Payton told us all about you and the shadow hunters. In a way, we have something in common. I'm the lone female in the pack and I take it you're the lone female hunter in your group."

Payton had told the pack their secrets. Tallulah bit the inside of her mouth and schooled her features not to give away distress. She wouldn't give Jillian the satisfaction.

"I suggest you find a suitable male in your group," Jillian said with false sweetness. "Just as I've done with Payton."

"And I suggest you go screw yourself."

Jillian drew up, finally dropping her calm, patronizing facade.

"That's right. Get the hell out of here," Tallulah snapped, out of patience.

Jillian gave an imperious lift of her chin. "Don't say you haven't been warned." With that, she turned and casually ambled out the door.

Tallulah seethed. She didn't believe half of what Jillian claimed, but there'd been enough there to raise serious doubts about Payton's true feelings for her. The man had some explaining to do tonight.

"Hand me that seventeen-millimeter wrench," Chulah said.

Payton grabbed it from the set of tools Chulah had

spread out on the concrete floor next to the Honda Gold Wing. He handed it to Chulah and watched as he loosened the bolts to the two front disc brakes. "I can help you with that."

Chulah brushed his long hair back from his forehead and scooted away from the bike. "Give it a go."

Eagerly, Payton set to work. Ever since Chulah had mentioned he owned a motorcycle shop, Payton had been dying to come down and check it out. He loved fixing all things mechanical. With a minimum of effort, he efficiently removed the disc pads from the brake calipers and replaced them with new ones by bolting them back to the front fork of the motorcycle. "That should do it."

"You're really good with bikes. You ever own a Gold Wing?" Chulah asked.

"No, used to have a Harley, though. Sold it a couple of years ago. Got to be too much of a hassle hauling it every time I moved. Besides, none of my other friends had bikes."

"I can loan you one while you're here. No charge. Me and a couple other hunters ride most Saturdays. Join us whenever you're free. Lots of scenic back roads 'round here."

His blood tingled at the offer. Funny, he hadn't even realized how much he'd missed the feel of the open road until Chulah mentioned riding.

"Let me show you what I've got." Chulah motioned him over to where he stood by a row of used bikes.

His eye was immediately drawn to a gold-and-white, two-toned Harley-Davidson Heritage Softail Classic with soft-mounted, studded leather bags that matched the seat. He let out a low whistle. "Love the huge retro-looking fenders and the whitewall tires that match the paint."

Payton inspected the pristine engine and checked out the odometer—sixty thousand miles. Not bad for a 1995 model. "This one for sale?"

"Sure. But Tallulah mentioned you're only in the bayou temporarily. So if you don't want to drag it along when you move, then I can just loan it to you."

The reminder of the move deflated his newfound excitement over buying the Harley. Leaving Bayou La Siryna, leaving Tallulah, would be the hardest goodbye yet. But it was the nature of his pack to keep on the road, to prevent detection and attachment to regular humans.

With an effort, Payton shrugged off the discomfort. Tomorrow's worry would take care of itself. "I wonder if Lulu likes to ride motorcycles?" he mused aloud.

"You mean Tallulah?" Chulah's lips twitched in amusement. "She lets you call her that?"

"She didn't like it at first, but it'll grow on her one day."

"I've never even heard Tombi call her by a nickname. You're brave, dude."

"Or crazy." Payton tread lightly. Tallulah had told him that Chulah had once proposed to her.

"Nah, she's cool. Just had a string of bad luck the last few years. Bound to make anyone a little edgy." Chulah gazed at him curiously. "Guess she told you I used to have a thing for her?"

"She mentioned it."

"Glad that never worked out. We would have driven each other nuts. Besides, one look at April and I was a goner."

Payton grinned. Chulah's wife was a stunning blonde

that stopped traffic in Bayou La Siryna. He climbed onto the Harley seat, testing its feel. "Does your wife ride with you?"

"April loves it. She'd be mad if I rode without her. Says riding makes her feel like she's flying."

Payton patted the motorcycle's studded driver and passenger seat. "How much for this baby? I want to buy it."

"About eight thousand bucks. I just rebuilt the motor. Take it for a test ride this weekend. If you like it, we'll work out a deal."

"Perfect."

The front door of the metal shop opened and Tallulah strode in, her mouth set in a grim, tight line.

Uh-oh. Trouble was brewing.

"Hey, Lulu," Chulah called out, slanting Payton a sideways wink. "What's the good news?"

Payton stifled a grin.

"Oh, great, see what you've started, Payton? Before long, everyone's going to start calling me that stupid name. And then—"

He ignored her grumpy greeting and cast a cheery smile, pointing at the Harley Heritage. "Look what I'm getting. I heard you like to ride, too. We'll have fun cruising together."

Surprise distracted her complaining spew of words. "Nice. I've always liked this one. As a matter of fact, I've thought of buying it myself."

"I gotta get back to work, guys," Chulah interrupted. "Payton, you know where I store all the motorcycle keys in my office if you want to take that Harley for a spin."

"Thanks, man." He faced Tallulah again. "I didn't know you could drive a motorcycle."

"Does that bother you?" she asked sharply.

"'Course not. Why would it?" He pictured her wearing chaps and tearing down the road on a bike. Damn, she'd look sexy as hell. What a turn-on that would be.

"I never bought one but I've driven one a time or two."

"Too expensive a toy?" he asked.

"No, it wasn't that." She hesitated a heartbeat and then plunged on. "Bo was dead set against me having my own bike. Said he was afraid I'd get hurt. He let me ride on the back of his, though, while he drove."

The admission surprised him. If he'd dared lay down a law like that, she'd probably buy a motorcycle that day just to show him he couldn't tell her what to do. Not that he'd order any woman around.

"You look surprised," she observed.

"A little."

"Would it bother you if I bought one?"

"No. I think you should." Damn, now he sounded unconcerned and uncaring compared to Bo's edict. "As long as you're careful," he added quickly.

A slow smile lit her face. "I appreciate that about you."

"Appreciate what?"

"That you let me be me." She heaved a deep sigh. "Damn, I was all ready to light into you until just now."

"I noticed," he said drily. "What's up?"

She glanced across the shop at Chulah.

"He can't hear over the running equipment. Go ahead."

"Tell me about Jillian."

Heat flared in his neck and chest. The question was

completely out of left field and he was unprepared. "She's a member of the pack," he hedged.

"I know that." Tallulah waved a hand impatiently. "How close are you two?"

"We've...seen each other on and off. Mostly off." He shifted his feet, uncomfortable with her hard stare. "What made you ask?"

"Jillian says you two are a permanent thing. Mated forever."

His head jerked back. "Whoa. That's a damn lie," he said hotly. "She actually said that?"

"Sure did. Came to see me at work today and showed her claws. Let me know you were just fooling around with me, that you did this in every new town, but eventually went back to her in the end."

"It's not true," he denied. "I can't believe she'd come to you and say that crap." He'd never known Jillian to be anything but agreeable and nonconfrontational. Visiting Tallulah seemed totally out-of-character. Still, a tinge of guilt left him squirming. He had occasionally gone out with Jillian, trying desperately to rouse some romantic interest or passion. But it wasn't there. Not at all. But had he left her with the wrong impression?

"You've never had a...relationship with her?"

"We've gone out a few times. That's the extent of it."

"I haven't told you the worst yet."

What the hell? He stuck his hands in his jean pockets and let out a low whistle. "Go on," he said tersely.

"She claims you only moved in with me because Matt ordered you to keep an eye on me."

The semitruth sucker punched him in the gut. Matt *had* said that—but he'd moved in with Tallulah because he wanted to be near her every night, to make love with her and hold her in his arms.

"He did order me—"

"Damn it, Payton. How could you do this—"

He abruptly pulled her into his arms and planted a quick, fierce kiss on her forehead. "Shut up and listen to me a minute, Lulu."

"Stop calling me that." She scowled and glared, but the hurt was there, too, in the slight shimmer of her chocolate eyes.

"I'm with you because I *want* to be with you. No other reason."

"You're not just biding time until your crew leaves? A little fling before you return to your true mate?"

He sucked in his breath. Jillian had no right to mention mating, much less imply that's what the two of them were. Life would have been easier if fate decreed Jillian his mate—but Tallulah it was.

"Seems I've hit a nerve," she said shrewdly.

"Jillian is *not* my mate. End of discussion." It wouldn't be fair to tell Tallulah the truth. Not unless he intended to stick around Bayou La Siryna after the pack moved on. For the past few weeks, they'd danced around the issue, never directly confronting the end of this timber job assignment.

He was in an untenable position. Leaving the bayou meant forsaking his true mate. No other female would ever be wholly satisfactory to him. Staying in the bayou meant breaking with his pack, his only family, his blood brothers that shared his wolf bond.

Tallulah crossed her arms. "Hell no, we're not done talking about this. Who do you think—"

"Hey, Chulah," he yelled across the noisy room. "I'm going to get the keys and take the Harley for a spin."

"You can't up and leave while I'm talking—" Tallulah sputtered.

Chulah nodded and gave him a thumbs-up. "There's extra helmets in the office. Help yourself."

He went to the office and grabbed two helmets, ignoring Tallulah's stream of complaints as she followed him.

"Why are you getting two of them?" she asked.

He exited the office and grinned at Tallulah as if they weren't in the midst of yet another argument. "C'mon. Let's get some fresh air."

She planted her feet. "I'm not going anywhere until you finish answering—wh-what do you think you're doing?"

She gasped and slapped at his chest as he lifted her in his arms.

"You're my girl," he said firmly. "Forget Jillian. We're going to ride and you're going to love it." He kissed her soundly on the mouth.

Loud applause and whistles erupted, and he looked up to see Chulah and his employees grinning and cheering.

"You're making a spectacle of us," Tallulah mumbled, but her voice had lost its sharp edge and her lips curved in a soft, feminine smile.

"Who gives a damn? Let's go have some fun."

Payton had forgotten how much he loved the feel of the wind on his face, the rumbling vibration of the road underneath his body. Tallulah's arms wrapped around his waist was a bonus. Her breasts pressed against his back, and her thighs hugged the outside of his legs. His sexy baby.

His *mate*.

She squeezed him, a gentle press of her arms on his abs. She was enjoying this as much as he was. He wanted to ride forever, the two of them wild and carefree with no worries of the future. Every day that the job progressed toward completion, a weight pressed down on his heart and chest, until some nights he woke from dreams, restless and full of worry.

Not today.

They drove down a lonely county road. It wasn't the mountainous, sparse environment out west with its stunning vista. But it had a unique, green lushness at the edge of the calm gulf waters. It was a magical, mysterious place that was ancient and wise.

He rode until the heat of the afternoon released most of its humidity and a hint of lengthening shadows crept into view. Payton pulled over to the side of the road. "Want to break and have a drink?"

"Yep." Tallulah slid off the motorcycle and stretched her arms over her head.

Payton hopped off the bike and opened one of the leather bags, where he'd packed a blanket and a couple of water bottles. Thank the gods that Chulah kept everything at the ready in his office for impromptu rides.

"We need shade." He grabbed the blanket and tossed her a water bottle.

They followed a small trail that led to a creek with a sandy embankment.

"Perfect." Payton spread out the blanket, took a long swallow of water and stretched out on the colorful woven rug.

Tallulah kicked off her shoes and also laid down, her head by his feet. Idly, he grabbed one of her feet and rubbed a delicate arch.

"Mmm," she mumbled appreciatively. "That feels amazing."

He hid a smug smile. This was so much better than arguing in Chulah's bike shop. The idea to take a ride had been an inspired one. He kneaded her heels and grinned at the pink polish on her toenails. Pedicures appeared to be her one feminine vanity.

Thoughtfully, he observed the wooded area. It was deserted, well-hidden from view if anyone should pass by on the county road. Which gave him an idea. He patted the blanket by his side. "Face this way and I'll rub your shoulders."

Tallulah obediently shifted her position and lay alongside him. He massaged down her slender shoulder blades. She arched into his hands, craving his touch as much as he loved the feel of her body.

"Why don't you take off your shirt?" he asked, voice husky.

Tallulah rolled onto her side and stared at him, her brown eyes darkening to black with desire. Wordlessly, she sat up and peeled the T-shirt over her head, exposing her golden, glowing skin, which was enhanced by the simple, white cotton bra she wore. Tallulah laid back down and he kissed her neck. Chill bumps flooded her skin.

"You're so beautiful," he whispered in her ear as he rubbed her neck and shoulders again. Being out in the woods, exposed to the elements, made his inner wolf howl with need—as if his human side didn't already crave her fiercely. His hands knowingly traveled up and down her spine, stopping near the bottom. Tallulah especially enjoyed being rubbed low in her back, just above the flare of her hips.

Heat, the kind not caused by the southern sun, licked his gut and his hands roamed up her back, stopping at her bra. Expertly, he unsnapped the hooks and tossed it aside. He'd never seen her topless in the sun—it only exposed more of her beauty in pristine detail. Her breasts were full with nice, dark rosy-colored nipples that were already tight and hard. He ran a hand over one, ever so slightly pinching the nipple between his index finger and thumb.

She moaned in pleasure. "Payton," she whispered.

He rolled her over to face him, admiring the view, thrilled with the way she was so open with him. Everything physical with Tallulah was so natural.

He kissed her. Wild, needy kisses as her tongue met his. Payton fought the urge to lose all thought and succumb to an all-consuming lust. Instead, he concentrated on her moans, aching to fill her with pleasure.

Tallulah's hands were on his erection, rubbing up and down its length through his jeans. She unzipped his pants, freeing his manhood. Her direct stare at the evidence of his desire turned him on even more. He ran a hand down her long, lean stomach muscles that disappeared into the waistband of her jeans.

Impatient, she undid the button and zippers and pulled off her pants. The sight of her entirely naked body in the sunlight made his mouth go dry. He splayed his hands across her flat abdomen and then reached one of them lower, massaging her core. She pressed against him and he slipped a finger into her soft folds. Her moans grew louder, more frequent. He quickened the tempo and depth until he felt the evidence of her need.

"Now," she said in a ragged voice.

"Not yet."

He slid down her warm, lean body, trailing kisses down her chest and stomach and lower still, until he kissed and tasted her intimate essence. She writhed underneath and her moans reached a fever pitch. Tallulah slipped out from his grasp.

"Your turn," she said.

Her mouth slid over his erection, her long, black hair settling around them like a veil. The things she did to him! No one could ever please him more. She was his destined mate, whether she knew it or not.

"Stop. I need to be inside you."

Tallulah quickly straddled him and he watched as her body quivered and her breathing grew fast and labored. And when her core clenched against his manhood, Payton lost all control, allowing himself to climax along with her.

Afterward, drowsy and content, he stroked her hair.

When the time came to move on, how could he ever leave Tallulah?

Chapter 14

"We need to talk."

Jillian smiled, then sobered as she read the serious expression on his face.

Payton leaned against the kitchen counter and folded his arms. "Heard you paid a recent visit to Tallulah."

"I was curious about the Native American Cultural Center." Jillian looked down and smoothed a hand over her apron. "She happened to be working there at the time."

"That's not the way I heard it."

Jillian's face hardened. "What did she tell you?"

"You told her we were mates. That I always returned to you after I had a fling."

"It's true. I'm always here and we're always on the move." She stepped toward him and touched his arm, doe-eyed and clingy. "So when you tire of the others, and you do, you come back to me in the end."

"Jillian. Don't. We've gone out a few times, but—"

She threw herself against his body and kissed him, pinning him with his back to the counter. The sudden assault took his breath away.

"Excuse me."

Jillian jumped back and patted her hair. "What are you doing in here, Matt?"

He grinned and headed to the fridge. "Just getting a soda. Carry on."

Damn, of all the people to walk in and misjudge the situation.

"This has to stop," he told her sternly. "You and I are not an item. And if you confront Tallulah again, we won't even be friends."

Her green eyes narrowed. "What are you doing? We'll be leaving this backwater bayou before long. You have no future with her or anyone else."

Her words hit like sucker punches and by the smug look on her face, Jillian knew it.

"That may be true, but it doesn't mean the two of us will get together."

She opened her mouth to speak, but he shook his head. If he needed to be cruel to be clear, then he'd do it. "I don't love you. I'm sorry. That's not going to change no matter what."

"But why? We're perfect for each other. Our children will be perfect, too. And we're in the same pack and know each other's friends and lifestyles and—"

"None of that matters. Tallulah is my mate."

Jillian paled and her lips trembled. "No."

"Yes. I really am sorry. But you're a beautiful woman, anyone in the pack would love to mate with you." He paused. "Except for me."

Jillian picked up a glass on the counter and threw it to the floor, shards exploding everywhere. He'd expected a scene, but a tearful one, not this show of temper.

He shoved off from the counter, brushing glass fragments off his jeans. "Have fun cleaning that up." Payton got to the kitchen door and turned. "And don't you ever speak hatefully to Tallulah again. I won't have it."

Jillian picked up a plate and he ducked out.

The full moon was barely visible under the cloud canopy. A stiff wind sent the tree limbs moaning, leaves slapping against bark.

Hell of a night for hunting. Tallulah sighed and stared into the bonfire that madly danced and flickered like a demon-possessed spirit.

"Something wrong?" Payton asked in a low voice.

"Not really. Just worried about the incoming storm."

"Can't you cancel the hunt? Just for this one night? We've been hunting several times without waiting on a full moon. I can enjoy getting in the woods and shape-shifting any night. I'm not dependent on the rise and fall of the moon."

"But cancel the first night of our full-moon hunt?" she asked, voice rising. "That's when the ancient shadow spirits are most active. No way!"

Heads turned in their direction.

"He doesn't understand our traditions," she explained hastily to the gaping men. Over a dozen shadow hunters had turned out for the first night of the full-moon hunt. They'd already performed their traditional song and dance rituals and now it was time for a short prayer and reflection before entering the woods.

Chulah slapped Payton on the shoulder. "A little rain's not going to hurt anyone. We're used to temperamental weather on the gulf."

"Won't be a problem for me, either," Payton said with a shrug.

If that wasn't an understatement. Tallulah stifled a grin. When Payton shifted to wolf, his thick fur kept him much more insulated from the elements than she was. Not that she could tell the others that, not even Tombi. Payton's secret was safe with her. During full-moon hunts, they kept well away from the other shadow hunters' territories. It was one of the few times Payton indulged freeing his inner wolf into physical form. His concern tonight was only for her; he'd be terribly disappointed if the hunt was canceled.

Tallulah smiled at the camaraderie Payton enjoyed with her friends. He'd easily won their acceptance, especially since her share of the wisp and Ishkitini kills had more than doubled since Payton fought by her side. They didn't understand how Payton helped, but the results were undeniable.

A car pulled into Tombi's driveway and they glanced at one another in surprise. Anyone who knew Tombi and Annie wouldn't interrupt their ritual. Vehicle doors slammed and a trio walked to the bonfire. Tallulah recognized them immediately: Koi and Shikalla Chase and their teenage daughter, Nita. Koi and his wife had tried to have a child for years and when they were finally blessed with a baby girl, they named her Kwanita, which in Choctaw meant "God is gracious."

Nita was a striking girl. Petite and animated. Whereas most of her peers kept their black hair long and straight, Nita opted for a layered bob that she often spiked with purple streaks. Her parents' unwavering devotion could have turned her into a spoiled, entitled brat, but Nita appeared sensible and sweet, if a bit head-strong at times.

Tonight, evidently, was one of those times.

Nita's face was set and she strode several feet in front of her parents, coming to a halt in front of Tombi.

"I want to join your group," she announced, lifting her chin. "I want to be a shadow hunter."

Nobody snickered, but Tallulah caught the amused grins and sly glances of the other hunters. Her heart went out to the girl. How well she remembered being that age and longing to became part of the hunters, a group that easily accepted her twin brother, but not her at first. Not until Hurricane Katrina hit and the situation became dire. The hurricane had kicked up something evil, had stirred the ancient spirits with new vitality. Even then, desperate for shadow hunters to combat the spirits, the group only accepted her because of Tombi's insistence. As their leader, the rest of the hunters eventu-ally acquiesced to his wishes.

Koi apologetically shook his head at Tombi. "Sorry to bother you, but Nita was more insistent than usual."

"Our daughter feels called to serve," Shikalla ex-plained.

Tombi crossed his arms and frowned at Nita. "What makes you think you're called?"

Nita stood her ground. "I can see in the dark. It started a year ago and just gets better and better. Plus, I can see and smell really good."

"You're too young. It's dangerous work." Tombi nodded at Koi. "Maybe when she's older, if she's still interested, then—"

"I want to hunt *now*."

The hunters frowned. Chulah spoke up. "The first thing a hunter must do is learn discipline and respect. Tombi is our leader. You don't interrupt when he speaks."

Nita's mother hung her head and Koi put a hand on his daughter's shoulder. "We'll go now," he said.

Nita's lips trembled and frustrated tears shimmered in her eyes.

"Wait," Tallulah called out. "I wasn't much older than Nita when I discovered my abilities. I think we should give her a chance."

Amidst the disapproving glances, Tombi's surprised face and Nita's eyes flashing with sudden hope, Tallulah felt Payton's hand in hers. A warm, soft glow lit deep within her soul.

"A very wise man that I respect urged me to follow my own instincts." She squeezed Payton's hand. "And that's what I'm doing. I feel Nita deserves a chance to show that she can serve along with us."

Nita clasped her hands. "I can prove it to you. Please!"

Tombi shot her an exasperated look. "Since when did you start championing kids?"

Chulah nudged Payton with his elbow. "Somebody's changing Lulu into a kinder, gentler person."

"Only Payton can call me by that ridiculous nickname," she whispered fiercely.

Chulah snorted. "On second thought, maybe you haven't changed that much."

"Back to the matter at hand," Tombi said, admonishing them. "I can give you a couple of easy tests."

Tallulah guessed from his tone that he didn't believe Nita would pass.

"Let's go farther out, away from the fire's light, and we'll test this sight of yours."

"Thank you." Nita was nothing if not confident.

Tallulah hoped that confidence was well-founded. Should Nita fail, she'd have stuck her neck out only to end up looking foolish. And if there was one thing she hated, it was losing face in her community. She'd never gone to bat for a new hunter before.

Tombi led Nita and her parents to the edge of the woods. All of the hunters followed, curious to see if Nita was capable enough for the job.

Payton bent down and whispered in her ear. "No matter what happens, you did the right thing."

Every day, he seemed to grow more attuned to her thoughts and feelings—to the point that it could be downright scary. What would she ever do without him when he left town? Fear twisted her gut.

Thick darkness settled upon them like a cloak.

Tombi hung his backpack on the lower branches of an oak, its black fabric blending almost seamlessly into the night. "Tallulah, hand Nita your slingshot and a few rocks."

Quickly, she gathered the weapons and pressed them into Nita's trembling hands. "Good luck," she said re-assuringly.

"Step back a good twenty yards," Tombi commanded. "And shoot at the backpack."

One of the hunters motioned to Nita and she walked in place beside him as he marked off the distance and then came to a halt. "This is it."

Nita nodded and assumed her stance. Feet planted sideways, she stretched the slingshot's band and loaded. She released the band and the rock flew like a missile.

With a dull thud, it landed unerringly in the middle of Tombi's backpack.

"Huh." Tombi rubbed his chin. "No doubt she has some talent."

Tallulah hid her triumphant grin. Nita's parents beamed with pride.

"This time we'll go forty yards out," Tombi said.

Again, the distance was marked, and again Nita hit the bull's-eye on the first attempt.

"Excellent job," Tallulah called out.

Nita grinned and triumphantly raised the slingshot as if it was a gold medal.

Tallulah surreptitiously watched the other hunters. Begrudging respect had grown on their faces. Even Tombi gave Nita a nod.

"Now let's see how you do from sixty yards."

Tallulah sucked in her breath and spoke up. "That's hardly fair. Sixty to seventy-five yards is pushing it even for an experienced hunter."

"It's okay. I can do it," Nita declared.

Chulah shook his head. "Pride goeth before a fall."

"My money's on the kid," Payton countered. "A steak dinner on me if she misses."

"On the first shot?" Chulah laughed. "Easy win for me."

"I didn't say first shot, but what the hell. Okay."

The other hunters picked up on the wager, all betting against Nita. Tallulah shook her head at Payton. "Trying to go bankrupt? Tough shot coming up."

"Have some confidence. I've got a feeling."

Nita took her stance and sent the rock flying.

It missed.

Loud laughter rang through the field and into the woods.

"You owe me, Payton," someone said.

"I'm ready for my steaks," another joked.

Poor Nita. Tallulah watched the girl closely. Her shoulders hunched slightly and she shot her parents a look of misery. Tallulah walked over and handed her several more rocks. "That's a hard shot for anybody. Keep trying. If you want to be a shadow hunter, you have to demonstrate courage and persistence."

"I—I usually make it," Nita stammered.

"Prove it."

The girl nodded, reloaded and shot, hitting the backpack dead center. Again and again, she loaded the slingshot and pummeled the target.

"Enough!" Tombi held up a hand and they all gathered around Nita.

"You can see and shoot in the darkness, I'll give you that."

"Can I join now? I want to hunt with you tonight." Her young face practically glowed with eagerness.

A reluctant laugh escaped Tombi's lips. "I admit you're good, but it takes training. And it's extremely dangerous. No place for a kid."

"We agree," Koi said quickly. "But if you would allow her to train with you until she reaches age eighteen, she'd appreciate the opportunity."

"Two years!" Nita's face fell and she pointed at Tallulah. "But you started hunting when you were sixteen."

Terrific. She'd helped the girl and now she was under attack. "That was because of a rare circumstance," Tallulah pointed out drily.

Nita hurried to speak. "I just meant that you're awesome! I've always wanted to be a shadow hunter like you. Even when I was little."

Okay, now she felt positively ancient.

Payton gave her an evil grin. "Old lady," he whispered.

"Which makes you a dirty old man," she muttered.

"Come back this weekend and we'll assess your trekking skills," Tombi said. "If they're half as good as your eyesight and shooting ability, we'll start your training."

Nita clapped her hands and jumped up and down. "Thank you, thank you. I promise you won't be disappointed."

She watched as Nita strode away with her proud parents. A sharp pain unexpectedly sliced at her heart, a stabbing longing to be with her mom and dad once more. Had it really been over a decade since Hurricane Katrina had struck? It didn't seem that many years ago since their family home had been blown into matchsticks and her parents had been killed. Tallulah closed her eyes. She could smell the scent of her mom's cornbread and melted butter in the kitchen; she saw her father's head bent over a small wood carving of a bird, his large hands capable of sculpting such delicate art.

Warm, strong hands rested on her shoulders, drawing her into Payton's hard chest where she rested her head. The steady beating of his heart pulsed under her cheek. It drummed and throbbed with reassuring regularity. But how swiftly everything could be taken away.

Mom. Dad. Bo.

She clung to Payton and grabbed onto his shirt.

"Hey, now. What's the matter, Lulu?" he whispered into the top of her scalp.

"N-nothing."

Horrified, she realized her tears had dampened his T-shirt. She let go of him and swiped at her eyes. This wouldn't do. She pasted a brittle smile on her face and played with the backpack handles at her shoulders. "Time we got moving. Ready to hunt?"

"If it will make you feel better. Yes." He gently brushed a lock of hair from her face.

Holy crap. Tender gestures absolutely undid her in this vulnerable state. She drew a deep breath. "I'm fine," she answered automatically with her fallback line. She winced at his rueful smile. "And I really mean it this time."

"If you say so."

Silently, they entered the woods, taking care to keep their distance from other hunters doing the same. Tallulah couldn't shake off the melancholy, and she carelessly stomped down the path, creating a ruckus of snapped twigs beneath her feet.

"For someone who says they're okay, you sure are in a temper," Payton said.

She turned and held a finger to her lips. "Quiet," she breathed.

He laughed. "Like you? C'mon, what got into you just now?"

She sighed. Might as well tell him, he'd pester the truth from her if she didn't. "Seeing Nita with her parents…it made me think of my own. I miss them."

"Understandable." His gray eyes turned dark and smoky. "Miss mine, too," he confessed. "Guess I always will."

What an ass she could be at times. She wasn't the only one who'd suffered tragedies. "Sorry," she murmured. She also wasn't good at apologies or offering comfort.

"I know. It's okay." Payton tipped her chin up with his fingers and gave her his easy smile.

Holy crap, he made her heart flutter with those smiles. Actually stole her breath away. Did she have a fraction of that effect on him? Highly doubtful. She turned away from his too-perceptive eyes and proceeded down the path. This time, with her usual silence. Payton's own footfalls were light and silent. How well they worked together, seamlessly fitting into a team. Again, Tallulah wondered how she would bear the loneliness when he left. Bracing her shoulders, she tried to push aside the thoughts. But they kept circling around, refusing to yield to her will.

Tallulah stopped abruptly, shock waves pounding her blood. Holy hell. How had she allowed this to happen? The truth mercilessly slammed into her consciousness.

She was in love with a wolf. A wandering wolf who would soon leave the bayou. What a stupid, stupid, stupid thing to do.

Yeah, she loved Payton Rodgers. And wasn't happy about it one damn bit.

Women.

Payton trudged through the swamp feeling like nothing more than sweaty mosquito bait. The hunt seemed to be dragging on forever. The opportunity to shift hadn't presented itself—too many hunters were too near. He slapped at the circling insects and eyed Tallulah ruefully as she continued on, barely even looking his way. What had he done now? Just when he thought he'd figured her out, she went and got her dander up about some other matter.

The cloud cover beneath the full moon did nothing

to satisfy his craving for release. His wolf nature was pulled to the moon's elemental force, as subject to its laws as it was to the ocean's tide.

Surely, he was being overly cautious in this lonely bayou. The need to shift overwhelmed and demanded release. Payton gave in to the urge, glad to roam and run. As a lone wolf, he didn't need to try and understand Tallulah, appease his alpha, or work a job. He just *was*. A creature of the night, his senses alive and tingling.

The earth vibrated beneath his four paws. A heavy tread—not Tallulah's. Too late, he caught a whiff of human, more than one.

"Someone's coming," she warned. "Hide!"

But it was too late.

Tombi, Chulah and the rest of the shadow hunters had stepped forward from a bend in the path just as he'd shifted. They stared, looks of wonder on their faces. These men had battled evil spirits in many forms… but he reckoned they'd never seen a man transform to an animal.

Two impulses clawed in his gut—to run into the cover of darkness and deny, deny, deny this had ever happened to anyone who ever mentioned it, or return to human form and ask them for their silence.

Payton shifted back to his two legs. He shrugged into his jeans and faced the tribe, arms crossed against his naked torso. Tallulah came to his side and stood in a silent stance of support. The men walked closer and he mentally braced himself, studying their faces for signs of anger or disgust. But their expressions were stoic, even if a little curiosity crept through the stern, angular features.

Payton focused on Tombi and Chulah, the leaders.

What would they do? What *could* they do? Whether they disapproved of him or not, it changed nothing. He'd stay with Tallulah and he'd always remain a werewolf shifter.

"I suspected as much," Tombi said flatly. "Even asked Tallulah if it were possible, but she can be tight-lipped and stubborn."

Of all the possible reactions that had raced through his mind, this calm acceptance had not been one of them.

"Well, I had no idea," Chulah said. "I thought we were friends—you could have told me."

Payton kept his wall of reserve in place. "I'm bound to secrecy by the pack. Of all people, you guys should understand that."

"There shouldn't be such secrets among friends," Chulah insisted. "If—"

"What about my sister?" Tombi interrupted, cutting off his friend.

Payton raised his brows. "Yeah? What about her?"

"How does this affect Tallulah? I want to know your intentions."

"Stop being an ass, you two." Tallulah rolled her eyes. "I'm standing right here. I can speak for myself."

Tombi scowled at her. "He's been living with you for weeks now. Is he committed to you or to his pack?"

Damnation. Tombi had nailed the quagmire in less than ten seconds. He didn't dare look at Tallulah.

"None. Of. Your. Damn. Business." Her words fell as hard and cold as ice cubes in the steamy swamp air.

Chulah cleared his throat, shooting Payton a sympathetic glance. "Maybe we're missing the bigger picture here. Who attacked and killed Jeb Johnson?"

The switch from commitment to murder should have ramped up the churning in his gut, but it actually freed him to take a deep breath and find his voice. "His name's Russell Hull. But he ran away from us when we realized he was the murderer and confronted him."

Chulah's brow furrowed. "Why'd this guy do it? You'd never hurt anyone that way."

His friend's unquestioning belief in his moral character staggered Payton. "Russell's infected with a lycanthropic fever that consumes his mind and body until all he can think about is sating his blood thirst."

Tombi's face grew sterner, a muscle working his jaw. "He bit Tallulah. If it wasn't for Annie, she'd have died. The same as Jeb."

"True." Payton couldn't deny it. "I'm forever in debt to your wife."

"And don't forget, Payton's the one who found me after Russell's attack," Tallulah quickly added. "I'd have died otherwise."

Tombi nodded and held out a hand. "We consider you one of us."

He accepted the peace offering and shook Tombi's hand. Tombi pulled him in close and whispered in his ear.

"Just don't hurt my twin."

"Hey, what did you say to Payton?" Tallulah asked, her hands on her hips.

Payton nodded at her brother, acknowledging his demand. He understood Tombi's concern. Hell, if he had a sister he'd feel the same.

Chulah stepped forward and shook his hand as well. "I consider you one of us." He grinned impishly. "Only a hairier version."

Everyone laughed and the tension was lifted. One by one, each of the shadow hunters came forward and shook his hand.

His chest tightened—in a good way. Had the situation been reversed, his wolf pack would have never accepted anyone outside of their own group. But these men had. They were so much more tolerant and open-minded—a true brotherhood.

And Tallulah. His mate.

Payton wrapped an arm around Lulu and pulled her to his side. Somehow, he had to make everything work out, convince the pack that the shadow hunters were special. Maybe they could even form an alliance of some sort and help one another—an unexpected home where they could grow roots.

The shadow hunters drifted off, done for the evening, until he was alone again with Tallulah. Roughly, he snatched her into a tight embrace, not knowing the words to tell her how much she and the others meant to him—that this night was one of the happiest of his life.

Luckily, she was no frail flower easily crushed. Tallulah hugged him back just as fiercely. Something unspoken hung in the air between them.

A black silhouette moved in the dark. Payton stared out at the trees, over the top of Tallulah's head, trying to pick out the shape. Had he imagined it? A low growl rumbled not twenty yards ahead. He zeroed in on the creature. Its white teeth were bared in a snarl, and two pinpoints of blue light glowed.

"What was that noise?" Tallulah loaded and raised her slingshot in five seconds flat. "How did it get so close, so quick?"

"Lower your weapon," he said quietly. "It's a wolf."

One he recognized immediately with the black hair and blue eyes. A lone wolf. Which meant the alpha's rule had been disobeyed.

By Matt, the alpha himself.

Chapter 15

The following day, Payton stayed well out of Matt's way, thankful for the confines of the skidder cab. For once, the sound of the lunch whistle brought him no pleasure. Matt had barked orders all morning and been edgier than usual.

Reluctantly, he scampered out of the vehicle, lunch pail in hand. He'd briefly considered eating inside the cab, but better to get the confrontation with Matt over with, unless his alpha wanted privacy when it came time to chew him out. After all, he'd been roaming the woods alone, breaking his own rules.

He swung a leg over the picnic table bench, joining the other men, who laughed and talked with ease. Matt was across the work site by the road, talking to a man dressed in a suit. Probably a city council member or something. How could anyone stand to be armored in a jacket in this heat?

Payton opened his lunch box and stared at the uninspiring offerings. He'd overslept this morning and at the last minute had tossed in a hodgepodge of food— a box of raisins, a case of saltines, a can of beef hash. Not great, but a man had to eat on a job like this. He set to work on the crackers, spreading them with dollops of canned hash.

Across the table, Adam signaled at someone in the distance, and then pointed at him. "Matt wants to talk to you."

Just what he needed. Payton chugged some water before ambling over to Matt, who now stood alone under the shade of an oak, one of the few trees that had been spared from their murderous saws.

Matt lit a cigar, a sure sign he was angry or stressed, or both. The boss didn't spare him a glance, instead gazing down at the tobacco's red tip.

"You got something you want to say to me?" Payton asked, vexed at the waiting.

Arctic-blue eyes landed on him like a blow. "I've got plenty to say to you. What the hell were you thinking, shifting in front of all those people?"

"Why were you alone in the woods?" he countered.

Matt blew out a haze of smoke rings. "Reconnaissance work."

"I call bullshit."

That got his attention. Matt faced him, eyes blazing. "Watch your mouth, kiddo."

"I'm not a kiddo anymore. And I'm damn tired of your orders." He could hardly believe his own ears. He'd never talked this way to Matt. Ever.

"I'm still your alpha. If I do something, it's always for the good of the pack. You got that?"

"Must be nice to set rules for everyone else to follow, only to break them if they don't suit *you*."

Matt jabbed a finger in his direction. "I was out there checking up on you. See what the hell you're up to these days with that strange girl and her kinfolk."

"Why? They aren't bothering you."

"She's got something to do with that damn sheriff who keeps hanging around us. The man can't prove anything, but he makes me nervous."

"Then let it go. We'll be on the road soon enough."

"Don't you *ever* tell *me* what to do."

Payton bit his tongue and kept his silence. No sense pushing this ugly scene with his alpha.

Matt threw down the cigar and ground it out with his work boots.

It felt like his hopes and dreams from last night were also being crushed. An alliance? Matt would never go for it. Neither would the shadow hunters if Matt demanded obedience. They were their own men.

He longed to join them, to be like them.

"I expect loyalty," Matt said, interrupting Payton's traitorous thoughts. "I took you in when no one else would have you."

"I'll never forget that," Payton answered quietly. "But what do you expect from me in return? A lifetime of servitude?"

Matt blinked. "Is that what it feels like to you?"

"Lately, yeah."

"I don't know anyone else who's got a problem with me."

"Maybe they do and they're afraid to speak up."

Matt swiped his hand in the air, dismissing the idea.

"It's that Tallulah." He raised his voice. "Your little piece of ass has got you brainwashed."

He flushed with anger, all caution gone. "Don't you ever call her that again," he said, advancing a step toward Matt.

His alpha didn't back down. "I call it like I see it. She's been nothing but trouble the first day she showed up here protesting our timber cutting."

"She has a right to protest it's—"

"Worse than that, she dragged the sheriff in our business and she's turned you against your own pack. Nothing. But. Trouble."

"To you, maybe. But to me, she's the most honest and brave person I've ever met. She's kind and—"

"Kind?" Matt sneered. "That witch? She's always scowling and complaining." He paused, his mouth twitching. "When you could have had someone like my sister, Jillian."

Uh-oh. So that's what this was about. He'd spurned Matt's sister. "So you heard about that?" he asked, finally chagrined.

"Everyone knows. There's no secrets between us." Matt winced. "Or that's the way it used to be."

He tried to explain. "About Jillian…it just wasn't there between us."

"Was on her end. She's been crying her eyes out for weeks now. Not that you care."

"Of course I do." He remembered her visit to Tallulah and the lies she'd told. Jillian wasn't all sweetness and light like everyone believed. "But at least now she realizes there's nothing between us. She can move on. Like I have."

"For someone like Tallulah? There's no future with

that female. Besides, Jillian's prettier, sweeter—a more suitable mate in every way."

Hah. Tallulah was striking and sexy and honest. Matt was obviously biased when it came to his sister.

"We can't always help who we fall for," he reminded Matt.

"Everything would have worked out fine if we'd never come to this hellhole," he said bitterly. "If you'd never met that bitch."

An angry haze fogged his mind and he grabbed Matt's shirt collar. "Take that back."

Matt shoved him away and they circled each other, fists drawn.

"She really worth fighting for?" he asked. "Or maybe you don't want to be part of us anymore—is that it?"

Payton was vaguely aware they'd drawn the attention of the pack. Men were moving toward them, no doubt ready to light into him for challenging their alpha. He tuned out everything but Matt's movements, ready to strike when the opportunity arose.

"Your last warning, kiddo. You're about to throw away everything for some piece of ass. Tallulah Silver is the biggest bitch I've ever met."

"Shut up," he growled. "She's everything I've ever wanted."

"I am?"

It took a few seconds for his brain to register the feminine voice coming from behind them.

Matt lowered his fists, a sheepish expression ghosting his features.

Payton slowly turned.

Tallulah held up a paper sack from Fat Boys BBQ,

a local restaurant favorite of his. "Thought you might enjoy a hot lunch for a change."

"Yeah, sure," he answered stupidly. He willed his raging temper to cool—which wasn't hard to do as he stared at the Tallulah. She wore a violet dress and her long black hair was as shiny as obsidian. Her cinnamon skin glowed. She walked toward him, hips swaying and long legs set off by black pumps.

But it was the shine in her eyes that arrested him—a glow of feminine grace and mystery and...love?

She canted her head in the direction of his hand, and he numbly lifted it, clasping the bag. "Thank you," he said simply.

"Hope y'all don't waste your lunch hour fighting." She stared directly at Matt, whose cheeks flushed red.

"Just leaving," he mumbled, gesturing at the men who'd gathered around them.

They were alone.

How much had she overheard? He flushed. Had he really blurted that she was everything he ever wanted? "Sorry you had to hear all that," he mumbled. "Matt's pretty touchy about his sister."

"So I gathered."

He held up the bag. "Uh. Thanks for lunch. Can you stay and eat with me?"

"I already ate. We're busy today so I need to get back to work. See you tonight."

She flashed a Mona Lisa smile and turned, heading back to her car. Payton admired her ass and hips, re-membering the magic feel of both in his hands.

Tallulah turned and blew him a kiss, a gesture so uncharacteristic he could feel his mouth hanging open.

He couldn't stop grinning for an hour.

* * *

"What's gotten into you with all the smiles?" Her boss, Laverna Finley, lowered the bifocals on her nose and stared.

Tallulah shrugged. "No special reason," she lied.

"Harrumph. Don't believe that for a minute, missy. I suspect this involves a man." Laverna's wrinkled face momentarily softened. "Whatever it is, it's a nice change."

"You saying I'm normally a grump?" she asked.

"Yes. But still a valuable employee. Now get back to work."

"Yes, ma'am." She hesitated a heartbeat. "Would it be possible to leave a little early? I'd like to...get a head start on dinner."

Laverna chuckled, her smoky voice as guttural as a man's. "You're wanting to get a head start on something all right, but I don't think it's cooking."

She blushed that the old woman could read her so well.

"First you start sashaying around in fancy dresses, all smiles, and now you're wanting to leave early when you're usually the last to leave the building." She waved a thin, veined hand. "Go. Enjoy your youth while you can."

"Yes, ma'am." Quickly, she grabbed her purse from under the counter and rushed across the cultural center's pine board flooring, her pumps clickety-clacking in her haste.

Laverna threw back her head and let loose a deep-throated laugh. "He must be damn good."

She pretended not to hear as she scurried out the

door. Oh, what the hell. Tallulah reopened the door and stuck her head inside.

"His name's Payton and yes, he's damn good."

Laverna raised her skinny hand in a fist pump. Tallulah giggled as she hurried to her car and started the engine, planning a special meal. Steak, baked potato, salad, pecan pie—all his favorites.

She's everything I ever wanted.

The words spun around and around in her brain, a carousel of joy. It was more than she'd ever dared dream to find again. He must love her, even if he hadn't said the actual words yet. Maybe tonight would be the night.

She practically danced in the grocery store and all through making dinner, picturing his surprise when he returned home to the smell of cooked rib eye. *Oh, that's right. It's your favorite, isn't it? I just kinda whipped this together last minute,* she'd claim.

A real catch, she was. Smokin' sexy in bed and hot in the kitchen. He'd never want to leave Bayou La Siryna when the project was finished. And here she'd been worrying herself sick over nothing.

Everything he ever wanted.

He was no Hanan. For over a year, she'd questioned her judgment in men. She'd been so totally duped by the shadow hunter betrayer. How often had she worried that Payton's ties to his pack were stronger than what they had together? So needless.

A disturbing scent of fur wafted through the aroma of steak and pie. Not Payton's. She glanced around the kitchen uneasily, and then walked through the cabin, looking for any sign of a disturbance. Everything was in place. Tallulah returned to the kitchen and inhaled deeply. The scent was gone.

She'd done this at least three times in the past week and it was annoying as hell. Some part of her subconscious must still be processing Russell's attack, even if she consciously had put it behind her.

Truck tires crunched on the gravel driveway, and she parted the kitchen curtain. It was Payton. Excitement zipped along her spine and she scrambled to set the table. Tonight was going to be so perfect.

He entered, looking sweaty and tired. She examined him closely for signs of blood or bruises. "You and Matt didn't come to actual blows, did you?"

"Nah." He ran a hand through his blond hair and sniffed. "Steak?"

"And potatoes and pie. What started the argument today?"

Payton sat down at the table and she poured him a glass of iced tea. He took a long swallow before speaking.

"Matt saw me last night."

"He was the wolf you saw? What bad luck it was your alpha. You didn't tell me it was him."

"Well, it was right before we left, and we were all focused on how I shifted in front of everyone. Unfortunately, Matt saw it all."

"So what?"

"So it pissed him off. I'd let my guard down. We aren't supposed to let anyone know we're werewolves, much less let them observe the shift."

She sat across from him and wrapped her fingers around the cold, damp glass. "It's no big deal. None of the hunters are going to talk about it outside of the group."

"Yeah, *we* know that, but Matt isn't exactly the trusting type."

"He'll get over it. Especially when he sees nothing bad is going to happen because of last night."

"I'm not so sure," he said slowly. "Things were said in the heat of the moment. Matt pretty much threatened to kick me out of the pack."

As far as she was concerned, that wouldn't be a bad thing. His allegiance to them demanded too much. It threatened their entire relationship.

"Would that be so terrible?" she asked. "After the way they treated you when you exposed Russell…well, they don't act loyal to *you*."

He pursed his lips. "You don't get it. We're a team, blood brothers in a way. Matt and the others took me in when I had nobody."

"Okay. Great. They helped you out once," she said, her temper rising. "Does that mean that now you have to spend your whole life with them, traveling all over the damn place? That's ridiculous."

The sharp words hung in the air between them and she wanted to bite her tongue. She should have broached the subject with a little more tact. Not something she was known for.

"How would you feel if you couldn't hunt?" Payton asked, breaking the tense silence. "If your brother and all the shadow hunters wanted nothing more to do with you?"

"It would hurt," she admitted. "But it wouldn't be the end of the world." *Not as long as I had you*, Tallulah wanted to say. But she didn't. If Payton chose the pack over her, then she'd still have her pride when he left. She'd never grovel for a man.

"So you say."

This was *not* how she'd envisioned their romantic evening. Her throat burned and her chest tightened. She had to know. "You told me your crew leaves at the end of the month. That's only two weeks from now," she stated past the choking sensation in her lungs. "Are you going with them?"

"I don't know," he said quietly.

She stood and began setting bowls of food on the table with enough force it was a wonder they didn't shatter.

"Lulu." He steadied her hand. "Let's not argue tonight. It's been a tough day."

"Don't let me be a downer." She sat down abruptly and speared a steak. Damn if she wasn't the world's biggest fool. She wasn't anybody's *everything*. Payton probably said that just to tick off Matt. He'd be gone soon and she'd be alone as always. Viciously, she cut into the rib eye and plopped a piece in her mouth.

With a sigh, Payton buttered his potato and they commenced eating. Only the sound of scraping utensils passed for dinner conversation. She'd gotten off work early for this? After eating only half the food on her plate, Tallulah threw down her napkin. Might as well have been eating sawdust for all the enjoyment in the special meal she'd prepared.

She stood and emptied the remainder of the food in the garbage can.

"Will you stop it, please? You know how much I care about you. It's just… I have a lot to think about it."

"Sure you do," she said bitterly. "Take your sweet time. You still have two whole weeks to decide if you're staying or leaving Bayou La Siryna."

She started out of the kitchen, but Payton jumped to his feet and came to her.

"Stop. I admit I'm confused as hell." He walked in front of her. "You're my mate, okay? It's not something I take lightly. When I—"

She placed a hand on her forehead, willing her brain to catch up to his words. "I'm your *what*?" she asked. Jillian had spoken of this. "But I thought…that was something among your own people."

"Usually, it is. But your true mate can be anybody. And you are mine."

He didn't look happy about it.

"Wh-what does that even mean? How long have you known?"

"It's hard to explain."

She steeled herself. "Try."

"It means no other woman but you will ever completely satisfy me."

She struggled to understand the implications. "Then what's the problem? Stay in Bayou La Siryna with me." She ground her teeth, bit back saying more. She'd vowed to never grovel for a man and she'd come dangerously close to doing so. If Payton was so unhappy to discover she was his mate, then that meant he didn't love her. "How long have you known this?"

"Since the first night we made love," he admitted.

"Why didn't you tell me right then? Is the idea so repulsive that you didn't want me to know the truth?"

"Of course it's not repulsive. Just surprising and unsettling. Staying with you meant a different kind of life from what I'd anticipated."

"One away from your precious pack. And I'm not worth it," she said bitterly. "Get out, then. Go home."

"Is that what you really want?"

She wanted him. Wanted his heart. When Payton left in two weeks, would his living with her until then make things worse or better?

Pewter eyes swirled to a mysterious, dark smoke as he gazed down at her. Would she ever truly understand this man and his wild wolf nature? Maybe his animal half compelled him in a way that was unfathomable to her human mind.

Or he could be playing her until it came time to get the hell out of Dodge.

"Two weeks," she said firmly. "Then make a permanent decision. If you go, I don't want any more communication with you. No letters, texting or phone calls. A clean break."

He nodded. "That's fair. I'd never string you along or deliberately hurt you."

But you already have, she wanted to scream. Perhaps if she stayed patient a little longer, he'd realize that he had choices in life.

She took a deep breath. "I'm going to get another plate of food. Let's finish eating our dinner."

Chapter 16

Six more days.

Every moment sped by much too quickly. Tallulah wanted to grab each second with a clenched fist and slow the steady progression of time.

The real kicker was that she was partly to blame for the early job ending. Sashy had finally convinced her husband, Hank, not to cut down any more trees on their land. April had spoken with Mrs. Potts and the fae charm had worked like…well, a charm. The couple would still make a profit on the cut timber, but the land would be reclaimed with trees instead of sold to a developer. So all that remained for Payton's crew was to clear up the timber that had been cut and load it onto transport trucks for sale.

Torn between opposing emotions of optimism and despair, her heart felt battered and confused. Glad she'd won the conservation battle, but broken that Payton might leave even earlier than planned.

And today's mission only pinched her heart more. But it must be done. Really, she should have done it long ago.

On the outskirts of town, she turned down Bosarge Lane, an area she normally avoided. She drove past the charming, older homes with their vibe from the arts-and-crafts era. Two more blocks and older homes, converted to duplexes, showed the wear and tear of time and landlords who neglected the finer details of home maintenance.

Another block and she pulled into the euphemistically named Magnolia Blossoms garden homes complex. Not a single damn magnolia tree or even a flower bed graced the shabby quarters. On the dead end of the last brick residential area, she parked and stared at house number 22A. One of the shutters hung precariously at a ninety-degree angle, although the paint was still crisp and neat. Weeds encircled the stunted shrubbery and although the small lawn was cut, grass grew high at the edges of the house and driveway. All of this wouldn't have been let go…if Bo hadn't died.

Sighing, she slid out of the car. Fala was at home, her old Plymouth Duster sat in the driveway. Tallulah tugged at the waistband of her shirt and marched to the front door. It swung open before she even had a chance to knock.

"What are you doing here?" Fala asked, eyes narrowed.

Same old Fala. "Nice to see you, too. May I come in?"

The old woman crossed her arms and hesitated, frowning.

Tallulah bit back a sharp retort. The last few years had not been kind to Bo's mother. More gray streaked her raven-black hair and the lines on her face had deepened. But the sharp beak of her nose and her dark, suspicious eyes were more accentuated, making her appear even more like her aptly named Choctaw moniker—crow.

And like a crow she just pecked, pecked, pecked away at people until they abandoned her. Like Bo's father had done.

Tallulah sat on the faded, floral-print sofa. In high school, she'd sat in this very spot with Bo, dressed in a formal prom gown as Fala took pictures, gushing over her handsome Bo and ignoring his unworthy date.

"No reason for you to come around now my boy is gone." Fala sank into a chair opposite her. "We were never on good terms."

"I did try." Tallulah's gaze swept the den. Nothing had changed. Photos of Bo hung everywhere. She stood and walked over to her favorite—Bo at age five, pulling back a child-sized slingshot, a huge grin splitting his face.

"Whatcha looking at?" Fala snapped. "Those are my pictures and I'm not giving you any."

"I didn't ask for one." She pointed at the faded black-and-white photo. "I was just admiring this one."

"My Bohpoli was well-named. He was the best shooter in the shadow hunters."

Tallulah went back to the sofa, hiding a small smile. Bo had always hated his name. It meant "thrower" in Choctaw, but over the years the name came to be associated with the Little People, or fairies, of the bayou.

"He was the best," she agreed.

Fala's prickly manner softened a degree. "Why are you here?" she asked again, though not unkindly.

She bit down on her lip to stop the trembling. Part of her wanted to run out the door and forget the whole thing. Her breath hitched. She wouldn't embarrass herself by trying to talk. Slowly, Tallulah slid the diamond ring off her right ring finger and then held it up. She had worn it one last time for this special visit. The small, solitaire diamond gleamed like a lit candelabra.

She held it out to Fala. "This belongs to you. Bo told me it was your mother's wedding ring and I want to return it."

Fala's head snapped back as if she'd been slapped. "Why? It wasn't good enough for you?"

Anger and hurt churned her gut. No one could push her buttons quite like Fala. *Be patient for one more minute and you can walk out.* "I treasured it," she said levelly. "But it doesn't feel right to keep it when it belongs to your family."

Fala's eyes flashed. "That's not it. You've been running around with a new guy in town. I still get out and about. I hear things."

"Bo's been dead over two years," she said drily. "Not like I'm cheating on him."

Fala snatched the ring out of her fingers. "If you don't want it, I'll take it."

"It's yours. You're welcome."

So much for gratitude. Fala might not appreciate the gesture, but it was something she needed to do. Bo would want her to move on and this was a final, symbolic step. Payton was her future now, if he chose to stay.

Tallulah stood, ready to take her leave. "I'll see myself out," she remarked drily.

At the door, she took a deep breath, saying good-bye to Bo's old childhood home. No need to ever return. Bittersweet, but it felt right.

"Wait."

Fala removed a photo from its frame and held it out. "For you."

It was the young Bo with his slingshot and impish grin. Her eyes watered as she felt a strange brew of happiness and sadness. Reverently, she tucked it into her purse. "Thank you."

On an impulse, she hugged a surprised Fala. The woman held her arms rigidly at her side, but that was okay. All her love had been wrapped up in Bo. He was the only one who brought out a warm side to Fala. Tallulah pulled away, but Bo's mom lifted an arm and awkwardly patted her shoulder.

Fala cleared her throat and stepped back. "*Chi pisa lachike*. I'll see you soon."

There was no literal Choctaw word for "good-bye," but they both knew this was an ending.

Tallulah hurried out and climbed back in her car, feeling lighter and ready to move on with the day's errands. Back in town, she drove past the same old shops, as familiar to her as the bayou woods, with the occasional new one cropping up. She pulled her vehicle into the Pixie Land shop, the newest business in Bayou La Siryna. It was small and quirky with its collection of mermaid and fairy figurines for sale, but the store had thrived surprisingly well. Local residents' tastes obviously ran to the unusual.

The scent of the ocean, underpinned with a woodsy herbal note, enveloped Tallulah as she entered. The proprietor, Chulah's wife, could stay in business just by selling the cologne and bath oils that replicated the aroma.

Long blond hair, with subtle pink and purple highlights, glowed in a way that no commercial product could ever deliver to human tresses, April Rivers spotted her and glided over in a graceful sweep, her long skirt swishing.

"If you weren't so sweet, I would just hate you," Tallulah said in greeting.

No wonder Chulah adored April. Even if she were a fairy from another dimension, the two made it work. She tried to take heart from that. Tombi and Annie were also opposites in personalities and supernatural gifts, and yet it only served to beautifully complement their relationship.

If only she could be so lucky with Payton.

April laughed. "What brings you here today?" Even her voice was melodic. Damn it. Tallulah glanced in a store mirror. They were as opposite as brilliant sunlight and a deep black abyss. Yet, at one time, Chulah had actually wanted *her*—Tallulah. Until one fine day April had wandered out of the bayou woods and stolen his heart.

Even though she'd long ago turned down Chulah's marriage proposal, Tallulah often wondered what her life would have been like had she accepted. She didn't love him like Payton, but he was one of her best friends growing up. A steady, reliable kind of guy.

"Why so sad?" April asked, putting an arm around her. "Did you have an argument with Payton?"

A guilty flush heated her neck. She had no right to be thinking of Chulah. "No. But he leaves in less than a week."

"He's really going to leave with the rest of the crew?"

The slight forehead furrow in April's creamy skin only made her look more adorable.

Tallulah shrugged, as if it didn't matter. "Maybe."

"Surely not." April withdrew her arm and tapped an elegant finger on her full, rosy lips. "Have you ever thought of moving with him?"

"Leave Bayou La Siryna?" The idea had never once crossed her mind.

"Much as you and the other shadow hunters love this place, it's not exactly the center of the universe," she pointed out mildly.

"Would you rather live someplace else, April?"

"Not at all. It's always been my home, too—of a sort. But Payton isn't from these parts, he doesn't have roots tying him down."

"But I do."

Move from the bayou? Away from the land of her ancestors and her life's calling to hunt the ancient, evil spirits?

"Something to consider," April said mildly. "I chose to be with Chulah and left my fae realm."

"But the other fae hated you," she blurted. "No tough choice there."

"It still meant leaving my own kind and a world I was familiar with—even for all its imperfections."

Her mouth twisted. "Guess you have a point," she admitted with an ungracious sigh.

"From everything you and Chulah told me, Matt is probably a father figure to Payton. And we have no idea what the bond is like for a pack member. It might be deeply ingrained in his DNA to live with other wolves.

At one time in years past, their lives depended on group habitation."

"You always make so much sense." Tallulah huffed and crossed her arms. "I won't argue with your logic. But Payton can't keep me hanging forever. It's not fair. I told him if he leaves me and moves away for the next job, that's it. We're done."

"Perfectly logical," April agreed. "But sometimes one person in a relationship has to give more than the other. And it's not fair. But don't you want to be happy?"

She shook her head. "Are you saying I should offer to move away with Payton? It's not like he's even asked me to."

"Probably figures you would say no. Or that it wouldn't be fair to ask you to give up your lifestyle."

"You think I should go with him. That I'm asking too much when I gave him an ultimatum to pick me or his pack." Tallulah placed her hands on her hips and scowled, uncomfortable with the doubts April had raised in her righteous anger against Payton.

"Not at all." April smiled. "Just pointing out a few issues for you to consider. You do what's best for you."

Thankfully, her temper didn't affect April's happy bubble of equilibrium. She looked around at the store's shelves, idly searching. "I've got a ton of errands to run today, including picking out a gift for Nita's birthday. I understand she's horse-crazy. You have anything besides fairies and mermaid stuff in here?"

"Of course I do," she replied, turning and heading to the back left corner of the store. "Nita's the young girl wanting to join the shadow hunters, isn't she?"

"Bingo." She marveled at the colorful, delicate merchandise on display as she followed April. Even though

Tallulah been a tomboy as a child and a warrior as an adult, there was something magical about everything April purchased and touched.

Once, she'd laughingly asked April where the store's stock was manufactured. "Are there fairy factories cranking out collectibles?" April had only smiled mysteriously and shrugged.

"Here we are." April pulled something down from a high shelf and turned around. "Think Nita would like this?"

"Oh. My. Word."

April held a large war-horse mustang molded from resin. On top of it rode a Native American woman, also molded from resin, and dressed in full regalia. Her face was beautifully fierce and captivating.

"I'll take two."

April winked. "I love when people buy a gift for someone and then another for themselves."

Tallulah exited the Pixie Land store carrying the heavy figurines—minus a wad of cash in her wallet. They were worth every penny. Quickly, she locked them in the trunk of her car, gathered her dry cleaning to drop off, and walked down Main Street. The streets were crowded as many of the shops set out their wares for a sidewalk sale. Next to the dry cleaners, raucous yipping and meowing noises sounded from a few people dragging reluctant pets to the veterinarian's office.

A scent of fur and musk slammed into her awareness. This wasn't from one of the domesticated animals about to see the vet. And it wasn't the faint, masculine scent that was part of Payton's intoxicating scent.

This was pungent, warped...*off*. She'd smelled it only once before.

Russell.

But where? The crowd all looked local and vaguely familiar. She quickly scanned bodies and faces, ruling out children and women. No Russell. Her scalp prickled as she spotted the back of a man wearing a dark brown uniform and swinging a large, pump canister. He was the same height as Russell, same medium brown hair. She scurried after him, dry cleaning forgotten. The man picked up his pace, weaving through a throng of customers picking among discounted clothing racks.

The scent left a trail behind him. He slipped into an alley and there was an explosion of metal on pavement.

Tallulah ran, reaching the side street moments later. The pump canister rolled harmlessly in the narrow alley, but the man had vanished. Unless he was hiding behind one of the large garbage bins scattered about haphazardly. She walked silently—nose, eyes and ears alert for signs of life.

An explosion of claws clattered at the far end of the alley. A wolf sprang from behind a bin, toting brown pants and a brown shirt in its mouth. A flash of brown fur, and it vanished on the far end.

Her heart beat loud and strong and her senses fired up in a primitive desire to pursue, as strong as if she'd encountered one of the ancient spirits from the woods roaming in the late afternoon sun.

Tallulah dropped her armload of clothes and ran down the alley, emerging into the next block of shops and offices. A young couple with a barking dog on a leash pointed down another side road. She ran again, only in time to see a flash of wolf tail racing toward the tree line at the edge of town. Too late. Two legs couldn't compete with four.

Her chest heaved from breathing hard—part exertion, part fear. "Damn it," she muttered.

"Did you see that huge dog?" the woman yelled above the cacophony of her dog's howls.

"Yeah, I saw it all right." She headed back to the alley to gather her belongings.

The man walking the dog with her shook his head, a dazed expression on his face. "Could have sworn it was a wolf."

"Shouldn't be wolves in south Alabama," she said to them in passing. But *were*wolves—oh my, yes.

Russell was back.

Tallulah hit the accelerator, driving well over the downtown speed limit. She had to warn Payton and the others. Matt certainly wouldn't be happy to see her, much less hear the news. But it had to be done. Of all the worst timing for Russell to appear... But, of course, Russell knew that—had probably been slinking around, watching and waiting. Hell-bent on revenge.

The pack had gathered for a full-moon wolf run. They'd become testy and temperamental after months of suppressing their animal urge to roam as a pack. But, at last, they felt it safe to run as one. Sheriff Angier had relaxed his patrol over the weeks. With no more dead bodies and no proof that Jeb had been murdered, he'd been forced to turn the majority of his attention back to other crimes.

So Matt had at last granted a return to their old ways. The pack was holding a supper meeting now to go over safety precautions, and the need to try and avoid shadow hunters who might be in the area.

At first, she'd been resentful of Payton's happiness

on being included, but if the pack moved on without him next week, this could be his last pack run. She could hardly begrudge him that opportunity.

She checked her phone for the umpteenth time—still no reply from Payton to her texts and voice mails. Tallulah slammed her fist on the dashboard. "Idiot!" she screamed. Arrogant, control-freak Matt had probably demanded the pack turn off their cell phones while he lectured them on the need for safety tonight.

The irony didn't escape her.

Tires squealed as she rounded a curve too fast and bumped over a curb. Too late, she saw the line of cars stopped at a traffic light. She slammed on her brakes, but realized it wouldn't keep her from rear-ending the other vehicle. At once, she turned the steering wheel sharply to the right, hoping to avoid a collision.

Metal crunched metal. She'd managed to avoid a fender bender with the other vehicle, but had demolished a US mailbox in the process. Freaking terrific. Like magic, a siren wailed nearby. With a sigh, she removed her driver's license out of her wallet for the cop, and got out of the car to inspect the damage.

Forty-five minutes later, she hit the road again, driving at a much more sedate rate until she reached the county road to the farmhouse. The cops never bothered with speed traps in this remote area so she sped up. Now that she was close to the house, doubt suddenly assailed her confidence.

Was it really necessary to crash their meeting? Matt wouldn't be thrilled, and Payton might be annoyed. They already knew Russell was a potential threat until—or if—he was captured. If only she'd had her slingshot with her today. She could have injured Russell and called Sheriff Angier to arrest him.

You couldn't have known, she chided herself. Wasn't like she'd ever before needed to carry weapons on a downtown shopping trip.

Up ahead, the usual hodgepodge of cars and trucks littered the driveway and front lawn of the large farmhouse. Payton's faded red Chevy truck was there. Slowly, she pulled into the driveway and parked. More doubts assailed her. If all these men stayed together tonight, what could Russell really do? His real beef was with her, Payton and Matt. And they each knew it. She drummed her fingers on the dashboard, debating.

What the hell. If she ticked off Matt, so be it. Payton could hardly get too annoyed for her interruption. She had their best interests at heart.

Resolutely, she flung open the car door and started up the driveway. Payton's truck motor made a faint clanking sound, as if he'd arrived to the pack meeting late—only minutes ahead of her. So Payton was okay. The tight knot in her stomach unwound.

Halfway up the sidewalk entry, she noticed a brown van parked at the side of the house. That didn't look familiar. Curious, she walked across the lawn for a closer look.

A business name was painted on its side in a bold yellow font—Clean Sweep Pest Control.

Chills crept along her nerves like a clutter of spiders. Could Russell's brown uniform have been that of an exterminator's? She'd instantly assumed he'd worn a janitorial outfit.

The pump canister.

Of course. Tallulah grabbed the cell phone out of

her purse to text Tombi. Come to farmhouse. Possible danger. Call sheriff.

Strong arms grabbed her from behind and squeezed her ribs so tight she couldn't breathe. A putrid scent of fur and disease watered her eyes. Bile rose in the back of her throat.

"Curiosity killed the cat," he said in high-pitched glee. "You're always causing me trouble. Poking your nose in everybody's business. You'll die like the others."

The others. Jeb's bloody, torn flesh flashed through her mind. *Don't let him bite you. He'll finish off what he started months ago when he attacked you.*

"I was going to come after you later," Russell continued. "But this worked out for the best. Now Payton can watch when I snap your neck in two with my bite."

His hands shifted on her arms and then the unmistakable sound of ripped duct tape came from behind. Fear shivered down her arms and she struggled anew. In seconds, he'd bound her hands behind her back at the wrists.

"You're a sick asshole." She kicked at his shins and he yelped, loosening his hold. She wiggled out of his grasp a fraction, only to have him jerk her roughly back against him.

Russell panted as he struggled to keep her captive. She kicked him again, but he only grunted, absorbing the pain without weakening his grip on her forearm. Whether it was his werewolf nature, or his job carrying timber that developed his muscles—or possibly some combination of both—he overpowered her.

She tried to scream, hoping—however remote the possibility—that Sheriff Angier might be wandering close by.

"Shut up," he said roughly. He slowly moved her, thrashing and kicking, onto the porch, evidently wanting to get her inside the farmhouse before killing her. She could only hope all the men weren't already deep in the woods, that Payton or some others were still hanging around.

Russell was lost in a fever, but he had enough sense to try and avoid any witnesses to murder.

Chapter 17

It was unnaturally quiet. Had the pack left for their outing without him? Payton wondered. He wasn't *that* late. Besides, Matt and Eli had asked to meet with him privately for a few minutes before the wolf run.

"Anybody home?" Payton called out. "Sorry I'm late."

The silence weighed heavy. His voice echoed indecently and his steps sounded obscenely loud on the hall's wood flooring. He paused, the hackles raising on his arms and scalp. Everyone should have been home already. Some primitive instinct seemed to slow time as his senses sharpened to pick up clues—but there was nothing. No sound. No scent. No movement.

Cautiously, he returned to the entry and picked up the baseball bat they always kept by the front door. He trudged back down the hall, gripping the bat and ready to strike at the slightest provocation.

Almost to the kitchen, a sickly sweet scent cloyed the air. It had a faint hint of something medicinal, totally out of place for a home. He walked into the room, bat raised high, but the only thing unusual was a large blue cooler on the table. Payton lowered his bat and raised the cooler lid.

Vials of blood in premeasured syringes lay scattered atop squared ice cubes like a macabre Picasso work of art. What the hell? He counted. Thirteen syringes…one per pack member. But…why?

Several syringes containing a clear liquid lay beside the cooler. Drugs? Poison?

He started toward the den, a knot of dread in his stomach. Whatever awaited in that next room wasn't going to be good. He breathed in a toxic miasma that numbed his lips and coated his tongue and throat.

Matt and Eli lay draped across the sofa, bound and gagged, their bodies as inert and lifeless as ragdolls.

He rushed over to Matt, whose chest rose and fell with shallow breaths. At least he was still alive, though his face was pale and his lips were turning blue. Payton placed his fingers on the side of Matt's neck and detected a faint heartbeat. A quick glance at Eli confirmed he was also still breathing.

This had to be Russell's work. They had no enemies—no outside friends, but no enemies, either.

The pack avoided doctors and hospitals like the plague, afraid lab tests would uncover their strange DNA. But in this case, an exception was justified. With shaking hands, Payton pulled the cell phone from his pants pocket to dial 911.

Scuffling and a male human voice sounded by the

front door. Had Russell returned, wanting to pick them off one by one as they returned home?

He suddenly realized the purpose of the blood vials. Russell's revenge on the pack would be to inject each of them with his tainted blood, a fit punishment for banning him from the group. He wanted them all to be outcasts like him, a tribe of infected misfits.

The bastard.

A female voice rang out, although he couldn't make out the words. Fear burned up his spine and momentarily short-circuited his brain. Tallulah. What the hell was she doing here? He threw down his phone and leaped to his feet, his wolf heart clamoring to fight and protect.

A blast of wood and steel, and Russell burst through the front door, Tallulah clasped tightly against him in a stronghold, hands bound behind her back. He held a knife against her throat.

But it was Russell's eyes, not the knife, that speared Payton with terror. Rimmed with red and shining with madness, they held the promise of death. The lycanthropic fever had reached an advanced stage where no remnant of his friend still existed. Diseased werewolf and man had merged to form a frightening beast, one without a soul.

Payton took in Russell's long ragged hair, the fresh streaks of blood where Tallulah had scraped one cheek with her fingernails. Too bad she hadn't been able to gouge out an eye.

The large carving knife twitched at the vulnerable hollow of Tallulah's throat. One wrong word or move on his part, and how easily Russell could plunge in the sharp blade, slicing through soft flesh and into her lungs and throat.

He swallowed hard and forced his gaze away from Russell and onto Tallulah. How frightened she must be.

If she was, not a hint of it showed on her face. Her dark eyes were narrowed with fury and determination. His girl wouldn't go down without putting up a helluva fight. Damn, he loved that about her.

He loved everything about her.

He loved *her*.

Now, when it was too late, he acknowledged the truth within himself. All that mattered now was saving Tallulah's life. Even if the residents of the farmhouse turned into a den of murderous wolves, Payton wanted her to escape their doom. After all, it was his fault she was in this position. Meeting him had been nothing but bad news for her.

"This is between the two of us, Russell. Let her go."

He grinned. "Why the hell would I do that? I want you to see the bitch bleed out."

Payton fought to control his urge to strike. He'd never reach Tallulah before the knife did its job. "You've already got to Matt and Eli and now you've got me. We're the ones responsible for kicking you out. Not Tallulah."

"She knows too much." Russell wasn't budging an inch.

"C'mon, let's fight. Winner takes all. Unless you're afraid to fight like a man," he challenged, appealing to his old friend's pride. "You're so sick with fever, you've probably grown too weak for fighting. Best you can do now is sneak up on other men. Or attack females."

Russell's expression grew tight with crafty suspicion.

"I know what you're trying to do. But it *would* be fun to torture your female instead of letting her die quickly. Unfortunately, it's too risky."

He read it on Russell's eyes before his arm moved an inch. He was going to kill her—right here, right now.

"Wait! I've got an idea," he said desperately. "I saw the vials in the cooler. Let's go in the kitchen. I'll inject myself if you let Tallulah go."

Russell hesitated.

"That's what you came here for, right? Thirteen vials for each of the thirteen pack members." He backed down the hallway toward the kitchen, hands held high in surrender. "See? I'm not going to make any sudden lunges at you."

"No," Tallulah screamed. Real terror spiked her voice at last. "Don't do it, Payton. Please don't."

"It's okay, baby. Everything's going to be okay," he said soothingly.

They made slow progress. The hallway seemed twice its original length. Tallulah dragged her feet, offering passive resistance, delaying the inevitable. He dared not get too far away from the two of them in case he had to make a sudden last-ditch move to save Tallulah.

His back slammed against the edge of the kitchen table. Russell moved into a corner, an eager smirk tightening his face. "Go on. Do it. Shoot it up."

"No, don't," Tallulah begged. "I called Tombi. The hunters will be here any minute."

A bluff, or had she really called her brother? No way to know.

"Hurry," Russell growled, looking nervously out the kitchen window.

Payton slowly opened the cooler lid, buying every

second possible. "Is there enough blood in the shots to kill us or just make us infected?" he asked, trying to draw out a conversation.

"How the hell should I know? Do I look like a damn doctor to you?"

Payton tried again. "What's in the other syringes? The clear liquid?"

"Anesthesia." He threw back his head and laughed. "Stole it from the vet's office when I went in and sprayed for bugs. Supposed to be strong enough to knock out a horse for surgery."

Payton shuddered to think of the damage done to Matt's and Eli's bodies—should they recover. "I'm curious. Would you rather us dead or did you envision us all living together with the same fever?"

"I want you and Matt and Eli dead," he said flatly. "I'll be the new alpha."

Russell's brain had turned to complete mush. Maybe he could poke holes in the guy's logic and reach some kind of compromise with him. "None of the pack will accept you as alpha. They'll hate you for turning them."

He frowned. "No. You're lying. I'll be their true leader. They'll look to me for guidance as the fever grows hotter and deeper."

"Russell, listen to me. This won't work. Let me give you money, as much as you want. Take it and run. Get as far away from Bayou La Siryna as you can. There's bound to be more of your kind out west. Find them and start your life over."

"My life *is* freaking over. So hurry up. Get one of those syringes."

Now what? Payton reached in the cooler and pulled out a syringe. Tallulah shuddered and squirmed harder in Russell's arms. He held it up to the overhead kitchen fixture, as if interested in examining its putrid contents. Time to make one last effort at trickery before leaping at Russell.

"How long did it take you to fill all these vials?" he asked, keeping his voice light. "Seems like you lost lots of blood. If it…" He turned swiftly toward the window. "What was that noise?"

Russell's hand slacked as he followed Payton's gaze.

It was all the cue Tallulah needed. She stomped on Russell's foot with enough force that Payton heard a bone crack.

Russell screamed. Tallulah cut out of his grasp and ran to Payton's side.

Thank the heavens.

He kicked at Russell's right hand, sending the knife clattering to the floor. "Run," he screamed at Tallulah.

Russell slammed into him and he went flying across the table, knocking over the cooler. Ice, broken glass and needles scattered and fell. Payton grabbed Russell's T-shirt and dragged him down with him as he tumbled to the tiled floor.

Tallulah's feet were nearby, trying to kick at Russell. Of *course*, she hadn't taken the opportunity to run and save herself. Aggravating woman.

Russell's breath was hot against his neck.

No. Don't get bit.

Hardly a fair fight if he had to stay constantly on the defensive. He'd rather take a stab wound or bullet than get bit and overcome with lycanthropic fever. Only one way to even the playing field. Payton yielded control of his body to his wolf, effectively shrinking away from Russell's mouth.

* * *

Tallulah desperately scanned the kitchen, seeking a sharp edge to cut through the binding on her wrists. Knives were everywhere, but they did her no good. An old-fashioned meat cutter mounted on the counter caught her eye. That might work.

She heaved herself up on the counter—no easy feat—and awkwardly tried to position the back of her hands to the metal cutter.

Snarls and growls erupted below. She paused in her struggle and gaped at the two men—er, wolves—who bared their fangs at one another. Each crouched and had their ears pressed flat against their heads. Quickly, she focused on the task at hand. If she didn't get her hands free, she'd be reduced to watching from the sidelines.

That didn't sit well with her hunter instincts.

A howl erupted, loud and unnatural in the room's close confines. Was it Russell or Payton?

Again and again she contorted her body and arms to fit her bindings over the circular meat cutter until she finally felt a loosening of the bonds. It was working. Her hands stung as she misjudged and accidentally cut into her flesh, but she didn't slow her efforts.

Freedom. Tallulah wiggled out of the remaining tape and tried not to wince at the number of bleeding cuts that covered her hands and wrists. Luckily, it didn't appear she'd severed a major vein. Hopping down from the counter, she recklessly pulled open drawers until she'd located a large boning knife.

Only then did she return her attention to the snapping wolves. Both of their hackles were raised, and lips curled back to expose fangs and gums.

Their eyes were locked on each other in what appeared to be a stand-down competition. Perfect. She hid the knife behind her back and silently eased behind the brown wolf with the patch of black fur between its ears—Russell.

Russell leaped, his giant paws extended toward Payton. Tallulah swing the knife down, stabbing him in the hindquarters.

A yowl of pain erupted, so loud it felt like it pierced her eardrums. Instinctively, she jumped back, narrowly missing Russell's snapping jaw.

Payton took advantage of the opportunity to strike. At the last moment, Russell must have sensed the danger. He turned and the bite landed in his chest instead of the vulnerable neck area.

They commenced circling again. Payton flicked her the barest of glances, cocking his head to the right. Was he just trying to get her to leave? He did it again, more insistently. She kept the bloody knife in her hand and padded to the next room, just in case there was new danger.

Two dead bodies, bound at the wrists and ankles, were draped on opposite ends of the couch. Matt and another male that looked vaguely familiar. She pressed her lips tight together to stop their trembling. Were there any more dead bodies sprawled around the old rambling farmhouse? Tallulah rubbed the chill bumps on her arms.

Matt groaned and moved his head to one side.

Tallulah gasped and went to him at once. She made quick work of cutting off the bindings and then hurried to the second man. He appeared lifeless, in much worse shape than Matt. She gently laid a hand on his chest and felt the slight rise and fall of his breath. Whew…

he lived. Tallulah also cut him out of the bindings. If only they were well, they could help with the battle in the next room.

They needed medical attention ASAP. Where was a damn cell phone when you needed one? Russell had knocked hers to the ground when he'd attacked outside. Tallulah stood, caught between wanting to search for her phone outside and wanting to run back in the kitchen to help Payton.

She ran to the kitchen. The wolves were entangled, rolling and snapping on the floor, sliding on the melting ice. The table and chairs were upended and photos that had hung on the wall had crashed down. The floor was littered with broken glass, syringes and needles.

Incredibly, Russell appeared to have the upper hand as Payton increasingly struggled from being held to the ground and pinned. Tallulah raised her knife again, but dared not strike, as she was afraid of accidentally stabbing Payton.

Blood and foam spewed from both their mouths. A gaping wound bled on Payton's left rib cage.

He had been bitten.

The horror of it gutted Tallulah. She fell to the ground on her knees.

Russell pinned Payton and his jaw came down to clamp over Payton's neck.

He was going to kill Payton. He'd be lost to her forever, just like everyone else she had ever loved. White-hot anger washed through her grief, cleansing the stupefying paralysis. She raised her knife, ready to strike again.

A loud whizzing noise shot past her ear and she froze.

* * *

Bits of glass ground into Payton's back. His strength was spent. Every ounce of muscle and willpower he possessed wasn't enough to fight against Russell's crazed determination. The fever lent him a demented power, as if he could withstand any blow and keep fighting.

Bloodshot, fevered eyes bore into him, triumphant and smug. Russell's snout lowered, his breath hot and nasty. His lips curled back, exposing tongue and teeth.

Lower, lower…he couldn't move. Teeth scraped his neck, a gentle tease.

This is it. The death bite. Poor Lulu. He'd let her down. Like Bo, he was going to die and leave her alone to grieve. She might not ever recover from this loss. His girl would retreat back to her prickly shell for years, if not forever.

He closed his eyes. Let the end come. It was better this way. His body burned with a dozen bite marks. He was already infected, his life essentially over. Shudders raked his body. Better death than to become a monster like Russell. Better not to see Tallulah eventually look at him in disgust. Better not to be kicked out of the pack and condemned to a life of solitary banishment.

If only he had one more day. How differently he would spend it. He'd make love to Tallulah over and over and then hold her close. He'd finally admit that he loved her, would never leave her. Now that opportunity was lost. He'd brought her nothing but danger and sorrow. And she'd never even know he'd decided his place was here in Bayou La Siryna. The only thing she'd ever asked of him, and he'd dithered on a decision for weeks.

He moaned. *Love you, Lulu.* She couldn't understand, even if she were near. But the words were for him. They calmed his soul and filled him with peace. He repeated it once more as the pressure on his throat increased and fangs penetrated flesh.

Love you.

Chapter 18

An inexplicable thud sounded above. The vibration of it traveled through Russell's wolf and reverberated in his own belly. A howl of pain and rage butchered his ears. The pressure of Russell's fangs at his neck retracted, and a weight lifted off Payton's body. Quickly, he scrambled to his feet.

Tombi stood in the doorway, slingshot poised for yet another blow. Russell crouched and took a running leap, claws clattering like thunder on the floor. He searched for Tallulah. She caught his eye and waved a bloody knife in her hands.

She lived. Relief flowed through his veins like an opiate.

He had to help Tombi put Russell down. Tombi was an excellent hunter, but Payton questioned the effectiveness of the slingshot against the raging wolf.

The best way was to shift back to human form, allowing his most serious wounds to heal in the process. Payton commanded his wolf to give up the fight. Bursts of pain prickled his entire body as human blood and flesh replaced fur and wolf marrow. Renewed energy flowed through his cells.

"Are you okay?" Tallulah asked anxiously.

"Yes." He took the knife from her hands. "Now get out of here." Not that he expected her to listen, but it was worth a shot.

Tombi landed another rock missile to Russell's chest, but not before the wolf knocked him to the floor. Swiftly, Payton stabbed the side of Russell's neck, praying Tombi hadn't been bitten.

Russell howled and rolled away from all of them. In a blur of fur and limbs, he shifted to human form. Damn, it was exactly what he would do in Russell's shoes. The transformation would help regenerate the worst of his injuries.

His old friend stood before them, the one who'd been his best buddy.

"Don't hurt me," he pleaded, hands help up in surrender. Naked and bloody, he was a pitiful sight.

For a moment, his heart ached. Russell bled from the neck wound, the one he'd inflicted. *I had to do it.* His options had been to stab Russell, or allow him to infect Tombi. The choice was clear.

"Don't trust him," Tallulah warned.

"Get out—" he ordered.

"Go away—" Tombi said simultaneously.

"Please. I promise. I'll go get help," Russell begged, slowly backing toward the hallway. "I didn't mean for it to come to this."

"Keep your hands up high," Payton growled, hardening his heart. He nodded at Tombi, a silent signal to take Russell down.

They approached cautiously, each ready to grab one of Russell's arms.

Russell dropped his hands and bolted.

Son of a bitch. Russell made it out the front door, and down the porch steps.

Payton almost caught him, but he slipped away, as cagey as a wild creature hell-bent on escape. He rushed through the door after Russell, then stopped at the sight before him.

Shadow hunters formed a human barrier, encircling the front yard. At a signal from Tombi, they all raised their slingshots and aimed straight at Russell's heart.

There would be no escape for Russell this time.

Without turning around, he sensed Tallulah's presence. "Call a doctor for Matt and Eli."

"Already have. Finally found the landline phone."

Vehicles pulled up into the yard and side of the road. Doors opening and shutting and confused shouting filled the air.

"It's Russell!"

"What's going on?"

"Get him!"

His pack members had arrived.

Russell shifted his feet, eyes darting everywhere at the enclosed semicircle in front of him, and at Payton, Tombi and Tallulah at his back.

"Lay on the ground with your hands and legs spread," Payton yelled.

Sirens wailed from down the road. Damn. "Go get me some pants," he called over his shoulder to Tallulah.

"Get them yourself," she said, brushing past him and starting down the porch steps.

"You have to fight me every step of the way," he mumbled. He reached out an arm to stop her, but Tombi shook his head.

"We'll get him—Russell's outnumbered. Go get dressed."

He understood Tombi's logic, but the sight of Tallulah marching toward Russell and the ensuing fray didn't sit well. But the wall of people closed in on Russell and the siren wails drew closer. Sighing, Payton ran back inside to grab a pair of shorts. Going to be hard enough to explain the commotion without being naked. Swiftly, he slipped on shorts and stopped to snag a roll of duct tape from the kitchen cabinet. Moans erupted from the den.

"Matt?" he rushed to the den.

Both Matt's and Eli's eyes were wide with fright and confusion. Thank God they were conscious. With a little luck, they might even make a full recovery from whatever the hell Russell had injected in them.

"I'll send someone," Payton promised. "Help's on the way. Everything's going to be okay."

He ran back outside.

Russell lay spread eagle on the ground. Tombi held one of his arms and Tallulah the other. Chulah and Adam, the young buck of the pack, each had one of Russell's legs pinned.

Payton went to Tallulah's side and clamped both hands on one of Russell's arms.

"I've got him," she said.

"Do me a favor. Get someone to check on Matt and Eli inside. Someone else needs to hide the blood vials.

We don't want the cops seizing that as evidence. Too risky." He stared at the mulish set of her jaw. "Please."

"You said the magic word." She bent down and planted a quick kiss on his forehead. "I'll take care of it. Even talk to the cops and medics too."

"Tell them—"

She held up a hand in warning. "I can figure out a cover story. Give me a break. They'll arrest Russell and—"

"No. No arrest." Payton pointed to Riley and Jason, who stood by watching. "Riley, take hold of Russell's arm. Jason, bring your truck around here and let's get Russell in there."

He stood as Riley replaced the hold on Russell.

"Got it," Jason said. "Be right back."

Tallulah shook his arm. "What are you doing? The cops need to take him away."

"He needs treatment," Payton answered tersely. He held up the duct tape and waved over three more pack members. "Hey, let's get him bound."

"No," Tallulah stubbornly insisted. "The bastard has to pay for what he did."

He tried to reason with her. "The cops think Jeb was killed by an animal. We can't have them find out about our existence. You want to see us all hunted down and shot? Or end up caged in some lab-testing facility? Because that's what will happen."

"He can at least be arrested for assault and battery. Russell needs to spend time in jail."

"He'll be released one day and then what? You don't want him free to kill again."

Tallulah's lower lip stuck out. "I hate it when you're right."

Jason pulled the truck to a screeching halt beside them and the men lifted Russell's bound and naked body. He thrashed like a netted cat held over a pool of water.

"Son of a bitch, let me go. Please," he pleaded, his voice raised and high-pitched. "They'll kill me out there. Don't make me go. Please."

Unheeding of his pitiful cries, the men heaved him into the backseat. Someone even had enough presence of mind to find a blanket and shoved it in his hands.

Russell stopped struggling and gazed directly at Payton. "If you were ever my friend, treat me with a little respect. Don't leave me trussed and naked."

Payton shook his head. "Jason and the other escorts will get you some clothes." With that, he threw the blanket over Russell and slammed the truck door shut.

He faced Jason. "Pick out a couple of men to go with you. Take turns and drive straight through to the treatment compound," he instructed.

"Gotcha." Jason nodded.

"Why'd it take so long for you to get here?" he asked.

"We knew Matt and Eli wanted to meet with you privately." He looked sheepish. "They were going to make you commit to the pack or else…"

"I get the picture," Payton said drily.

Jason stuck his head out the window and waved an arm. "Hey, Steve and Ash, come with me."

The two men scrambled in the truck. Everyone jumped out of the way as it headed for the road. The Englazia County's sheriff's vehicle passed it as it pulled up to the farmhouse. Payton swiped a hand over his brow. Talk about cutting it close.

Hunters and wolves alike closed rank around them. The duct tape made a mysterious disappearance.

Sheriff Angier approached, demeanor as austere as a member of the Secret Service. "What seems to be the problem tonight, men?"

Tombi stepped forward and flicked a thumb toward Payton. "Just a little scuffle between the two of us. That's all. We settled things."

Angier looked Payton up and down, evidently taking note of the bloody wounds. "Looks like you got the worse end of the deal. Anyone else hurt?"

Tombi caught his eye, brows raised. Payton involuntarily glanced at the farmhouse and almost did a double take.

Matt and Eli both sat sprawled on the porch steps, cans of beer in their hands. Their glazed eyes could easily be attributed to excess alcohol consumption.

"Everything's cool this way," Matt said with a slight slur, giving a thumbs-up signal.

Angier frowned. "Is that what's going on here? Y'all been drinking and fighting? Could have led to a brawl with this many people."

"Yes, sir. Won't happen again," Tombi said.

Angier still looked disgruntled. "Who called the ambulance?"

Tallulah spoke up. "That was me. I saw the blood and freaked out."

"What were y'all fighting about?" Angier evidently sensed something amiss and didn't want to let it go.

"I had a problem with Payton living with my sister."

Tallulah rolled her eyes and he shot Tombi a startled glance. Tallulah's brother had sure thought that lie up in a hurry. Maybe it really did bug the guy that he'd moved into his twin's place.

Medics ran to them, ambulance lights strobing red over the lawn. One of the EMTs pulled on a pair of plastic gloves and nodded at Payton. "Those wounds look nasty. We'll disinfect them and give you a lift to the hospital for stitches. Let the docs check you over good."

He looked down at the bite marks, heart sinking at the reminder he was infected. Damn Russell. But at least he'd lived long enough to see Tallulah through the crisis.

"I'm not going anywhere," Payton said firmly.

The EMT shook his head. "Can't make you go, but it would be foolish not to."

"Medical care is against my religious beliefs," he lied with a straight face. "Sorry you came all this way for nothing."

"Are you pressing charges?" Angier asked him.

"No. Everything's been resolved."

The sheriff shook his head in disgust. "Something strange brewing out here, but damned if I can figure out what's really going on." He nodded at Tallulah. "Take a walk with me."

Tallulah followed Angier to the squad car. He leaned against the sedan and pinned her with a hard stare. "You want to shed some light on all this?"

She shrugged. "Nothing to tell, Sheriff. Just a little tussle. No big deal."

"You wouldn't lie to me, would you?"

"Never."

He didn't speak for several minutes and she rocked back and forth on her heels, wishing he'd hurry and leave. She needed to get Annie tending to Payton's bites ASAP. Before the infection spread and it was too late. She broke the silence first. "If there's anything else…?"

"I see you've clammed up as tight as the rest of these newcomers to Bayou La Siryna."

She had to give him something or the mystery would drive him nuts. "Tillman, everything's going to be okay now. The problem's been resolved. You're right about strange things happening in these woods. But the timber crew is leaving in a week and that's the end of that."

"You sure? No more suspicious deaths or mutilated animals?"

"Zero," she said firmly.

"What about justice for Jeb Johnson? A man is dead after all."

"Justice has been served," she assured him. "I promise."

With a sigh, he straightened and ran a hand through his hair. "I don't like it, but I see that's all I'm going to get from you. Always were a stubborn thing."

She flashed him a genuine smile. "As you once told me, we all have our own secrets in the bayou. I suspect you have one or two yourself."

Angier didn't deny or confirm. "Later, Tallulah." He got in the car and then rolled down the window. "One more thing."

"Oh, crap, are you pulling a Columbo on me?"

"No." A faint smile tugged at his lips. "A word of advice. That Payton dude? My instincts say he's a good guy. But I don't blame Tombi—he needs to put a ring on your finger if he stays in town."

Tallulah let loose a loud moan, which was unfortunately wasted as Angier had already rolled up the window and started backing out of the driveway. The ambulance left as well and a relative peace settled in the yard. She hurried to Tombi's side. "We need Annie."

Her brother held up his cell phone. "Already done. She's on the way to your cabin. Be there in less than ten minutes."

Pack members and shadow hunters mingled, discussing the night's events. Any other time, she'd have been delighted to see their worlds coalescing, but she needed to whisk Payton away. Annie always claimed that the sooner a person came to her for help, the quicker the cure.

But getting him away from the crowd could be a problem. An excited buzzing group of men surrounded him.

A loud whistle erupted from the porch and in the sudden silence, Matt wobbled to his feet. "I have something to say. Payton, I didn't give you permission to send Russell away."

Tallulah's palms itched, wanting to slap him. How dare he insult Payton like this? That arrogant, pompous ass...

"But you did the right thing," Matt continued. "If not for you and your friends, Eli and I would be dead. And no telling how many others in the pack Russell might have killed before we eventually overpowered him." He paused to wipe perspiration from his forehead. "Anyway, I'm sorry I've given you such a hard time lately. I've talked it over with Eli. I'd like to offer you a position as second-in-command of our pack."

Payton turned, searching the crowd. His eyes connected with hers and he came to her side at once, putting a hand over her shoulders.

"Thanks for the offer, but I'm going to have to discuss it with my significant other before I make any major decisions."

Significant other. She could feel the heat in her cheeks and her mouth splitting into a grin like some besotted teenager. She turned her head to the side, letting her long hair shield her face like a veil. "We need to go," she murmured. "Annie's on the way to the cabin. She can take care of your bites."

He nodded and kissed her forehead. Raising his head, Payton waved at Matt and the crowd. "We've got to go. See you all later."

Tallulah hurried him to her car and sped like mad to her cabin. A whoosh of relief escaped her at the sight of Annie's car already parked in the driveway. A light glowed at the window and she could see Annie bustling about in the kitchen. Most likely boiling water for one of her herbal concoctions.

She pulled up in the yard, close to the door. "Can you make it up the steps alone?"

"Of course I can," he said with a trace of irritability. He eased out the passenger side and she walked alongside him up the porch steps. By his stiff gait and pale face, she realized the adrenaline rush had left his body and pain and fatigue were setting in. She opened the door for him.

"Sit on the couch," she said, then straightened and called out to her sister-in-law. "We're home, Annie. Thanks for coming."

He sighed. "Yes, ma'am. Any other orders?"

"Shut up and be a good patient." She kissed his cheek and led him to the couch. "And no matter how nasty Annie's medicine, you have to swallow every drop."

He gave a mock salute and sank wearily down onto the cushions, at the last minute pulling her arm so that she fell into his lap. "We need to talk. Now. While we still have some privacy."

The intent, sad look in his gray eyes made her tremble. Whatever it was, she wasn't going to like it. Tallulah smoothed a lock of his blond hair from his forehead. "Okay," she whispered. "Spit it out."

"I'm infected. I don't want you to be disappointed if Annie's remedies don't work. Russell bit me multiple times."

"It *will* work, just like it did for me," she insisted. The alternative was too horrible to even consider.

"I say the chances are slim. We need to face facts." He took a deep breath. "If I contract the fever, I'll change. Very rapidly. The bloodlust eventually can't be sated by small animals. I'll crave bigger prey."

Her throat went dry. "No. You could control it."

"Be brave, Lulu. The facts are that I'd slowly change into a monster."

"You could *never* be like Russell. Never."

"Yes."

"No."

He gave an exasperated sigh. "We don't have time to argue. The worst thing about the fever is that it changes your thinking. So as the physical need for fresh meat increases, the brain starts justifying the killings. A vicious circle."

She wanted to clamp her hands over her ears, refuse to imagine her sweet Payton turning into a murderer with no conscience.

Payton tapped her lips with a finger. "I'd like to think I'd never hurt anyone. Especially you. But I won't take that chance. At the first sign of craving raw meat, I'm committing myself to treatment."

"But why? There's no cure. Sounds like this treatment center is a prison."

"For now," he admitted. "But the doctors are making progress to slow down the progression of the disease. One day, soon, they may find a cure."

She couldn't bear the thought of him living alone and isolated in some godforsaken military-like compound. "No. Stay here. Me and the hunters can keep you supplied with wild game. We'll make it work."

"Just promise me one thing. When I leave, I want you to forget me. You understand? Don't hope I'll be cured and return one day. It might never happen. I don't want you waiting or grieving for me like you did Bo."

Too late to guard her heart. It had belonged to Payton for weeks, if not longer. She smiled through her tears, determined to lighten his mood. "Remember the first day we met?"

"When you stood in front of my skidder and blocked me? How could I forget?" He chuckled and then sobered. "In hindsight, I might have half fallen in love with you at that very moment."

She hardly dared breathe. "Are you saying...?"

"That I love you. There. I didn't want to, but I do. You deserve to know it."

She kissed him, long and hard, unmindful of his injuries and the consequences.

"Ahem." Annie stood a few feet away, a tray in her hands. "Sorry to interrupt, but the sooner we get started, the better."

"Of course." She scooted out of Payton's lap as Annie

set the tray on the coffee table. "I'll fetch some clean washcloths and bandages."

"Perfect." Annie held out a cup of tea to Payton. "Drink up."

He shot Tallulah a pitiful look and she snickered as she hurried to gather supplies.

The door opened and shut and Tombi's deep baritone filled the room. Tallulah returned to the den and stopped short at the cozy sight of the three people she loved most in the world—her brother, the only family she had left, Annie, who had come to feel more like a sister than a friend, and Payton. Her chest squeezed. This wasn't enough. She wanted more nights like these.

Quietly, she set the medical supplies on the coffee table and watched as Annie did her usual work, a combination of prayer and hoodoo and first aid. She lent her own silent prayers in an agony of waiting and hoping.

After cleansing, applying an herbal salve and bandaging the wounds, Annie placed a hand over Payton's heart and closed her eyes. Her lips moved in a silent chant. A crease formed in her brow.

Something was wrong.

Annie opened her eyes and sadly shook her head. "It's not working. Not completely."

Tallulah rose to her feet. "Then don't stop. Keep doing—" she waved her arm, at a loss for words "—whatever it is that you're doing."

"It's no use. It's beyond my abilities. There's a dark presence within him that's blocking the saints' healing. Too strong for the likes of me to fix."

"But you have to," she cried out.

Payton stood and extended a hand to Annie. "Thanks for all your help." He turned to Tombi. "Thanks, bro."

"We can try something different," Tombi offered. "We have a Choctaw healing man that's exorcised evil shadow spirits. Maybe he could exorcise this fever."

Her heart lightened. "I didn't even think about Nash! Great idea, Tombi."

Payton shrugged. "Guess it's worth a shot. Although I have to be honest. I don't have much faith in that kind of thing."

"You don't need to have faith for it to work," she said.

"A shaman might not want to help me."

"He's not exactly a shaman," Tombi explained. "He learned a variety of techniques from his grandfather before the old man died. Draws on different traditions of several nations, depending on what he's led to try."

"Why do you think Nash wouldn't want to help you?" Annie asked.

Payton shifted uncomfortably. "Well, I'm not, you know…one of you."

Tallulah wrapped an arm around his waist. "You are at one with us in our hearts."

"Doesn't matter to Nash who seeks his help," Annie assured him. "I've sent him several people from all walks of life. He helped them all."

"Okay, okay," he conceded. "I'll give it a go."

Tallulah nudged him. "Werewolves shouldn't be so cynical about the supernatural."

"Got me there."

Tombi and Annie took their leave. As soon as the door shut behind them, Tallulah stepped into Payton's open arms, burying her face in his wide, strong chest. "You can't leave me, not like everyone else, Payton."

"I won't unless it becomes necessary." He rubbed her

back and kissed the top of her scalp, sending a bitter-sweet longing through her body.

Bo would always have a special place in her memories, but Payton's love brought out the softer, gentler side of her. Bo had always been in full warrior mode, a fierce and uncompromising shadow hunter. With Payton, she could relax. He made her feel confident and vulnerable all at the same time and he trusted and respected her—always encouraging her to follow her instincts, just as he did with his werewolf nature.

She lifted her face. "I've been wanting to tell you for a long time. I love you, Payton."

His eyes softened and he raised her hand to his lips, tenderly brushing a kiss against her skin. "I already knew that, even if you didn't."

She laughed and hiccupped at the same time and swatted his chest.

"Ouch." He stumbled backward, a hand over a bandage.

Her hand flew to her mouth. "Oops, sorry! Did I hurt…?"

He laughed.

"Not funny." But her mouth and lips betrayed her and she laughed along with him.

It was better than crying.

Chapter 19

If the fever didn't kill him, this sweat lodge would, Payton thought. It was hot enough in south Alabama without entering an artificial sauna.

And he had to sit in this primitive contraption for an entire hour? Payton guessed that only five minutes had passed so far. If this heat was supposed to draw him closer to his spiritual center, it was failing miserably. Right now he'd trade his soul to jump in a pool of cold water.

He drank greedily from one of the water bottles Tallulah had supplied and glanced around the wood-framed dome structure. In the center, hot rocks steamed in an earthen, dug-out pit. Nashoba Bowman had promised to come in periodically to check on him and to pour water over the rocks.

The man inspired confidence. He promised no miracles and was very matter-of-fact about explaining the healing ritual and why he practiced the traditions he'd be using. Payton had no worries he was in good hands, if still skeptical of the notion of a spiritual and physical cleansing. Tallulah off-handedly mentioned that Nash's name meant "wolf" in their language. Nashoba's grandfather had held him in his arms, outside, on the day of his birth, and had a vision of a wolf.

Payton wasn't sure if he believed in such a thing as spirit wolves, but he'd felt an immediate connection with Nash.

Lethargy swept his already weakened body. In the space of twenty-four hours since being bitten, he'd observed a few subtle changes—irritability, fatigue and a slight ache in his stomach, no matter how much he ate at a meal.

The bent tree limbs that framed the leather coverings looked too fragile to lean against and bear his weight, so he laid on the dirt. He'd expected the ground to be a few degrees cooler, but the sandy soil was baked hot. But he needed to lay down. A nap would be so convenient. Maybe if he could manage sleep in the heat, he'd wake up and the ordeal would be over.

He closed his eyes, feeling and thinking of nothing but the sweat pouring out of every pore on his skin. The science behind sweating out toxins was controversial, but he'd try anything to get rid of the lycanthropic fever. For Tallulah's sake, he'd tried to minimize his fear and downplay the danger, but contracting the fever was a death sentence.

So sweat it was. He licked his parched lips and raised up on one elbow for another swig of water. Sighing, he laid back down and closed his eyes.

A gentle touch on his shoulder roused him. He bolted upright and looked at the unfamiliar surroundings, the smoke so thick he felt he couldn't breathe. "What? Where am I?"

"All is well, Payton. It's me, Nashoba. You are here for a healing, remember? Drink more water."

His heart rate returned to normal and he accepted the cup of water Nash held out, drinking deep, long draughts.

Nash had his fingers pressed against a pulse point on his wrist. He nodded. "You're doing fine."

"Is it time to come out?" Payton asked hopefully.

Nash's lips softly curled. "It's only been fifteen minutes."

"Are you kidding me?"

"Nope. Tallulah's sitting outside the lodge. Yell out and let her know you're okay. She's worried."

"Hey, Lulu," he said in a loud voice. "You been hanging around?"

"I'm here. You doing all right?"

"No. Your friend's trying to kill me," he joked. "Wish you could join me in the funhouse."

Nash had explained the need for the treatment to be private. The healer found this to be more effective for those in need of intensive intervention.

That would be him all right. He laid back down, watching as Nashoba exited. For two seconds, the cooler breeze from outside washed over him like a balm. Cooler being relative—after all, it was summer in the deep south. The only good thing this lodge had going for it was that the smoke and heat kept the bugs far at bay.

Again, he closed his eyes and drifted into a void.

Time had no meaning. Three minutes or thirty minutes might have passed. Mind and body acclimated to the intense heat. He was past the discomfort, past the ties that bound him to the earth and to the living. Every sense was amplified—the perspiration dripping on his skin, the shuffle of feet from outside, the wind rustling through pine and magnolia.

He was wolf, and yet he was not. He was human, and yet not completely. He was in a between realm of sensation and spirit. A loud flapping of wings erupted nearby, yet it didn't scare him or seem unusual.

All is well.

Nashoba's deep voice echoed reassuringly in his mind. He was floating, the air cushioning him, and it felt as natural as walking on ground. A white owl screeched and flew away, chased by a golden eagle.

He laughed, the sound reverberating in his brain. If the herbs he'd ingested earlier were hallucinogenic, they'd produced quite the show. The eagle returned, its large wings spread in glory as it glided on the wind. Payton stared into the eyes of his protector. A wise, powerful intelligence bathed him. Someone close by spoke in a foreign tongue, but he couldn't understand a word they said.

His body lightened and he, too, flew, gliding in the bayou breeze with a freedom that transcended anything he'd ever experienced.

"Payton. Payton? Payton!" A voice called from below. A familiar, beloved voice.

He had a choice to make. Fly with the eagle, or return to Tallulah.

Brain and body whirled in a downward spiral—falling, falling. Her voice pulled at him, tethering him from air to land. *Hold on, hold on, hold on.* A chanting began, still in the foreign tongue—a promise, a lifeline.

Down, down, down, returning him to his body and awareness.

"Payton? Are you all right? Talk to me."

He struggled to open his heavy eyelids. Two blurry faces hovered nearby, male and female. Brown eyes filled with concern drew his attention.

"Lulu," he said weakly.

She gave a shaky laugh. "That name's never sounded so good to me."

From the side, strong arms pushed him upward to a seated position. Tallulah held out a cup of water.

"Drink."

"Always bossing me around," he joked, licking his parched lips.

The lukewarm water revived his sense of lucidity. It was Nashoba behind him, supporting his back. Payton tensed his body and rocked forward, preparing to stand. Nash and Tallulah went to either side of his body and supported him by the arms. He stood, a momentary blackness arose, and he swayed.

"Sit back down," Tallulah ordered. "You're going to fall."

"Sassy woman. I'm fine. Ready to get out of here." He turned to Nashoba. "No offense. It was an amazing experience."

Nash nodded. "It worked. I felt the fever lifting from your body. The eagle took it away when he chased the white owl from your spirit."

"Wow," he breathed. How did Nash know the details of his vision? He had the utmost respect for the man.

"We're not done yet," Nashoba cautioned. "The fever

is gone, but now we need to finish the ritual by restoring your strength and offering protection from further evil."

What new torture did they have in mind? Payton squelched the thought immediately. He was cured. It was worth whatever discomfort lay ahead.

"Are you sure he's really cured?" Tallulah asked.

Nashoba nodded at Payton. "Let him tell you."

"Is it true?" she asked.

"It's true."

The tension in her face melted and she closed her eyes for a moment. He suspected she had realized all along the danger posed by the fever.

With their help, he walked out of the lodge and into the cool of night. He lifted his chin, savoring the breeze on his face. His sweat-drenched body felt renewed and he walked without assistance, not the least bit dizzy.

"This way." Nash directed him to a large circle bordered with seashells. Tallulah had explained earlier that this was a medicine wheel blessed by Nashoba and consecrated to the four elements, the Great Spirits and the four spirit animals—the bear, the buffalo, the eagle and the mouse.

Inside the circle, Nashoba commenced to brushing the outside of Payton's body with a large brown-and-white turkey feather. This, he'd been told, was the final cleansing aspect of the ritual. Nash replaced the turkey feather with a red cardinal feather.

"For vitality to all your blood cells and to boost your energy," Nash said.

Whether it was from the feathers or just plain relief from being outside the sweat lodge, Payton felt his strength rapidly returning. The mental anguish was gone, too, replaced by the peaceful certainty that all would be well, just as Nash promised.

Nash removed a seashell necklace from around his neck and placed it on Payton's. "Wear this for the next forty-eight hours. It will continue to invigorate and protect you. For the last step, we offer tobacco to the spirits to thank them for their goodness in answering our prayers."

They all took a pinch of tobacco from a leather pouch and threw it in the air. Tallulah and Nash spoke something in Choctaw.

"Thank you," he chimed in.

The faintest rustle of wings sounded from far away, an acknowledgment of his gratitude.

Nash faced him. "It is done. Go home tonight and drink plenty of water and get lots of rest."

That part sounded like a typical doctor. Payton took Tallulah's hand and they silently exited the sacred circle. Once out, he felt free to speak. His old friend had weighed heavy on his heart. Russell and every other infected wolf out west needed the same help he'd received. "Nash, they sure could use you in Montana."

"It was a near thing with you," Nash said soberly. "If you don't get help quickly—"

"Right." The others had been in darkness too long.

"It's not just the physical progression of disease," Nash explained. "It's the spiritual darkness that often descends at the same time. I believe healing comes when both physical and spiritual are addressed together. Not only that, healers like me draw power from the land itself and our work is also stronger when we treat people that also have that same connection to our land."

"Like me," Payton agreed. He turned to Tallulah. "Bayou La Siryna feels like home."

"It can be your home," she said simply.

It was. But he wanted that conversation for when they were alone. He extended a hand to Nash. "Thank you isn't enough."

"Thank the spirits, not me." Nash briefly clasped his hand. "Be well, my friend."

Tallulah insisted on driving and he didn't put up a fight. He reclined in the passenger seat, letting the air-conditioning chill his sweaty skin. They were both silent, consumed with their own thoughts and processing tonight's miracle. They arrived at her cabin, where a light left on glowed from within, cozy and welcoming.

He pushed out of the car and took her hand. When she started past him to open the door, he tugged at her arm. "Let's sit on the porch for a bit."

Surprisingly, she agreed with no complaint. He gazed up at the stars, filled with awe and humble for the second opportunity in life. A comfortable silence stretched between them.

He spoke at last. "I meant what I said earlier. Bayou La Siryna is my home. I'm not going anywhere."

"But what about your pack?"

"They're leaving this weekend. Without me."

"Are you sure that's what you want?"

"Very. I'll always be grateful that Matt took me in when I was alone in the world. But I must have lived like an outcast for too long with my parents. All the rules of the pack and having to obey the alpha eventually became…oppressive."

"But you're the only wolf here in the bayou. You don't think you'll be lonely?"

"No. I can hunt shadow spirits with you and your people. Besides, I can always visit the pack out west from time to time."

"I don't want you staying because of some misguided sense of obligation. I mean—"

He kissed her. Kissed her until she moaned and wrapped her arms around his neck. "You know what your problem is, don't you?" he mumbled against her ear.

"I'm in love with a werewolf?" She giggled.

"No, you talk too much."

She playfully bumped her knee against his and he hugged her close to his side. "That's okay, I love talkative women."

"And I love hairy guys."

"Witch."

"Wolf."

She snuggled into his side and he picked up her hand and ran his fingers along her soft palm, tracing her lifeline, and then along the band of pale skin circled her right ring finger. "Do you miss wearing Bo's ring?" he asked, touching the delicate skin.

"No. And I don't even have it anymore. I returned it to Bo's mother. It had belonged to her mother and I thought she should have it back in the family."

"Can I ask you a question?" he said hesitantly.

"Anything you want."

"Do you still grieve over Bo?"

"No. I'll always have fond memories of him. But it's time for me to move on. I realize I went overboard, obsessing over him and always visiting the place where he died." She stopped and caressed his face. "Now I can seek my happiness with the living. With you."

It wasn't enough. It should be, but he needed more reassurance. Needed to feel that she wasn't settling for him only because Bo was gone. Needed to know that she loved him with every bit of her heart. He hated feeling so insecure, but he had to ask.

"This is unfair, but I want to know. Is your love for me as strong as it was for him?"

Her sharp eyes blurred. "Yes. A million times yes. You said when we made love the first time that you knew I was your destined mate." She traced his lips with her fingers. "We were meant for one another and I've never been so happy, so in love."

He buried his face in her hair. Damn if he wasn't the luckiest man in the world. "My sweet Lulu."

Another kind of lethargy stole over him, but so different from the one in the lodge. This time, he felt drunk on happiness. He really should get up and take a shower, but he was loath to leave the sweet embrace of her arms. Apparently, she felt the same, as she lazily ran her fingers up and down his back. They sat a spell longer until she raised her hand and regarded him curiously.

"What happened in the sweat lodge?" she asked, her head canted to one side.

"Haven't you ever been in one?"

"Never. I've always been healthy as a horse."

"At first, it was miserable. Then you get used to it and…you completely relax and your mind fills with strange images and sounds. Hard to explain…"

She laid a finger on his lips. "Shhh, you don't have to give me all the details. Especially about spirit animals visiting. That's between you and the spirits. I was mainly curious about what you said in there."

He furrowed his brow. "I don't remember saying anything. I did hear other people talking though, some foreign language that was gibberish to me."

"I don't know what you mean by *other people* but we sure heard you talking."

"Me? What did I say?"

"You kept repeating *hold on*."

"I said that out loud? Well, I dreamed you were calling me. Right at the same time the eagle in my vision offered me the opportunity to keep flying with it." He watched her face closely, but Tallulah didn't laugh or express skepticism. "Somehow I knew that flying away meant going to the After Life. And then you were calling my name and I needed to get back to you. I was afraid you'd give up on me, but you continued saying my name." He squeezed her hand. "If not for you…well, I owe you my life."

She shook her head slowly. "How strange. I *was* calling your name from time to time, making sure you hadn't passed out from the heat. But the really weird part? When you asked me to hold on, you spoke in Choctaw."

He pulled back to stare at her. "What? That couldn't have been me you heard. I don't know any Choctaw."

"I'd know your voice anywhere," she insisted. "It was you."

He shook his head in wonder. "I'll be damned."

Tallulah lifted his hand and kissed it, her lips soft and smooth on his calloused skin. "Thank you for coming back to me. You could have followed the eagle to the After Life. And thank you for not leaving with your pack, for staying here in Bayou La Siryna with me."

He lifted her chin with a finger and stared deep into eyes as dark and mysterious and gentle as the night.

"I'd choose you every time."

Chapter 20

"Our women are finally on the way over with sustenance," Tombi announced. "We should cut out after lunch and all go for a ride."

Payton looked down at the oil staining his hands, and the smear of grease on his work clothes. Normally, he didn't care about the mess. Working at Chulah's motorcycle shop was the best job he'd ever had. He'd been working there for nearly a month now and was used to oil stains. But today…well, he'd just have to wait until this evening and a good clean-up before he took action.

Yet the circle of gold in his uniform pocket nagged at him like a child with a few bucks to spend in the candy store.

Chulah handed them each a soft drink from the vending machine and they sat in his office, taking a break.

"Thanks for helping out today, Tombi," Chulah said. "I'm game for a ride. We're all caught up here."

"Full moon tomorrow night," Payton said. "Are we camping out tonight, too?"

"Let's just wait until tomorrow. The shadow spirits have been quiet lately," Tombi said.

Perfect. Much as he loved roaming as a wolf and hunting with them, this evening should be special. A kind of special that required privacy. A final bonding with his true mate.

But first things first. Chulah knew his game plan, so Payton shot a significant look at his friend, who nodded in understanding and got to his feet.

"Got to, um, check on something. Be back in a few minutes," Chulah said.

Not the cleverest of exits, but it would do. He was alone with Tallulah's brother. His palms dampened and his throat went dry. This shouldn't be so hard. After all, they were great friends and he'd been living with the man's twin for months.

"That night we captured Russell—" he began.

"Hell of a fight that guy put up," Tombi interrupted. "I was worried he'd escape from your pack buddies that drove him to Montana."

"Worried me, too," he admitted. "But they arrived without incident. Russell's getting the best care available."

"Sorry if your friend's health doesn't matter to me," Tombi said drily, taking a swig of his drink. "My concern is that he's in a secure facility where he can't hurt anyone else again."

Payton couldn't blame him. Tombi had never met the Russell he once knew and had called friend before the lycanthropic fever destroyed his soul. "No telling how many of the pack might have died that night if not for you, Tallulah and the rest of the shadow hunters."

Tombi waved a hand in dismissal. "Catching Jeb's killer was the least we could do for our former neighbor. Besides, we're sworn to protect the people of the bayou from all supernatural beings. I would say that a werewolf qualifies as such."

Just the opening he needed. "Does it ever bother you that Tallulah is living with a werewolf?" he asked.

"I trust you. I do have a couple of concerns, though, now that you brought the subject up."

"Spit it out."

Tombi leaned forward. "It deals with the first part of your question. The one about *living* with my sister. Are you going to marry her or not? Our father's dead, so I feel like I have the right to ask in his place."

Payton pulled the ring from his pocket. "I'm proposing today."

"Excellent." Tombi nodded and smacked a fist down on the office desk. "About time, too."

"I take it you approve then? Your blessing's important to me, especially since you're the only family she has left. Tallulah would be hurt if you opposed the marriage."

"'Course I approve. Tallulah's crazy about you. You'll make her happy, without letting her strong personality run all over you." He raised his soda can in a toast. "No easy feat. Kudos."

One problem down. "You said you had two concerns. What's the other?"

Tombi flushed. "Again, you might think this is none

of my business, but remember that I'm acting like a surrogate father here."

"Go on."

"What if you two have kids? Are they going to be werewolf shapeshifters like you?"

Payton went still, preparing himself for the worst—human prejudices against their species was well-documented through history. Marriage and children always brought the issue to the forefront. "Yes. As half wolves, the urge to shift won't be as strong, but it will be there. I'm hoping you and the rest of the shadow hunters would accept them as you have me. Is that a problem?"

"Tallulah know about that?"

"She does."

"And she's okay with it?"

"Yes."

"Then it's not a problem for me, either." Tombi extended his hand. "Welcome to our family."

Their men were going to be thrilled with the impromptu picnic lunch. The scent of fried chicken, cheese biscuits and potato salad made Tallulah's mouth water. "You sure they're all going to be in the shop?" she asked.

"I just talked to Tombi," Annie said.

"And Chulah's always at the shop," April said from the front seat of Annie's car. "I swear if he didn't own that shop, he'd pay someone for the chance to work there."

"Payton loves working at the shop," she said. "He's always wanted to do something mechanical like this instead of working with that damn timber crew that destroyed land."

"Does he miss the pack yet?" Annie asked. "I know

they've only been gone a short while, but they all seemed so close."

"A little. But we plan to visit out there occasionally."

Privately, she still considered Matt a bit of a jerk, even after his apologies to Payton. But she'd learned she didn't always have to share her opinion on his old buddies. Made life easier. And with them living hundreds of miles away, very doable.

April smiled at her. "I'm glad things worked out for you and Payton and that you're so happy, Tallulah. I know it's been rough for you the last couple of years."

Annie winked. "Lulu mostly has a smile on her face these days."

"Still hate that name," she muttered. "I haven't changed that much, have I?"

"Don't worry. You're still you, just a better version," April said.

Annie pulled the car up to the front door of the shop and they each gathered supplies—food, drinks, paper plates and napkins.

The noise in the place came to a halt as the men watched them enter. Payton was the first one over. "You're all angels of mercy. Do I smell chicken?"

"You do."

Tallulah kissed his grease-smeared cheek, uncaring of the dirt or the knowing smiles of their friends. "All your favorites."

He peeked in the wicker basket and rummaged through the containers. "What? No pecan pie? Or chocolate chip cookies?"

She put her hands on her hips. "Of all the ungrateful…" She sputtered. "I spent over an hour with

Annie and April peeling potatoes and battering chicken and…"

She caught Payton's wink at the others just as he bent down to cut off her complaints with a kiss. Geez, that man knew how to push her buttons. She shoved at his chest and gave a mock frown. "You'll eat what we cooked and love it."

"Yes, ma'am. But can I ask a question first?"

"Shoot."

He dropped to one knee.

What the hell? He couldn't be…not here in the most unromantic of settings… Not now…in front of everybody? How embarrassing. She leaned over to tug at his sleeve, signaling him to stop and stand up.

Undeterred, he reached into the pocket of his shop coveralls, producing a large diamond ring that shone with an incongruous purity in the greasy shop.

"Will you marry—"

To hell with what anyone else thought. Tallulah sank to her knees in front of him and threw her arms around his neck, almost sending them both toppling to the cement floor.

Payton grinned and raised a brow. "I take it that's a *yes*?"

"Let's hurry up and make this official," Tombi said.

Everyone laughed, and she didn't care a bit. Dignity be damned.

A sudden doubt assailed her and she leaned in, whispering in his ear. "Are you sure you won't leave me to rejoin your pack one day?"

"Never." He set her back a foot to gaze into her eyes. "My place is with you. Always. You and the shadow hunters are my family now."

Holy spirits, she was going to totally disgrace herself and cry. Payton cleared his throat and glanced at Chulah, who gave him a slight nod. What was this about?

"Chi hollo li," he said slowly and carefully.

A swelling of joy bubbled inside her. He'd taken the time to learn the Choctaw phrase.

"I love you, too."

Payton rose to his feet and scooped her in his arms, swinging her a full three-hundred and sixty degrees.

"I still haven't heard you say *yes,*" her brother called out.

She pretended annoyance and frowned at Tombi. "Yes, yes, yes, yes, *yes*! There. Happy now?"

Because she was. Payton had come into her life and changed everything. She ran her fingers through his blond hair and stared into his pewter eyes.

"Kept me guessing there for a minute," he joked, then his face sobered. "I'll love you forever."

"Same here," she whispered around the hitch in her breath.

After a long, long darkness of the soul, Payton's love was *onnat minti*—the coming of daylight.

* * * * *